John Morris

Notes of Spiritual Retreats and Instructions

Volume 2

John Morris

Notes of Spiritual Retreats and Instructions
Volume 2

ISBN/EAN: 9783337332259

Printed in Europe, USA, Canada, Australia, Japan

Cover: Foto ©Andreas Hilbeck / pixelio.de

More available books at **www.hansebooks.com**

THE INTERIOR

OF

JESUS AND MARY.

TRANSLATED FROM THE FRENCH

OF

THE REV. J. GROU,

Of the Society of Jesus.

BY

A MEMBER OF THE URSULINE COMMUNITY,

BLACK ROCK, CORK.

Authoress of the " Month of Mary," " Practical Reflections for the principal Feasts of the Year," &c. &c.

IN TWO VOLUMES.

VOL.

DUBLIN:

PUBLISHED BY JAMES DUFFY,

10, WELLINGTON QUAY.

1847.

Printed by THOMAS I. WHITE,
45, Fleet Street, Dublin.

CONTENTS.

CONTENTS.

CONTENTS.

INTERIOR OF JESUS.

PART FIRST CONTINUED.

CHAPTER L.

Jesus never sought his own glory.

ALL glory was unquestionably due to the sacred humanity which the word had mercifully assumed; in fact, the dignity imparted to it by the hypostatical union, was in itself so sublime, that any attainable degree of external honour, must have dwindled into nothing by comparison. To human view, it appears, that consistently with the demands of strict justice, Jesus Christ should have exalted his humanity in the eyes of mortals, —the more so, as it was incapable of appropriating that glory, which would have reverted in its fulness to his divinity. But widely different are the views of God, from those of men! It was decreed in the eternal counsels, that at an appointed time, the Incarnate Word should re-

ceive supreme honour in heaven and on earth,
but that until that period arrived, he should
devote himself exclusively to the promotion of
his Father's,—the great object which had brought
him from heaven: far from seeking his own, he
was to renounce it absolutely, and thus to merit
that his Father should at a future day, interest
himself in its restoration. Such was the connection of the events pre-ordained from eternity
by the Almighty.

Never were ordinances obeyed with more
punctual exactitude, or more loving submission.
Not a word, not an act, not a miracle of the life
of Jesus Christ tended to the diffusion of his own
renown. Before his passion, he prayed, " Father
glorify thou me with thyself, with the glory
which I had, before the world was, with thee,"—
(St. John, xvii. 5.) But this petition was intended
only to enliven the faith and fortify the courage
of his apostles, and was moreover offered on the
eve of his ignominious death, when he had ceased
to consider himself an inhabitant of earth. He
prayed that his humanity might be glorified only
after its resurrection from the dead, and restoration to immortal life, and he implored the
favour as the reward of his sufferings, and in
virtue of his Father's previous promise. In fact,
the words convey less a petition for, than a prediction of the glory destined to recompense his
humiliations, and his obedience unto the death of
the cross.

But his habitual mode of expression, was

totally different. " I seek not my own glory ;"
said he to the Jews : " if I glorify myself, my
glory is nothing."—(St. John, viii. 50—54.)
How clear and emphatic this assertion of the
Son of God, who in one sense possessed the
strongest possible title to glorify himself! What
right can we have to personal exaltation, after
Christ has distinctly acknowledged that he had
none ? And if " his glory was nothing," what
are we to think of that we attribute to ourselves ?
Shall human pride and vanity now dare to lift
their heads ? Shall we not henceforth despise
the contemptible honours we have hitherto ido-
lized, ambitioned, and pursued even at the peril
of our immortal souls ? Shall we claim the distinction of a Christian, and yet aspire to the
vanishing glories of earth ?

Jesus Christ assures us of the astounding fact,
that had he given testimony of himself as man,
his testimony would not have been true. " If I
bear witness of myself, my witness is not true."—
(St. John, v. 31.) And although a contradiction
appears to exist between the foregoing assertion,
and the following, " If I give testimony of myself,
my testimony is true : for I know whence I come,
and whither I go ;"—(Ibid, viii. 14,) the apparent
inconsistency is removed by remembering that in
the first instance, Christ spoke as man ; in the
second, as God. How delusive then, whatever
be its subject, is the praise we arrogate to ourselves, either in the secrecy of our own hearts,
or before human witnesses ! Should our con-

duct really merit approbation, the self-esteem it excites, is not the less reprehensible, because the glory of our good qualities belongs essentially and solely to God.

This indifference for his reputation, Jesus Christ adduced as an argument in favour of the truth of his words. " He," said he, " that speaketh of himself, seeketh his own glory, but he that seeketh the glory of him that sent him, he is true, and there is no injustice in him;"—(St. John, vii. 18,) thus admitting, that to convict him of labouring for his own renown, would be to prove his doctrine false, and establishing his claim to truth and justice on the measure of his zeal in extending the glory of his Father.

What ample grounds of self-condemnation are here unfolded to those preachers of the Gospel, who teaching the heavenly lessons of Christ, and bearing the title of his apostles, render their sacred functions subservient to the acquisition of perishable fame! While supposed to speak by the inspiration of God, their words flow in reality from the abundance of their pride, and having no view but personal reputation, they are neither upright in intention, nor veracious in words. Faithful souls, who in sincerity seek a guide filled with the spirit of God, and who are apprehensive of error in your choice, closely observe the ministers of his altar, and if you detect in them any covert view to their own glory, be assured that God, infinitely jealous of his, will grant them neither his light nor grace for your direction. I do not mean that a transient emotion or passing expression of vanity, is incompatible with genuine piety and sincere zeal, but I do maintain that no true apostle of Jesus Christ will systematically labour for his own exaltation, and that to pursue such a course, is totally to derogate from the sanctity and dignity of the sacred ministry.

Jesus Christ was so utterly indifferent to his reputation, that he never rendered instrumental to its diffusion the glorious testimonies he received from his Father. Having once publicly prayed, " Father, glorify thy name, a voice came from heaven : I have both glorified it, and will glorify it again." Upon which, he observed to the surrounding multitude, " This voice came, not because of me, but for your sakes."—(St. John, xii. 28—30.) From the same indifference to human applause, he exacted secrecy of those he restored to health ; he recommended that the gratitude due for his miraculous benefits, should be transferred from himself to God ; he imposed silence on the evil spirits who proclaimed his praises ; he forbade Peter, James, and John, the witnesses of his transfiguration, to disclose the splendid scene, until he should have risen from the dead ; he reprehended the individual, who considering merely his human perfection, called him " good master ;" " why," said he, " askest thou me concerning good ? One is good, God ;" —(St. Matt. xix. 16, 17,) he took flight, when the multitude for whom he had miraculously multiplied the loaves, would have elevated him to the regal dignity, and in his triumphant entry to Jerusalem, he totally dispensed with the pomp usually attendant on similar public pageants.

St. Paul, who thoroughly understood the spirit of his divine Master, had assuredly ample grounds for asserting that " Christ did not please himself;" for imputing to him the words of the Psalmist, " the reproaches of them that reproached thee, fell upon me ;" (Rom. xv. 3,) and for declaring that " Christ did not glorify himself that he might be made a high priest;" but that he was glorified by " him that said unto him, thou art my Son, this day have I begotten thee."—(Heb. v. 5.)

Since the Son of God so absolutely renounced the glory due to him, we may infer how hateful in the sight of heaven, is the deliberate pursuit of ours.   Yet, the desire of exaltation is the most deeply seated feeling of the human heart ; it is the propensity whose perilous consequences man most ingeniously conceals from himself, and to whose injustice he is least alive ; it is the inclination he combats with least energy, and never so completely subdues, as not to retain at least an involuntary bias towards it.   Those who make it their study to observe and rectify the secret movements of the heart, must be aware that man is ever inclined to convert his interior and exterior gifts, even the most vain and fragile among them, into a source of self-complacency ; that this tendency constitutes one of the chief obstacles to the exercise of true piety, and the acquisition of an interior spirit ; that temptations to vanity, to self-seeking, to the open or disguised pursuit of fame ; to secret satisfaction at external evidences of approval or deference, are among those to be resisted most vigorously, most frequently, and most perseveringly ; that the desire of renown, is the first instinctive impulse of the human heart, and that only deep meditation, followed by long practice, can establish the habit of giving to God, what belongs to God, and losing sight of selfish interest.

So subtle is the venom of this fatal propensity, that it insinuates itself into the innermost recesses of the heart, and unless arrested in its devastating progress, destroys the germ of virtue, engenders hypocrisy, and other spiritual vices, and becomes at last the efficient agent of the soul's destruction. We have a forcible illustration of this truth in the sad fate of the Pharisees, which should strike us with awe and terror. Jesus Christ attributes their incredulity and obduracy to the indulgence of this one passion alone. "How can you believe," said he, "who receive glory from one another," employing mutual flattery to attain your own selfish ends, "and the glory which is from God alone, you do not seek ?"—(St. John, v. 44.) St. John the Evangelist, filled with astonishment that the wondrous miracles of Jesus Christ should have failed to impress the people with belief in his Divinity, accounts for their obstinacy, by observing, that "they loved the

glory of men, more than the glory of God."—
St. John, xii. 43.) When God is pleased to
exalt his creatures, vanity is not likely to ensue,
for he elevates none but the truly humble, who
fully and faithfully restore to its Donor, the glory
derived from him. The proud man despises such
glory as this, precisely for the reason that
he cannot appropriate it; his desires are wholly
centred in earthly honours; he loves them, he
revels in them, he values them beyond all treasures; in his headlong pursuit of them, he forgets God, and ends by offering the incense of
idolatry at the shrine of his own ambition. Let
us henceforth apply with active energy and ever
increasing earnestness to the eradication of this
detestable vice, adopting the most effectual measures to close the avenues of our heart against
its approach.

CHAPTER LI.

Jesus washes his Apostles' feet.

THE details left us by St. John of the washing
of the apostles' feet by Jesus Christ, and still
more, his description of the imposing preparation
for that most solemn ceremony, cannot fail to
excite deep emotion in the reflecting mind.
"Jesus," said he, "knowing that his hour was
come, that he should pass out of this world to
the Father: having loved his own who were in

the world, he loved them unto the end. And
when supper was done, knowing that his Father
had given him all things into his hands, and that
he came from God, and goeth to God."—(St.
John, xiii. 1, seq.) Why is the mind held in
suspense by this magnificent preamble, and to
what does it lead? Doubtless to the narration
of some splendid achievement of Jesus Christ;
some astounding illustration of his power. Such
at least is the natural anticipation of every
reader unacquainted with the sequel; an anticipation confirmed by the knowledge that no
other portion of the history of Christ's life is
similarly introduced.

But what follows the sublime preface? " He
riseth, from supper, layeth aside his garments,
and having taken a towel, girded himself. After
that, he putteth water into a basin, and began
to wash the feet of the disciples, and to wipe
them with the towel wherewith he was girded."
(Ibid, 4, 5.) St. John must have been deeply
impressed with the sublimity of this seemingly
debasing act, to enter with so much precision
into the detail of its most minute particulars; his
aim was doubtless, to convey a similar impression
to all who should peruse the solemn and affecting
history. How incomprehensible the humility
here exemplified! A God stoops so low as to
wash the feet of his creatures, thus fulfilling in
their regard the office of a menial! Can we
wonder at St. Peter's reluctance to submit, or
at the exclamation prompted by the vivacity of

his faith, "Lord, dost thou wash my feet?"—
(Ibid, 6.) *Thou* to wash *my* feet! The contrast between the two extremes of supreme majesty and abject misery, is here clearly defined.
How natural his vehement protestation, "Thou
shalt never wash my feet!" (Ibid, 8.)_ "I cannot
permit that Thou, my Lord and Master, shouldst
thus degrade thyself." The reply of Jesus Christ,
and the menace by which he overcame the apostle's repugnance, all are familiar with.

Were the greatest monarch on earth, to render
a similar service to the last of his subjects, we
should say he had compromised his majesty as
a sovereign, or his reputation for judgment as
a man; and humanly speaking, the conclusion
would be correct, for humiliations like this are
inconsistent with the dignity of royalty, and
neither natural affection, nor any motive of the
kind can render them admissible. But such a
case would merely involve the humiliation of a
mortal, whereas in the present instance, it is a
God who stoops beneath his own creatures, and
who considers the degradation in no wise dero-
gatary to his infinite majesty. It was indeed his
humanity which humbled itself so low, yet, the
divine nature being united to that humanity, the
humiliation reverted to the Man-God, who eagerly
desired and voluntarily embraced its abjection.

What could have induced Jesus Christ to perform such an act? Love, which neither shrinks
from difficulties, nor hesitates at obstacles; which
seeks only to satiate its own ardour, and is

wonderful in its inventions. Love suggested the act, but who could describe the zeal, the fervour, the interior joy with which it was performed ? We are lost in astonishment, when we contemplate this manifestation of Christ's condescending goodness to the disciples who revered and cherished him; but when we behold him kneeling at the feet of Judas, washing and wiping them with as much affection and humility as those of his faithful followers, our minds are bewildered, our feelings rebel, and the sole conclusion left to us is, that only the heart of Jesus was capable of such heroism.

Jesus washed the feet of his apostles before he gave them his flesh to eat, for although pure, as he himself declared, they were not sufficiently so to participate with the requisite sanctity in the divine banquet; it was necessary that Jesus Christ should himself perfect that purity, by cleansing them from the least stain. The connection between this fact, and the dispositions for the holy Communion, is evident. It is not necessary to recur to the sacrament of penance, for the express purpose of manifesting to the minister of Christ, every slight blemish we may discern in our souls before approaching the holy table; but we should excite ourselves to sincere sorrow for even those trivial faults, and beseech Jesus Christ to blot them out before he enters our heart.

"After he had washed their feet, and taken his garments, being sat down again, he said to them: Know you what I have done to you?"

By the question, he invites reflection on the great scene just enacted, and solicits attention to the divine instruction by which it is to close. " You call me Master and Lord : and you say well, for so I am. If then I, being your Lord and Master, have washed your feet ; you also ought to wash one another's feet, for I have given you an example, that as I have done to you, so you do also."—(Ibid, 12, et seq.) How powerful an inducement to the practice of humility ! Can a true disciple of Christ require a stronger, or could a more irresistible be presented ? As our Lord and Master, Jesus Christ, was authorized to impose commands at his own option, while that two fold title assuredly dispensed him from giving to the world so astonishing an example of annihilation. But he knew how strongly our pride would revolt against this command, and therefore he would require nothing of us, which he had not first practised. Nature rebels at the very idea of performing a menial office for equals or inferiors, even though that act be ennobled by the motive of divine charity. To subdue our repugnances, and inspire us with nobler senti- ments, he displays to our view his own admirable humility ; he exhibits his divine person prostrate through love at the feet of his apostles, and in that posture, he says, " I have given you an example, that as I have done to you, so you do also." If we closely examine into the origin of human feeling, we shall find that pride is the great obstacle to the exercise of fraternal charity;

that it is pride which forbids us to anticipate
our neighbour's wishes; to bestow on him certain undefinable evidences of cordiality; to render him certain services, which would cost us
nothing more than the sacrifice of an inclination.
We glory in the display of benevolent compassion and noble generosity, but we shrink with
extreme repugnance from any act which seems
to lower us beneath our fellow creatures. The
example of Christ has not been altogether fruitless,
it is true, many persons of high rank, having been
stimulated by it, to devote their exertions to the
poor, the sick, and imprisoned. But without
instituting a minute inquiry into the secret
motives of these good works, we may hazard as
a general assertion, that humility of spirit, is not
always, as it should be, their vivifying principle,
and that if such charity were absolutely hidden
in God, totally veiled from public observation,
and accompanied as an indispensable condition,
no less by interior, than exterior self-abasement,
it would find fewer votaries. To enter into the
dispositions of Jesus Christ on this point, and in
sentiments like his, to cast ourselves at the feet
even of an acknowledged enemy, requires exalted
virtue. In religious communities, where perpetual opportunities occur of rendering mutual
services, dictated by humility and charity, what
an effort it costs to discharge the duty freely,
cordially, and generously towards those from
whom we have received annoyance, or between
whom and ourselves there exists reciprocal cold-

ness of feeling! How few are capable of such an effort! A community animated by the genuine spirit of charity, may unhesitatingly be pronounced an assembly of sanctified imitators of Jesus Christ. In some particular instances, it is as mortifying to the members of religious as of secular society to stoop beneath their fellow-creatures. Although the pride of the world may be banished from the cloister, pride of another species is to be found within its walls; a pride more subtle, more fastidious, more prompt to take umbrage at every fancied slight. Scarcely in any case is humility loved and practised for its own sake.

CHAPTER LII.

Of the institution of the most Blessed Eucharist.

HEREAFTER, I propose to devote some observations to the eucharistic life of our divine Redeemer,—the most perfect model for the imitation of interior souls. In the present chapter, I shall confine myself to the institution of the holy Eucharist, refraining, however, from any elaborate details on a subject which has already engaged the pen of so many authors.

What is the Eucharist? A sacrament, and a sacrifice; the most excellent sacrament, and the only sacrifice. In the Eucharist, Jesus Christ renews and perpetuates to the end of time, the

sacrifice of the cross. He immolates himself on
the altar by the ministry of his priests, really,
though in a mystical and unbloody manner. He
offers to his Father in his own name and ours,
the only homage acceptable to God; he adores
his sovereign majesty; returns him thanks for
his benefits; satisfies his justice for human guilt.
and obtains for man all necessary graces. Of
ourselves, we can neither honour God adequately,
nor thank him for his favours; nor obtain, or
dispose ourselves to obtain the remission of sin,
nor merit the smallest grace. But all these defi-
ciencies are amply supplied through the sacrifice
of Jesus Christ, which eminently fulfils these
various ends.

The Eucharist is the most excellent and august
of the sacraments. In the other sacraments,
Jesus Christ is present by his power; in this, he
resides personally. In the rest, he communicates
grace, but in this, he gives us his flesh, and with
it, his soul and divinity. He could not bestow
a stronger pledge of his love, nor contract with
us a more intimate union. The Eucharist is truly
an extension of the Incarnation, imparting to our
souls the effects of that adorable mystery, and as
the humanity of Christ is divinized by its union
with the Word, so we in a manner participate in
the divine nature by being incorporated with
him. His flesh is truly united to ours; he is not
transformed into us, but he transforms us into
himself. By a miracle in the natural order, the
food we partake of, becomes part of our sub-

stance ; by a miracle in the supernatural order, participation in the holy Eucharist incorporates us with Jesus Christ. In a word, he communicates to our soul and body, the same divine virtue which sanctifies his own.

To effect this ineffable union, he performs the most astounding prodigies. This sacrament is the combination of miracles so countless and so wonderful, that it surpasses all other manifestations of divine power, and may be called the crowning effort of omnipotence. It is the production no less of love than of power, and because that love is incomprehensible in its attributes, so is its master piece likewise. Can language more forcibly express the extent and depth of the tender love of Jesus than in the words, " He gives us his flesh to eat, and his blood to drink !"

The one he bestows under the form of bread ; the other under that of wine, to show us, that as bread and wine are the ordinary nourishment of the body, so should his flesh and blood be the habitual food of the soul. " My flesh," said he, " is meat indeed : and my blood is drink indeed : Except you eat the flesh of the Son of Man, and drink his blood, you shall not have life in you."— (St. John, vi. 54—56.) How could we have life, while separated from Him who is the only source of supernatural existence ? That life is conferred at Baptism, when sanctifying grace is bestowed, and after being unhappily lost, it may be recovered in the sacrament of penance ;

but the holy Eucharist alone imparts its plenitude, and soon would it be altogether forfeited, without participation in the adorable body and blood of Jesus Christ. The use of corporal food pre-supposes existence,—but that food preserves, invigorates, and supports the life previously enjoyed. The effects of the holy Eucharist on the life of the spirit, are precisely similar. To partake of it with advantage, the soul must be alive, but if she abstain from it, she will languish and die. " As I live by the Father," said Christ, " so he that eateth me, the same also shall live by me."—(St. John, vi. 58.) The Son receives his gifts from the Father, by whom he is be-gotten, and as he could not exist, if he would possibly be separated from him ; so neither will the soul retain life, if she neglect to partake of the body of Christ. The intimate and inse-parable union formed between the Father and the Son by eternal generation, is produced in a proportionate degree between Jesus Christ and the faithful, by participation in his adorable flesh. As the Father abides in the Son, and the Son in the Father, one by communication, the other by reception of the divine essence, so Jesus Christ abides in us, by giving us his body, and we abide in him by partaking of it. Does it seem difficult to yield implicit faith to expressions so forcible? Yet, the saints, the truly interior disciples of Christ believed them unhesitatingly. If we have never felt their truth, it is because we do not approach the august sacrament with

requisite dispositions; because we do not place
our happiness in habitual union with Jesus Christ.
Where is our love for him?   Alas! that love is
wholly centred in self.   Where is the similarity
between our sentiments and his?   Shall we venture to assert that our thoughts and judgments
are conformable to his?   Where is our recollection, our spirit of prayer?   Jesus Christ,
living by his Father, is ever absorbed in him;
are we absorbed in Jesus Christ from one communion to another?   If not, we do not live by
him, or at least our spiritual life is weak and
languishing.

The moment selected by Jesus Christ for the
institution of the holy Eucharist, was that immediately preceding his passion.   He was on the
eve of death, and like a tender parent, he provided by his last will, for the wants of his children.
What had he to bequeath to them?   He had
never shared this world's affluence; his garments, the only possession he could call his own,
were to become the property of his executioners.
What, then, had he to bequeath?   He gave
himself wholly and entirely to every individual
of the human race, thus to indemnify for the
privation of his sensible presence, the faithful
disciples from whom it was about to be withdrawn, as well as the generations to come, who
had never enjoyed its advantages.   His love
forbids him to forsake us; he will remain among
us to the end of time, substantially, although
concealed by the veil of faith.   We are not

merely to behold him corporally, but by a surpassing favour to receive him into our souls, and
that, not once alone, but every day of our existence, if we correspond with his intentions by
rendering ourselves worthy of so great a happiness. Surely the excess of love alone, could
suggest to the mind of the Incarnate God a
legacy like this !

Jesus Christ selected for the institution of the
most holy Eucharist, the period assigned by the
law for the solemn sacrifice of the Paschal lamb,
and he chose the hour of supper, the only repast
of which the ancients partook in common. His
motive in the first arrangement, I shall not now
advert to ; his design in the second, was to show
us, that, as to eat at one table, is a sign of unity
among men, so participation in this heavenly bread,
distributed in common to his apostles, and afterwards to the faithful, should tend to cement that
union, and to maintain the vigour of charity.

On this account, the celebration of the holy
mysteries, in which every individual participated,
was followed in the primitive ages by a repast,
of which all partook indiscriminately,—noble
and obscure, rich and poor, master and servant :
this repast was appropriately designated *agape*,
or the feast of charity. Even the pagan world
admired the mutual love of those first, fervent
Christians. Charity has grown cold among the
faithful, in proportion as their recourse to the
holy communion has become less frequent; its
true spirit is maintained only in communities and

families, wherein the holy table is frequented with fervour and assiduity.

There is an incessant demand for new forms of preparation for Communion, and devout methods of hearing Mass. These will never be found while sought only in books, for they must be established in the heart, and books are useful only as far as they tend to effect this object. Because a prayer-book was employed in early years, as a help to the discharge of these two essential duties, does it follow that the same assistance is to be always necessary, and no effort made to dispense with it? The best method with which I am acquainted, is the following, derived from the nature of the Eucharist itself.

In the adorable Eucharist, considered as a sacrifice, Jesus Christ offers himself and us to his Eternal Father; we have but to unite in that twofold oblation, adopting at the same time intentions and dispositions similar to his. The nature of those intentions and dispositions we are already conversant with. Let us render them personal, not by a multitude of varied acts, but by one act, most simple and intimate. Let us ask him to impart them to us; let us vigilantly preserve the spirit of holy recollection, and leave to his grace to suggest our interior occupation during the celebration of the holy mysteries. He requires that we avoid bringing to them minds pre-occupied by profane and distracting thoughts, and that by restraining the senses and imagination, we remove the two great sources of distraction. He will regulate the rest, if we place our trust in him. If at the commencement of Mass, we said with simplicity and earnest fervour, " Lord, since I am incapable of assisting worthily at the holy sacrifice enable me thyself to do so ;" I am convinced from experience that we should feel the beneficial effect of such faith and humility. Jesus Christ would then act in us ; he would instruct us in the holy silence of respect and love, and we should bring from the altar a strong impression of his grace, easily retained throughout the day.

In the holy Eucharist, considered as a sacrament, Jesus Christ gives himself to us in the plenitude of love, let us sincerely give ourselves to him in the same spirit. He burns with ardour to communicate himself to us ; let us cherish an equal desire to be united to him ; his delight is to be with us ; let ours be to remain with him. Many acts are not necessary for this ; the interior disposition suffices. If such be not our disposition, let us pray to Jesus Christ to bestow it. Let us calmly humble ourselves at the sad spectacle of our coldness and indifference ; let our preparation be an earnest intreaty that he would himself prepare us. Cannot his grace do so more effectually than our own most eager exertions ? And why not expect that it will ? Let our thanksgiving consist of docile submission to his interior inspirations, with silent love and adoration. We are never satisfied unless we feel the operation of our own ungoverned activity ; unless we experience certain sensible and consoling emotions, to excite which, we exert impetuous eagerness. We forget that true devotion can never spring from our own hearts; that we should await it with humility and confidence, and never desire it with a view to the gratification of self-love. We wish to feel satisfied with our Communions, whereas our only wish should be to content Jesus Christ. We should ever aim at identifying our satisfaction with his, and then our peace would be more deep, more solid, and more perfect, than we can now comprehend.

It is an excellent preparation for the interior life, to hear Mass, and dispose ourselves for Communion in the manner I now propose; repressing our own precipitate eagerness, and allowing unbounded freedom to the inspirations of Jesus Christ; having once attained an interior spirit, we shall acquit ourselves with abundant profit of these two essential duties of religion, solicitous only to submit to the operations of the Holy Ghost, and to obey his grace.

CHAPTER LIII.

The Passion of Jesus Christ pre-ordained in the eternal counsels.

It does not enter into my plan to enlarge on the details of the passion of Christ, which are to be found in numerous works, particularly that so extensively known under the title of the "Sufferings of Jesus." I shall merely touch on those points most calculated to reveal his interior dispositions, and more especially proposed to our imitation.

From the commencement of his public life, our divine Redeemer entailed on himself the envy and hatred of the Pharisees, priests, and doctors of the law, to whom his doctrine and his conduct were hateful, because a condemnation of their own. Their resolution to destroy him was quickly formed, and its execution delayed only because the "hour was not come."—(St. John, viii. 20.)

God had foreseen the malice and blindness of the Jews from eternity; conformably with that anticipated view, he had pre-ordained the sufferings to be endured by his divine Son for the glory of the Godhead, and the salvation of the human race, and those sufferings he had announced by his prophets. St. Peter formally declares this truth, in his first discourse to the Jews. "This same being delivered up by the determinate counsel and foreknowledge of God, you by the hands of wicked men have crucified and slain."—(Acts, ii. 23.) You would have had no power over him of yourselves. It was necessary that God should deliver him up to you, and this he resolved to do, notwithstanding his perfect knowledge of your evil intentions, aware of the benefit which would result from so great a crime. The prayer of the assembled faithful, after the Jewish counsel had forbidden the apostles to preach the name of Jesus, is thus worded, " There assembled together in this city against thy holy child Jesus whom thou hast anointed, Herod, and Pontius Pilate, with the gentiles and the people of Israel. To do what thy hand and thy counsel decreed to be done."—(Acts, iv. 27, 28.) In his second discourse to the Jews, St. Peter attributes to God himself " the fulfilment of those things which God had showed by the mouth of all the prophets, that his Christ should suffer."—(Ibid, iii. 18.) The Jews in satisfying their jealousy and rage, became unconscious instruments in the accomplishment of the divine designs. " This," said Jesus Christ, to the miscreants who seized his person, " this is your hour, and the power of darkness."—(St. Luke, xxii. 53.) Hitherto you have not dared to apprehend me, though you could easily have done so, because the hour appointed by my Father had not come. Now that it has arrived, exert, in concert with your instigators the demon, the authority allowed you by my heavenly Father. To Pilate, who boasted of his power to pardon or condemn him, he declared, " Thou shouldst not have any power against me, unless it were given thee from above." (St. John, xix. 11.) In the exercise of that power I recognize the will of God, and to that, I submit. To the disciples of Emmaus, he said, " Ought not Christ to have suffered these things, and so to enter into his glory ?" (St. Luke, xxiv. 26.) Why

ought he to have suffered? was it from impotence
to elude the pursuit of the Jews, who had determined on his destruction? No; he had already
frequently escaped their snares, and as he himself
assures us, he had but to invoke the aid of his
Father, who would have armed twelve legions of
angels in his defence. The necessity arose, not
from compulsion, but simply from his own generous resolution to drain the chalice presented to
him by his eternal Father.

It was of vast importance firmly to establish
this point, without which the meaning of the sacred
volume would not have been clearly apparent,
nor the connection of God's designs over Jesus
Christ fully developed. No event of our divine
Redeemer's life arose from hazard ; all were foreseen ; all pre-concerted. He was destined to be
the martyr of truth and charity ; to seal with his
blood the religion he came to establish; to receive
for his great mercies the return of heartless ingratitude, and thus to invest his sacrifice with a surpassing excellence, in which it would otherwise
have been deficient. It was ordained in the eternal counsels, that the Incarnate God should offer
to the Deity, the highest degree of glory within his
power to procure for it, and for this end, it was
requisite that his passion should be exactly what
it was—the outpouring of demoniac vengeance
and human fury ; the combination of extreme
suffering and unparalleled humiliation, including the treachery, the denial, and the flight of
his apostles, with a pang yet more intense than

any of these,—his interior dereliction by his Father, who exercised on him the rigorous justice due to the greatest of criminals. Thus, Deicide, the most atrocious crime ever perpetrated, gave occasion to the exercise of the most heroic virtue ever practised, and the most perfect homage which ever has been, or ever will be offered to the majesty of God.

Hence results a truth most comprehensive in its practical application, and which it is important we should fully understand; viz, that sin, although not willed, is foreseen and permitted by the Almighty; that it enters into the plan of his providence, and contributes to the accomplishment of his designs, for his honor, the good of his church, and our individual perfection. The passion of Jesus Christ clearly proves, that God makes use of sin to manifest his attributes and to promote his glory. If the sanctity of the Deity was outraged by the crime of the Jews, it shone with a glorious lustre after the sufferings of the Man-God had solemnly repaired the insults offered to it by our iniquities. If the rights of divine justice appear to have been set at nought, by the iniquitous sentence which doomed to death the most holy and innocent of men, it amply exercised its prerogatives and satisfied its claims, in the atonement of the spotless Lamb, who substituted himself for his guilty creatures, and became the voluntary ransom of insolvent debtors. If his mercy semed in a manner eclipsed on Calvary, where he appeared to forget and forsake his only Son, it displayed

its exhaustless riches, by generously and gratuit-
ously pardoning for his sake, the sinful race which
had rendered itself unworthy of his forgiveness. If
when we behold Jesus Christ expiring on the
cross, the victim of death and hell, it seems to us as
though the wisdom of God had miscalculated its
end, we shall behold the triumph of that wisdom on the day of the resurrection, when Christ
shall trample on the devil and death, tauntingly
applying to each the words of the prophet, " O
death, I will be thy death ; O hell, I will be thy
bite." (Osee. xiii. 14.) God having derived his
glory from the Deicide of the Jews, what other
species of iniquity is there which he will not render instrumental to its advancement? That glory
he will infallibly attain, either in this world or
the next. Let us have zeal for it; let us promote
it by every means in our power, but let us not
indulge anxious solicitude on the subject, as if
human efforts could mar its interests. Sinners,
who here below refuse to glorify God's mercy,
will assuredly hereafter glorify his justice.

With regard to the external trials and persecu-
tions of the Church, which it almost staggers our
faith to witness, we should remember that Jesus
Christ has purchased her by his blood, and that
as his spouse, she is entitled to no other fate than
his own. Like him, she must glorify God by her
sufferings, and then he will render her a partici-
pator in the triumphs of his Son. Her afflictions
have ultimately tended to her exaltation, even
here below ;—persecution has increased her sta-

bility, and heresy confirmed her faith; it has fallen, while she still stands erect: what she loses in one respect, she recovers in another, and, whenever her children have been least numerous, they have invariably been most fervent. The course of events seems sometimes to presage her downfal throughout a whole quarter of the globe, as for instance, when the torrent of infidelity which deluged France, appeared ready to pour its foaming waters over the face of Europe;—yet, however threatening the aspect of affairs, we may ever confidently rely on the promises of Christ to his chosen spouse, and without indulging vain speculations on the manner of their fulfilment, firmly believe that he will faithfully accomplish them, as he has invariably done, even at the most tempestuous periods of her existence. The elect shall be tried, but not one of them shall perish; to this the word of Jesus Christ is pledged.

Particular devotion to God's service, infallibly entails contradiction, calumny, injustice, and various trials from creatures; and that not only from the wicked, but even from the virtuous, or at least, those reputed such. Is this to be wondered at, after Jesus Christ became the victim of false devotees seated on the chair of Moses? All such trials are foreseen by God; permitted as regards their authors; willed, as regards their object. They are destined for his glory and our sanctification, which they will infallibly promote, if we take Jesus Christ for the model of our sentiments and conduct. Nothing but our own opposition can render the designs of God abortive, and provided we co-operate with those designs, the sins of others, far from impeding, will contribute to our perfection: their reprobation may become the source of our salvation. How consoling this reflection!

In fine, our own sins, the remembrance of which so often fills us with despondency and alarm, may become, through the grace of God, a means of our sanctification; he has permitted them with no other view. They are destined to draw forth the display of his great mercy; to produce in us great confidence in his goodness, affectionate gratitude for his benefits, with humility and distrust of self: they are likewise intended to stimulate us to those heroic acts of virtue, necessary for their expiation or reparation. How many illustrious saints were once great sinners! How many of the Jews who took an active part in the death of Christ, were afterwards converted, and formed the church of Jerusalem, the most perfect of all churches? Their affectionate repentance contributed immeasurably to their sanctification; why should not ours lead to the same result, provided it be equally sincere? The distance between a great sinner and a saint, is often less than between a tepid and a fervent soul. All depends upon the sincerity and generosity of the heart, and the measure of its correspondence with grace. It is a dreadful misfortune to offend God, but it is in our own power to convert the calamity into a blessing.

CHAPTER LIV.

The sacrifice of Christ was perfectly voluntary.

THE sacrifice of Jesus Christ would have been essentially deficient, if it had not been perfectly free. He was the Lord of life, and absolutely exempt from the dominion of death, which owed its origin to sin alone. Union with the Divinity, had imparted immortality, as well as impeccabilty to his sacred humanity, which was no less free from the penalty of pain, than from the law of death, and could suffer only by the express choice of its own will. To opprobrium and humiliation, Jesus Christ had as little claim as to corporal suffering; union with the Word had elevated his soul and body to a dignity incomparably superior to that of the blessed spirits; therefore he was on the contrary, worthy of supreme honor.

" He was then offered," as the prophet declares, "because it was his own will." (Isa. liii. 7.) To repair his Father's glory, and redeem the human race, he need not have submitted to a violent death, preceded by unparalleled torments and ignominy; a prayer, a tear, a sigh, a wish would have sufficed. The further manifestation of his zeal for these ends, proceeded wholly from love of his Father and love of us; and this generous love it was, which rendered his oblation infinitely precious in the sight of God; this, which should render it infinitely dear to the heart of man. " Therefore the Father doth love

me," said he, " because I lay down my life that
I may take it again. No man taketh it from me:
but I lay it down of myself, and I have power to
lay it down; and I have power to take it up again.
This commandment have I received of my Father."
(St. John, x. 17, 18.) He has not imposed a precept, but merely testified a wish: he has declared
his will, and I have cordially submitted to its decrees. It is because I love him, that I obey his
ordinances, and for the same reason it is, that he
cherishes me so tenderly in return.

Interior souls, how instructive is the lesson
which Jesus here conveys to you! Many points
of the evangelical morality are only of counsel and
perfection; among these may be ranked the interior life itself, with the practices it includes. Salvation, and even a certain degree of sanctity are
attainable without it; but when God gives a decided vocation for it, should not this intimation of
his desires suffice to a soul which prefers his will
before all things beside, and proposes to herself
to imitate the perfection of the sacrifice of Jesus
Christ? Would she evince the love she owes to
God, would she deserve his special predilection,
if the anticipation of difficulty, subjection, and
mortification deterred her from meeting his advances—if she were ungenerous enough to argue,
" God desires, but he does not command; I
shall not endanger my salvation by refusing to
obey the grace which attracts me onwards?"
Let us leave sentiments and conclusions like these
to selfish souls, who will not renounce themselves

to please God—to mercenary souls, who serve him from dread of punishment or desire of reward, but never view him as a Father worthy to be obeyed from affection. Let us rather rejoice at having adopted a line of conduct more worthy of the God we adore, more conformable to the example of the Redeemer we honour, more advantageous to ourselves in every sense; and let us incessantly thank Him for having inspired and strengthened us to embrace it.

These sentiments are especially appropriate to those persons whom God calls to the religious state. The principal merit of the engagement contracted by the religious vows is, its entire freedom; for, in granting a vocation, God leaves the soul at liberty to follow it or not. To gain the will, he frequently suggests motives connected with personal interest, such as the desire of securing salvation and the fear of forfeiting that all-important blessing in the world. But the love of God is almost invariably the crowning argument which terminates irresolution, and, provided the duties of the state embraced be afterwards discharged with an interior spirit, love ultimately becomes the pervading principle of existence. Thus, the sacrifice of religious persons resembles that of Jesus Christ only as far as it is accompanied by similar dispositions; and its sole claim to the title of a sacrifice, consists in the freedom of will with which it is offered.

But the sacrifice which bears the closest resemblance to the oblation of Jesus Christ, is that of certain privileged souls on whom the Almighty has peculiar views and for whom he destines extraordinary trials. Having first inspired them with the resolution of generous and unreserved devotion to his love, he gradually disposes them for his designs, which he at length reveals, by presenting the cross they are required to carry and asking their consent to bear the burden. Notwithstanding the extreme repugnance of nature, they finally yield to grace ; they embrace the cross, on which, if they are faithful, they have the happiness of expiring, at least in a moral sense—dying to self, and then mystically rising to a renewed existence. A sacrifice of this description is usually accompanied by external crosses, such as corporal suffering, persecution, calumny, contempt, and humiliation. Sometimes the very demons conspire against the servants of God, inflicting incredible torments both on soul and body. As these sufferings have been previously proposed and accepted, at least in a general manner, their privileged objects are in one sense entitled to say with Jesus Christ, that the Father loves them, because they have voluntarily immolated themselves as victims to his glory, never uttering a complaint under the crucifying operation, but resolutely clinging to the altar, until the perfect consummation of the sacrifice.

CHAPTER LV.

Agony of Jesus Christ in the Garden of Olives.

THE first scene of Christ's Passion occurred within his own soul, and was witnessed only by his Father. Scarcely had he entered the Garden of Olives with his disciples, and withdrawn to a short distance from them to pray, than he was seized with terror, desolation, and mortal sadness. He confided the secret of his anguish, to his apostles Peter, James, and John, and conjured them to watch with him, as if he had stood in need of their assistance. Independently of many other convincing arguments which might be adduced to support the point, his divine discourse after the last supper, sufficiently proves that these sensations were supernatural in their origin; that the impression they produced on his sacred humanity, was owing to the subtraction of the sensible support of the Divinity, and that the measure of violence they were allowed to attain, was regulated solely by his own will. He who had so often comforted and encouraged his apostles, now fell prostrate before them, overwhelmed with grief and terror. Was it the anticipation of approaching death which thus affected him? In any one else, similar emotions might naturally be attributed to that cause; but how could it be so with him, who had forewarned his disciples of the excruciating torments and ignominious death in reserve for him, assuring them that his fate was not one to be deplored? Undoubtedly, those agonizing impressions were not produced by the view of his humiliations, for he had ever eagerly desired the moment of his passion, and he welcomed its arrival with joy. The divine fortitude he displayed throughout the awful scene, proves how far his courage surpassed his pangs.

Other causes combined to create the feelings which oppressed his soul in the garden of Olives; to produce the terrific struggle which convulsed his frame; the incomprehensible agony which the strengthening presence of an angel was required to calm; the sweat of blood, which flowed from every pore, and trickled in large and heavy drops to the ground.

First, all the sins of the universe, which had become his own, presented themselves to his mind, in colours more vivid than they had ever worn before; their number and enormity oppressed him with agony; their heinous guilt covered him with confusion; and as a criminal, he submitted to the chastisement they merited. Secondly, he beheld his Father armed with the terrors of Almighty vengeance, at one time averting from him his eyes, at another casting on him a glance of indignation; he saw his arm raised to strike, and he felt that he was to be treated as an object of malediction. Thirdly, he forsaw the ingratitude of men, who would derive no benefit from his sufferings, but on the contrary, convert them

into a source of reprobation. Many more were
the sorrows which pierced his heart. Those
already enumerated, would have sufficed to deprive him a thousand times of existence, had he
not exerted his omnipotence to support his
sinking frame, and sustain life until all should
be consummated.

Feeble and exhausted as he was, he passed
nearly three hours in prayer, and interrupted it
only to awake his sleeping disciples. Prostrate
on the earth, he exclaimed, " My Father, if it
be possible, let this chalice pass from me. Nevertheless not as I will, but as thou wilt."—
(St. Matt. xxvi. 39.) The inexplicably bitter
ingredient of that chalice, that which mingled its
bitterness with each drop of the loathsome
draught, was his dereliction by his Father. How,
indeed, could he resign himself to be forsaken
by the Father who possessed his undivided love?
the Father who had ever reposed in him his
complacency, which, though now apparently
withdrawn, was in reality still centred in him?
To understand the reluctance of Jesus Christ to
expire thus abandoned by his Father, we should
know and love God, as Jesus Christ knew and
loved him. Yet he submitted to this surpassing
trial, asking every time he prayed, that his Father's will, not his own, might be accomplished.
St. Luke further observes, that he redoubled his
prayer, as the violence of his agony increased.

Personal experience of interior suffering, can
alone convey an idea of the Saviour's agony in

the garden. Generous as may have been our consecration to God, and unreserved our anticipated acceptance of tribulation, yet—when the blow has really fallen, when suffering has attained a certain degree of intensity, when the support of natural courage fails, when the operation of grace, although real, becomes imperceptible,—there necessarily arises a species of agony, caused by the rebellion of the passions, and the revolt of nature, unable to submit without a struggle to its destruction. The soul is subjected to this painful ordeal, only to impress her with profound humility, and to convince her that her strength comes from God alone. In this violent struggle, although she seems to herself to repulse with horror, the cross she had embraced with love; although she is a prey to dreadful temptations, she must not imagine that her submission is at an end, because she exclaims, "Father, if it be possible, let this chalice pass from me," but let her add with Jesus Christ, "nevertheless, not as I will, but as thou wilt." Two wills are at that moment in operation within her; the will of nature, which may be more correctly designated a blind instinct, than a will; and the will of grace, which may be termed a superior will, ever united to the will of God, from which it would not for any earthly consideration be severed. The influence of this superior will is not always discernible, for its action does not come under the senses, and moreover, the soul is forbidden the support she might derive from reflection on her state. But the existence of that will is incontestibly proved by her inviolable fidelity to grace, and by her unhesitating rejection of all alleviation of her sufferings.

Jesus Christ submitted to this extreme of weakness, and this apparent interior rebellion, that under a similar trial, his servants may never yield to the desponding thought that God is offended in consequence. No; he is not offended, for the trial originates with him, and is intended to exhibit the power of his grace, and to deprive us of all confidence in self.—Again, Jesus Christ submitted to it, that experience might inspire him with compassion for our weakness, and render him more prompt to succour us. Of this, St. Paul himself assures us in his epistle to the Hebrews, (ii. 17, 18.)

The repugnances of nature, and the revolt of the passions should not excite alarm ; the struggle is but temporary ; a simple act of submission suffices to calm the troubled waters. The tranquillity of the soul suffers no real interruption ; the consoling impressions of heavenly peace are even sensible at intervals. If our own efforts prove insufficient to subdue our mental agitation, we should at least derive comfort from the decision of an enlightened director, whom God himself has qualified to understand our interior dispositions ; and who is a better judge of our case than we can be, because enjoying the tranquillity of mind we have lost. By submission of judgment, faith, and obedience, we shall not only escape uninjured from the storm, but even derive benefit, from exposure to its rigours. If, owing to the ignorance and prejudicial counsels of their spiritual guides, some souls are borne down by its violence, a far greater number lose courage, and retrace their steps in consequence of obstinate adherence to their own opinions.

CHAPTER LVI.

Of the treachery of Judas, and the meekness of Jesus Christ.

ONE of the deepest sorrows of Jesus, must undoubtedly have resulted from the treachery of Judas, which formed the opening scene of his passion. The Jews panted for possession of his person, but they feared to seize him while surrounded by the people, from whose reverence for him as a prophet, they anticipated open resistance to their designs. Judas offered for a small sum of money to deliver him to them at night, and this infamous resolution he executed with the assistance of a troop of men, armed with swords and clubs, as if prepared to apprehend a robber. To guard against the mistakes likely to arise from the obscurity of night, it was arranged that Jesus should be identified by a pre-concerted signal,—that signal, a kiss from his ungrateful apostle!

We cannot too deeply meditate on the charity and meekness displayed by Jesus Christ towards the traitor, as well before the commission of his crime, as at the moment of its completion, and after its consummation. Previously to selecting Judas for one of his apostles,—nay, from all eternity, he knew that he would betray him; yet he admitted him not the less to his society and intimate familiarity; he laboured not the less to enlighten his mind, and to form him to the evangelical ministry. He ever treated him with the utmost tenderness, and even granted him a particular evidence of his confidence, by intrusting him with the money destined for his own support and that of his disciples, as well as for the use of the poor. Independently of these external marks of kindness and love, it cannot be doubted that he interiorly visited his heart by the powerful impressions of grace. It was with a view to touch that obdurate heart, that he discovered to him his perfect knowledge of its evil dispositions. " Have not I chosen you twelve :" said he to his apostles, "and one of you is a devil?"—(St. John, vi. 71.) What a lesson these words should have conveyed to Judas! At the last supper, he washed his feet, as well as those of the remaining apostles, and according to the general opinion of the holy fathers, founded on the sacred text, he gave him his flesh to eat, and his blood to drink. Then it was, that for the last time, he endeavoured to dissuade him from his crime. " I know," said he, " whom I have chosen : but

that the Scripture may be fulfilled, ' He that
eateth bread with me, shall lift up his heel
against me.' " A moment after, " he was troubled
in spirit," at the thought of the crime Judas was
about to commit, and he declared, with his usual
asseveration, " Amen, amen, I say to you, one of
you shall betray me."—(St. John, xiii. 18, et seq.)
The consternation of the apostles ; the apprehension of each least this prediction might regard
him personally ; their earnest inquiry on the
subject, and the audacious demand of Judas, all
prove that hitherto the Saviour had never directed
suspicion towards him. What kind consideration
for the reputation of a wretch, about to con-
summate a crime, which his divine Master could
so easily have prevented ! He informed Judas,
it is true, that he knew him to be the traitor,
but that with so much caution that the rest did
not observe it. To St. John alone, who at that
moment reposed on his bosom, he distinctly
pointed him out, saying in a low voice, " He it
is to whom I shall reach bread dipped." This
last mark of love having produced no impression,
Jesus said to him, " that which thou dost, do
quickly." The direction was unintelligible to
the rest, and after having received it, " Judas
went out immediately."—(Ibid, 26, et seq.)

A few hours after, he entered the garden of
Olives with his armed band, and approached
Jesus, saying, " Hail Rabbi : and he kissed him."
The Saviour did not reject the treacherous em-
brace, but merely said with incomparable meek-

ness, " Friend, whereto art thou come?"—(St.
Matt. xxvi. 50.) Judas, dost thou betray the
Son of Man with a kiss?"—(St. Luke, xxii. 48.)
What heart but that of Judas, could have resisted
such an appeal?

The next day, " seeing that he was condemned,
repenting himself, he brought back the thirty
pieces of silver to the chief priests and ancients,
saying: I have sinned in betraying innocent
blood."—(Ibid, xxvii. 3, 4.)   What but the grace
of Jesus Christ inspired that repentance?   He
was still willing to extend forgiveness to the
unhappy sinner, and he would have done so, had
not Judas added to his already enormous crime,
the double guilt of despair and suicide. We have
here a faithful representation of the efforts daily
made by Jesus Christ, to rescue sinners, who
impelled by despair, rush on with determined
obstinacy to destruction.

Sensibility is among the most excellent of
natural endowments, but while on the one hand
the source of the heart's sweetest joys, it is on
the other, that of its most bitter emotions. When
pride and self-love arouse it into activity, how
lively and durable is the resentment it excites
for certain evidences of unkind feeling, certain
galling insults!   How difficult it renders the
pardon of such offences!   Jesus felt the hein-
ousness of Judas's treachery, more poignantly
than any human being could have done, but
although it signed his death doom, his regret for
it arose, not from personal considerations, but

from the offence against his Father, and the reprobation of the unfortunate being of whom he
declared that " it were better for him, if that
man had not been born. The Son of Man
indeed goeth," said he, " as it is written of him :
but wo to that man, by whom the Son of Man
shall be betrayed."—(St. Matt. xxvi. 24.) I have
foreseen and accepted my fate ; I do not apprehend it on my own account, but I deplore the
misfortune of him by whom it is to be consummated.

The soul unreservedly devoted to God, and
destined for the honour of peculiar conformity
with Jesus Christ, must expect infidelity and
treachery from her friends, confidants, and spiritual children. But for this trial, God previously prepares her, and as, during its continuance, he insensibly diverts her attention from
herself, she views it merely in its connection with
God, and with those who unhappily offend him
by inflicting it. She has consequently no difficulty in pardoning those who afflict her ; in
praying for them ; in rendering them service,
and in granting them evidences of kindly feeling.
This degree of perfection she attains, after multiplied tribulations and sacrifices have laid prostrate the pride and self-love once so active.
The serenity of her countenance, and calmness
of her deportment, seem to indicate insensibility ;
but very different is the reality :—grace, far from
destroying, refines and perfects feeling, substituting the interests of God and man, for its

original all engrossing object,—self. Why should
we deplore those occurrences, which, tested by
the solid principles of religion, are not a real
misfortune? And why, on the contrary, should
we not lament those, which involve an offence to
God, and a dreadful calamity to our neighbour?

The generality of Christians are under the
impression, that dispositions so perfect are unat-
tainable: the reason is, that they are accustomed
to direct their sensibility to themselves alone,
and that the love of enemies, and pardon of
injuries, is in their estimation the most difficult
point of Christian morality. Some even pronounce it impracticable, and so it is for them,
while the wound of their pride bleeds freshly.
It would not be so, had they early understood
the necessity of acquiring an interior spirit, and
conquering pride, and self-love. Devotees, whose
piety consists in external practices, and self-reputed
spiritualists, who are ignorant of the true meaning
of the word, are invariably more sensitive to
annoyances, than Christians of an ordinary stamp;
it needs not the treachery of Judas, to inflict on
them a hopeless wound.

Those who aspire to perfection, and who are
obliged by their peculiar position or profession,
to give to others the example of perfect imitation of Jesus Christ, should cautiously guard
against the slightest emotions of sensibility, animosity, and resentment; they should never nur-
ture mortified feeling, by revolving in mind, or
confidentially imparting to others, their real or

imaginary grounds of complaint ; they should on the contrary, crush those feelings at their birth ; they should subdue self, on trifling and continually recurring occasions, in order that they may have grace to conquer on others more important and more rare. How shall we pardon insults, contempt, and injurious treatment, if we indulge so much sensibility about an inadvertent remark, or a slight want of attention ? Can we expect to live in society without encountering many annoyances which must be mutually overlooked ? And where shall we find the meekness required for Judases, if we have none for persons, whom we can tax at most, with trivial breaches of charity ?

CHAPTER LVII.

Denial of St. Peter.

THE denial of St. Peter, which God permitted to humble that apostle, and inspire him with salutary distrust of himself, is a source of much useful instruction. Of all the disciples of Christ, Peter was the most devoted to his person, the most zealous for his interests, the most prompt in testifying his love. Of this, the gospel furnishes many instances, which it is needless to enumerate. His sensible fervour, founded on grace, but also mingled with natural character, had engendered a presumptuous belief that his attachment to his Master exceeded that of the other apostles, and that stronger than his associates, he would not sink like them under temptation.

" All you shall be scandalized in me, this night," said Jesus, to his apostles, " For it is written ; I will strike the shepherd, and the sheep of the flock shall be dispersed." Peter, too much carried away by the impetuosity of his zeal, to reflect that he contradicted both the words of Jesus Christ, and the declaration of Scripture, presumed to answer, " Although all shall be scandalized in thee, I will never be scandalized." His rash presumption drew on him the personal prediction, " Amen I say to thee, that in this night, before the cock crow, thou wilt deny me thrice." Unabashed by the reply, he once again ventured to contradict his Master, and to assert, "though I should die with thee, I will not deny thee."—(St. Matt. xxvi. 31, et seq.)

The ardour of St. Peter lasted until the seizure of Christ, when he drew his sword to defend him, but soon after it vanished, and like the rest, he fled. He had afterwards the weakness to deny him three times, protesting with oaths that he knew not the man. It may be inferred from the narrative of St. Luke, that this scene occurred in the very presence of Jesus Christ, who from the position he occupied, could both see and hear his apostle. After the third denial, " the Lord turning looked on Peter."—(St. Luke, xxii. 61.) How efficacious that look, and how powerful

the interior grace by which it was accompanied!
It penetrated to the heart of St. Peter, who
overwhelmed with confusion and sorrow, with-
drew in haste, to shed bitter tears over his sin.

That glance of the Saviour, while it sealed
his pardon, confirmed his repentance. For life
he bewailed his crime, and the presumption
whence it had arisen. Had he been less presumptuous, God would not have permitted so
dire a fall in the prince of the apostles and head
of the church; but his spiritual malady required
a severe remedy, which became to him the source
of many great advantages. His love was rendered more tender, solid, and grateful, and at
the same time, more humble and vigilant: of
this he gave proof, when after the resurrection
Jesus Christ required him to retract his triple
denial by a triple protestation of love. To the
first inquiry, " Simon, son of John, lovest thou
me more than these?" he simply replied, " Yea,
Lord, thou knowest that I love thee,"—(St.
John, xxi. 15,) without asserting that his love
surpassed that of the remaining apostles. He
was grieved at the repetition of the question,
fearing, not that Jesus doubted of his tenderness,
but that his own protestations of love were deficient in sincerity. On no occasion did he say,
" I love thee," but " thou knowest that I love
thee," appealing to the omniscience of Jesus
Christ for the sincerity of his protestations of
love, rather than trusting to the testimony of his
own heart.

Truly worthy of admiration is the mercy displayed by Jesus to St. Peter! He foretold his fall, that distrusting himself, he might avoid its occasion; or that if inevitably placed in that occasion, he might have recourse to Him, who alone can support human weakness. For the prediction of Christ was conditional, not absolute; it was founded on the supposition that St. Peter would persevere in his expressed sentiments, and expose himself to a temptation which he was quite at liberty to avoid. Having once fallen so low, the apostle would never have risen again, without the special aid of Jesus Christ. While the enemies of the Saviour were conspiring his destruction, bringing forward false witnesses, proclaiming him worthy of death for having assumed the title of the Son of God, and overwhelming him with insults and outrages,—insensible to his own interests he thought but of his cherished disciple; he cast on him a glance more eloquent, more impressive, more pathetic than words; he pierced his heart with sorrow, and drew from that deep source of human emotion, a fountain of bitter tears. After his resurrection, he treated him with renewed tenderness; he distinguished him from the other apostles by a particular apparition; he conversed familiarly with him, without once reproachfully alluding to his fault, and after having inspired him to offer a reparation dictated by love, he confided to him the care of his lambs and sheep, and foretold the description of death by which he should one day glorify

God. His tender kindness to sincere converts
has on all occasions been precisely similar. Do
we thus make the first advance towards those
who have injured us ? Do we endeavour to gain
their hearts by cordial kindness and substantial
services ? Alas, no! And yet, how much we
ourselves require that Jesus Christ should anticipate our necessities, and pursue us in our wan-
derings ? Should not his charity be the model
of ours ?

The example of St. Peter's fall should serve
as a salutary warning to beginners in the spiritual
life. Like the apostle, they are but novices in
the service of God : in the first fervour of sensible love, they feel a courage, which inclines
them to presume on their strength ; to imagine
themselves capable of splendid achievements and
heroic sacrifices ; to suppose that no temptation
can conquer, no obstacle arrest them : all things
seem possible, nay easy, to their fervour. When
they read or hear of the repugnance endured,
and protracted struggles undergone by sanctified
souls before their acceptance of the cross, they
feel great surprise, not understanding the possibility of refusing any thing to God. But soon,
their ideas and language will undergo an alteration. As yet, they have had no experience of
their weakness; they are ignorant of its existence;
they have tasted only sweets, and consolations,
and with David they " say in their abundance, I
shall never be moved."—(Ps. xxix. 7.) But if God
should even partially avert his countenance; if

aridity should succeed to sensible fervour ; if the least storm should arise ; if a slight temptation is to be surmounted, or an emotion of human respect resisted ; if their resolution is tested, not by the frowns of authority, but by a word from a slave, their courage evaporates, their determination wavers, nature trembles, they are on the point of betraying the cause of God, and happy are they, if they do not in fact betray it. O man, how weak thou art! But how strong thou wouldst be, if thou didst not imagine thyself so! Do not rely on the impressions produced by a transient grace, and never form an opinion on your dispositions, until your ardour has cooled. Distrust of self should prompt you to avoid occasions of sin ; but if you are inevitably exposed to them, you should humbly implore, and confidently rely on God's assistance. Never seek the cross, which will surely come uninvoked. Seen from afar, in a moment of fervour, it appears so sweet and attractive, that you invite it by your desires ; whereas viewed more closely, under your ordinary state of feeling, it will assume a terrific and revolting aspect. There is much difference, said a holy and experienced soul, between sacrificing life in words, at the foot of the altar, and renouncing it in reality at the foot of the scaffold. How often have we said to God, with St. Peter, " I will lay down my life for thee," and yet afterwards refused him a trifle, a mere nothing! He is not deceived by our protestations ; neither should we suffer ourselves to be deluded by them; we shall not make so many, when we have learned to know ourselves. After the descent of the Holy Ghost, St. Peter exhibited superhuman fortitude, yet, not one word or feeling indicative of presumption ever again escaped him.

CHAPTER LVIII.

Silence of Jesus Christ before his judges.

WERE it my intention to write for the instruction of the worldling, I would accompany Jesus Christ in his various transitions from one judgment seat to another; I would follow him to the tribunal of the Jews, where prejudice and passion pronounced his condemnation; to that of Herod, where impiety scoffed at him as a fool; to that of Pilate, where policy sacrificed acknowledged innocence to human respect, and I would prove that in all ages, but especially in our own, Jesus Christ and his doctrine have been and are condemned by the prejudice, passion, impiety, libertinism, interest, or policy of the world. But as this subject more appropriately belongs to the chair of truth, I shall leave it to the preachers of God's word, and merely reserve for myself a few observations on the conduct of our Redeemer in presence of his accusers and judges.

The priests, scribes, and ancients, with their president, Caiphas, had long since pronounced the death warrant of Jesus Christ in heart and desire, and only sought to conceal the manifest injustice of the sentence under a legal formality. They accordingly suborned false witnesses, whose evidence proved contradictory. At last, two appeared, who accused him of having applied to the temple, the remark really referring to his own person; that if it were destroyed, he would rebuild it in three days. Hereupon the High Priest inquired why he made no reply to these accusations, but he still maintained silence. He could easily have embarrassed his accusers, and undoubtedly he would have spoken had he recognized in his judges a principle of uprightness and equity, or a desire of necessary instruction. But he knew that bent as they were on his destruction, any defence would have been useless, therefore he silently bore the imputation of crimes, of which He saw they were determined at all hazards to convict him.

Among Christians, and even among devout persons, many may be met, ever ready to censure the interior life, and its votaries. From the nature of their observations on the subject; from the strange intermixture of calumny and exaggeration which forms the peculiar character of those observations; from the high tone they assume, and the obstinacy with which they repel all attempts at explanation, it may easily be inferred that their prejudice is violent and firmly fixed. With persons of this description, silence is the only alternative.

We must allow them to decry the spiritual life with those who profess it, and even suffer them to include ourselves personally in the condemnation, should we be cited before them. We must refrain from any attempt at our own justification, for this would tend only to inflame their anger and increase their guilt. The defence of the divine interests seem sometimes to involve a necessity for breaking silence ; but were those interests apparently ever compromised to so great an extent as in the case of Jesus Christ ? Yet he opened not his mouth, because his silence, with its attendant consequences, was essential to the reparation of God's glory. Let us imitate that silence, even at the risk of forfeiting reputation and life.

No sooner had the high priest commanded Jesus, in the name of the living God, to declare if he were the Son of God, than he unhesitatingly revealed the truth. He acknowledged the claims of lawfully constituted authority, and evinced his respect for it by replying; he equally asserted the unimpeachable rights of the holy truth, by bearing testimony to it, although aware that the death of a blasphemer would be the award of his answer. Thus we learn that if the example of Christ sometimes imposes silence on his followers, it equally obliges them on other occasions to declare their sentiments openly, as, for instance, when interrogated by lawful authority, or on matters connected with the advantage of religion and morality. Neither the evident malice of the interrogator's intention, nor the personal detriment likely to accrue from the avowal, should then deter the disciple of Christ from intrepidly confessing the truth, deeming it an honour to be immolated in its defence.

Herod, an impious and voluptuous prince, who had imbrued his guilty hands in the blood of St. John the Baptist, had long desired to see Jesus, not to derive instruction or practical benefit from his lessons, but merely from curiosity to look on so remarkable an individual, to hear his words, and, if possible, to witness one of his far-famed miracles. He proposed many questions to Jesus, all prompted by a heartless love of exciting amusement, and precisely of the character to be expected from an infidel, destitute alike of religion, morality, and humanity. But Jesus deigned him no reply, because perfectly indifferent as to what opinion he might adopt concerning him. Of what consequence indeed was the sentence of a judge such as he? Would not the pardon sealed by his lips amount in truth to little less than an insult? Herod and his courtiers having amply gratified their taste for barbarous sport at the expense of the Redeemer, sent him back to Pilate invested with a public mark of their scorn, the white garment appropriate to a fool.

All who openly profess adherence to the example and doctrine of Jesus Christ must be prepared to rank as fools in the estimation of infidels and libertines, and patiently submit to their contempt. It is not advisable to enter into their arguments, or answer their captious questions, for in proposing them, they have no other end in view than to surprise their unsuspecting victims into discussions which may afford ground for the ridicule in which they so much delight. When divine things are made the subject of raillery, silence is generally speaking the safest refuge; the construction to which that silence is liable, should be set at nought. Happy they who are found worthy thus to share the opprobrium of Jesus Christ!

Pilate, to whose judgment the Jews were compelled to appeal, they themselves no longer possessing control over the law of life and death, clearly discerned the innocence of the reputed criminal, and easily traced the popular desire for his destruction to its true source—malice and envy. Having heard their accusations, he declared that they involved no cause of death. He exerted his ingenuity to save Jesus Christ, and, to effect this purpose, he first placed him in competition with the notorious malefactor Barabbas, and then condemned him to be scourged. But he was weak and politic; he trembled for his reputation with Cæsar, should he discharge a man who declared himself king; and finding that the Jews persisted in demanding his death, he resigned him to their power, first washing his hands, and proclaiming himself guiltless of the just man's blood.

Jesus knew the Roman governor to be upright, though weak; therefore, in answer to his inquiry, " Art thou the king of the Jews ?" (St. Matt. xxvii. 11,) he unhesitatingly informed him that he was, but that his kingdom was not of this world, thus preparing the way for Pilate's further instruction, in case he pleased to avail himself of the opportunity. "For this was I born," he added, "and for this came I into the world, that I should give testimony to the truth. Every one that is of the truth heareth my voice." (St. John, xviii. 37.) To a pagan, the words were unintelligible, but for that very reason it would have been only natural to ask their explanation. Pilate carelessly inquired, "What is truth?" (Ibid. 38,) and, without waiting for the reply, which would have shed supernatural light on his benighted mind, he abruptly left Jesus, to assure the Jews once more of his innocence. This was Pilate's first fault, and the fatal source of the many that followed it. Jesus was desirous to impart his grace to him ; the first ray of heavenly light had already beamed on his understanding ; gradually it would have burst into brilliancy, had the conversation been pursued, but, unhappily, Pilate interrupted it, and rendered himself unworthy of its future renewal. It was immediately after this first interview that he placed the Saint of saints in competition with the malefactor Barabbas, leaving it at the option of the Jews to release one or the other, and then condemned Jesus to a cruel scourging. Pilate's intention was, no doubt, a good one, yet no intention, however upright, could excuse two such flagrant acts of injustice. He should have adopted the more successful expedient of determined firmness, aware, as he must have been, that

passion becomes importunate, precisely in proportion as its unlawful demands are acceded to.
Vainly did he seek to arouse the compassion of
the Jews for the patient victim of their barbarity ;
that feeling was now banished from their hearts,
and with renewed vehemence they exclaimed,
" Crucify him, crucify him."—(St. John, xix 6.)
And when he bade them decide the point themselves, as he saw no guilt in him, they replied,
" We have a law ; and according to the law he
ought to die, because he made himself the son of
God." (Ibid. 7.) This was in their estimation
the real crime of the Redeemer.

These words must have recalled to Pilate the
previous observations of Christ, and led him to
surmise that the speaker was something more than
an ordinary mortal. The impression they produced was one of lively apprehension. Re-
entering the pretorium, he asked Jesus, " Whence
art thou ?" but Jesus gave him no answer, for he
merited none after his recent abuse of the light
vouchsafed him, otherwise the question would
have led to an exposition of the truth, by affording
Jesus Christ an opportunity of explaining whence
and why he had come on earth, and of revealing
both the mysteries of his eternal generation, and
the object of his temporal mission. Pilate asked
with surprise, " Speakest thou not to me ?
Knowest thou not that I have power to crucify
thee, and I have power to release thee ?" He
could not understand that a man whose life was
at his mercy, should evince so little desire to pro-

pitiate his clemency, and so great indifference for self-preservation, as to refuse him a reply. Actuated by compassion for the timid judge, who stood on the brink of eternal ruin, Jesus spoke once again, for the last time, and in a strain well calculated to excite serious reflection. " Thou shouldst not have any power against me, unless it were given thee from above; therefore he that hath delivered me to thee hath the greatest sin." You are convinced of my innocence, and unacquainted with my person, yet, through human respect, you are about to sentence me to death. In this you are culpable, but less so than those who, through malice and envy, have delivered me into your hands, and who know me not, only because they have obstinately closed their eyes against the light. As regards your power over me, it is given you from above, nor are you free to use it at your option. How irresistibly impressed must Pilate have been by such God-like firmness, such superhuman dignity, such total indifference for life, such cool contempt for a punishment at once agonizing and ignominious! Once more he desired to rescue the just one, but he had not resolution to encounter the unfailing argument of the Jews, " If thou release this man thou art not Cæsar's friend. For whosoever maketh himself a king, speaketh against Cæsar. We have no king but Cæsar."—(St. John, xix. 9, 10, 11, 12, 15.)

The true disciples of Jesus have daily occasion to struggle against that insidious enemy of the soul—human respect ; but, under this trial of their constancy, God never fails to impart his fortitude and wisdom to those who are ready to sacrifice all things for the defence of truth. Of this the heroism of the martyrs is a striking proof. As Christians, they deemed it their duty to submit like their divine Master to a death of torture, preferably to a renunciation of their faith. Their heavenly words, inspired by the Holy Ghost, and still more, their dauntless courage under excruciating torments, utterly confounded their judges, who, while convinced of their innocence, generally condemned them through servile respect for imperial edicts, and abject deference to popular prejudice. Although the terrors of persecution have given place to the mild reign of Christianity, how often does human respect still lead to public injustice, as well as individual resistance to grace ! How many souls has it plunged into eternal woe ! how many pious projects and saintly resolutions has it rendered nugatory ! If not always an impediment to salvation, it is generally an obstacle to perfection ; it is equally the enemy of the worldling and the recluse. The gospel precept requires that we conceal our virtuous deeds from men, never doing good in order to attract their observation ; but neither should the desire of their friendship, nor the apprehension of their enmity, deter us from executing all that duty demands, and grace inspires. We should openly pursue the path of rectitude, proclaiming our sentiments if needful, and never betraying the cause of God, whom we please and glorify by proving that, even in matters of trivial moment, his interests are of more importance in our eyes than all temporal advantages combined. It is in fact more difficult to resist human respect in trifles than in affairs of consequence, for the latter, of their own nature, suggest motives of courage and endurance not supplied to so great an extent by the former.

CHAPTER LIX.

Sufferings of Jesus Christ in his Passion.

WELL did Jesus Christ substantiate his claim to the title of *Man of sorrows,* conferred on him by the prophetic pen of Isaiah, for his sufferings, both of mind and body, attained the last possible extreme of intensity—his corporal pains exceeded only by his mental anguish. " From the sole of the foot unto the top of the head, there was no soundness" in him, (Isa. i. 6.) From every pore of his body trickled a sweat of blood, the miraculous effect of a strange and unnatural convulsion of the system. His head was crowned with thorns, driven deeply into the brain by forcible blows ; his face was disfigured with livid bruises ; his flesh was mangled, and his veins rent asunder by the scourging ; his wounds re-opened by the violent removal of his garments, first to give place to the robe of mock royalty, and again when his

lacerated shoulders were about to be laid on the
hard cross. What must he have suffered in car-
rying his cross through the streets of Jerusalem
to Mount Calvary ! How acute his pangs when
his hands and feet were pierced with sharp nails!
How violent the shock to his frame—how painful
the distension of his nerves when the cross was
elevated into the air, and then suddenly jerked
into the place prepared to receive it ! During
the three hours he remained suspended on the
fatal tree, his pangs gradually reached their
height, attaining the last degree of intensity
endurable by mortal nature. For fifteen or eigh-
teen hours, his sufferings were not only unremitting, but perpetually increasing. A particular
torment was assigned even to his palate—vinegar,
and wine mixed with gall being offered him to
assuage the burning thirst of which he so pathe-
tically complained.

On his interior sufferings I have already touched
in treating of the agony in the garden; but to
form even an idea of the reality is not given to
man. We can adopt but one conclusion concerning them, viz. that they reached the highest
excess endurable even by an incarnate God.

He had no consolation under his sufferings either
from God or man, nor did he even derive support
from his own Divinity. He suffered with the
impression that greater torments still were due to
him, and those additional torments he desired
through love of his Father and of us. He suffered
without evincing a wish for sympathy or compas-

sion. "Daughters of Jerusalem," said he to the holy women who accompanied him in his sad journey to Calvary, "weep not over me, but weep for yourselves, and for your children." (St. Luke, xxiii. 28.) His mind was more deeply engaged, his heart more profoundly touched with the calamities impending over the ill-fated city, than with his personal sorrows. He suffered with unexampled equanimity and serenity, seeming in a manner to derive happiness from his sufferings, and to treasure the aggravating circumstances of each.

We have now to consider the sufferings of Christ under another aspect that of their attendant humiliation, which was, if possible, more poignant, and therefore more dear to his heart than his sufferings themselves. It was, no doubt, a deep humiliation to see himself forsaken by his disciples, betrayed by one, and denied by another, as if in tacit acknowledgment that hitherto they had been the dupes of an impostor, to whom they would no longer concede the undeserved title of master. His enemies no doubt turned this circumstance to good account, and reproached him in his loneliness with the universal desertion of friends and followers. The insults to which he was subjected in presence of his three judges are known to every one conversant with the writings of the evangelists, who cannot be supposed to have exaggerated the sad record, No sooner had he spoken in reply to a question from Annas, than a servant struck him on the face, accom-

panying the blow with the insolent inquiry,
" Answerest thou the high-priest so ?" (St. John,
xviii. 22.) On his declaring himself the Son of
God, the mob clamorously accused him of blasphemy, spit in his face, and rudely struck him,
saying, "Prophesy unto us, O Christ, who is he
that struck thee ?"—(St. Matt. xxvi. 68.) Herod,
incensed at his silence, vied with his courtiers in
deriding him, and, after venting on him the full
measure of his scorn, he sent him away clad in a
white garment, the emblem of folly. Barabbas,
a bandit, a rebel, and a murderer, was preferred
before him, as a more deserving object of popular
favour. He was condemned to scourging, a
punishment peculiarly reserved for slaves. The
Roman soldiers made a heartless sport of their
helpless victim; they substituted a purple garment
for his own seamless robe ; they crowned his head
with thorns, and placed a reed in his hand as a
sceptre ; then, bending the knee before him in
derision they said, " Hail, King of the Jews ;"
(St. Matt. xxvii. 29,) they spat on him, and, taking
the reed from his passive hand, they struck his
sacred head with it. In this disguise, calculated
no less to excite the horror than the pity of the
spectators, Pilate presented him to the Jews,
hoping to arouse their obdurate hearts to mercy,
but with redoubled eagerness they cried, " Crucify
him, crucify him."—(St. John, xix. 6.) Vainly
should we endeavour to describe the pealing
laughter, the scornful shouts, the frantic execra-
tions which assailed him in his transitions from

one tribunal to another, and on his way to Calvary. For this end we should understand the extent of his enemies' fury, as well as the delirium of their triumph at its gratification. Never was a real malefactor treated with the cruelty exercised against the innocent Lamb of God. He was crucified between two thieves as the most guilty of the three; those who passed, insulted him both by word and gesture. The chief priests, the scribes, and ancients, recommended him, in scornful allusion to his miracles, to save himself as he had so often saved others: to come down from the cross if he were the king of Israel, and they would believe in him; and, among many other blasphemies, they suggested that the God, whose son he declared himself, should come to his rescue. Even the thieves who shared his punishment, added their raillery to that of the infuriated rabble.

In perusing the record of these atrocities, we find it necessary to arouse all the vivacity of our faith. That faith teaches us that the victim of such multiplied sorrows is the only Son of God; that those humiliations were decreed for him in the eternal counsels; that he joyfully accepted and endured them, to glorify his Father, and to expiate our pride, with the many other sins of which it is the source. It teaches us, that in this state, more than in any other condition of his life, Jesus Christ is our model; therefore that to subdue pride, the first and greatest of vices, we should aspire to love the contempt and humilia·

tion he so dearly cherished, and endeavour to view it as the livery, the ornament, and the distinguishing characteristic of a servant of Christ. It teaches us, that until we have attained this point, not merely in desire and resolution, but in practice, we shall not be the friends and favourites of our Redeemer; that the love of contempt is the highest degree of perfection inculcated by his doctrine; the infallible road to sanctity, or rather its summit and consummation.

Let us now examine our hearts in God's presence, and, without seeking to disguise or palliate the truth, let us sound our interior dispositions regarding suffering and humiliation. If we detest them—if the very prospect of them fills our mind and heart with horror, we may be assured that nature maintains her ascendancy undisturbed, and we may acknowledge ourselves unworthy of even the name of Christian. We have no alternative but to contradict the gospel, or avow this fact. If, notwithstanding extreme repugnance to contempt and humiliation, we esteem their intrinsic value, blushing at our pusillanimity, and alarmed at the contrast between our ideas and those of Jesus Christ, we begin to become Christians, at least in sentiment. If, in defiance of the revolt of nature, we resign our wills to the sufferings and humiliations it may please God to send us, we have made a considerable advance in the path of solid virtue. If, from resignation and patience, we proceed to joy under suffering—if we learn to esteem as the highest treasure what-

E 3

ever mortifies the flesh, and humbles the spirit, we have progressed far in the way of perfection; nothing remains but to desire the cross with all the ardour of the soul, preferring it, not alone to earthly honours and riches, but even to the consolations and favours of heaven. This Jesus Christ did, when " having joy set before him,"— and that joy the purest and brightest that heaven itself could give—" he endured the cross, despising the shame."—(Heb. xii. 2.) This many of his generous imitators have also done, choosing the cross in preference to the proffered bliss of God's celestial kingdom.

We are not to aim at acquiring these sentiments by the violent efforts of an over-excited imagination; grace alone can inspire them, and the progress of their ascendancy must be gradual. Let us humbly acknowledge our incapacity for good—let us embrace the trifling opportunities of practising virtue with which Providence strews our daily path—let us understand the great importance of repressing a casual emotion of pride, sensibility, or self-love—of renouncing a trivial gratification of sense—of silently bearing an inconvenience or a pain. When we have long been faithful to these minor practices, attributing the glory of that fidelity not to ourselves, but to God, steadily persevering meanwhile in the exercise of the interior life, perhaps we may then be judged worthy of a share in the chalice of Jesus Christ. Without aspiring to imitate what we admire in a small number of the saints, let us only beg of God the grace to accomplish the measure of sufferings and humiliations destined for ourselves, not stopping to consider whether it be little or great. The greatest are nothing compared with those of Jesus Christ, and the least are sufficient to overwhelm us, if our own powers of endurance alone be taken into consideration. Let us ever remember that the most profitable cross is not that we select for ourselves, but that which comes to us from the hand of God. Never shall we die to nature by entrusting the infliction of the death-stroke to the agency of our own hands, or regulating its force by the suggestions of our own will.

CHAPTER LX.

Prayer of Jesus Christ for his Enemies.

JESUS CHRIST well knew the depths of the malice, the hatred, and the vindictive fury of his enemies; he knew too how often he had signally proved to them the supernatural character of his mission, and substantiated his claim to the title of their long-expected Messiah—the only Son of the eternal God; he understood how powerfully the grace of heaven had wrought on their hearts, to touch, enlighten, and gain them, and he remembered the determined obstinacy with which they had resisted its appeals ; he saw their unrelenting resolution to work his ruin, and that, on the pretext of those very miracles whose truth they themselves acknowledged; yet, even amidst his excruciating pains, and still more galling humiliations, he felt no resentment at the consummation of their barbarity; he not only cordially pardoned them, but, in the excess of his charity, he besought his Father to do so likewise. " Father," he said, " forgive them, for they know not what they do."—(St. Luke, xxiii. 34.) They know not that it is the long-promised Messiah, the hope and expectation of Israel, the author of all being, whom they doom to death; the violence of passion has gradually obscured their understanding; their ignorance is culpable, because voluntary; I do not attempt to extenuate it, yet I know that it is from that ignorance alone their sin proceeds. They do not understand the enormity of the crime directed against thee, my Father, and against thy only Son; they do not consider that it is the Lord of glory whom they sentence to the chastisement of the slave; they do not advert to the terrific calamities their iniquity will entail on their doomed city and nation, nor do they reflect on the eternal woe into which it will plunge their own miserable souls. Foreseeing as I do the multiplied disasters impending over them and their posterity, how can I refuse them my compassion; how can I be insensible to their fate? Father! look thou on them with equal commiseration; open their eyes, and since it is now too late to prevent the commission of their crime, grant them at least to repent of it in sincerity.

The prayer of Christ was not confined to a verbal petition for mercy ; his wounds and sorrows were supplications more eloquent than words. He shed his blood for his enemies, and offered to his Father on their behalf the merits of his obedience and his death. He was well satisfied to lay down his life as the purchase-money of their pardon, which he considered an ample indemnification for the sacrifice.

The prayer of Jesus Christ embraced each sinful member of the human race; for us, no less than for the Jews, he implored mercy and forgiveness. Every Christian who commits mortal sin, " crucifies the Son of God anew in his own soul, makes a mockery of him, treads him under foot, and makes the blood of the testament unclean ;" such is the doctrine of St. Paul. (Heb. vi. 6. x. 29.) How few are the privileged souls who have not to reproach themselves with one or more grievous sins ! If we examine our interior dispositions, and sound our secret but deep antipathy to the doctrine of Jesus Christ, we shall be compelled to own, that had we existed at the period of his mortal life, we should have added to the number of the incredulous, and joined the Jews in demanding our Redeemer's death ; therefore as much as they, we needed his prayer for mercy.

After Jesus Christ has asked and obtained the forgiveness of our transgressions, can we refuse pardon to those who offend us ? Can we hate those for whom Christ has manifested the tenderness of his love ? As the disciples of a God whose expiring effort was a prayer for his persecutors ; whose last act was a voluntary sacrifice of the life they were violently wresting from him, can we retain and cherish feelings of revenge ? "Christians," said St. Augustine, "you seek revenge, although knowing that Jesus Christ is not yet avenged." The day of general judgment will be the day of his triumph over his adversaries; defer yours also until then, and meanwhile imitate his example by pardoning those who persecute and calumniate you, saying with him, "Father, forgive them, for they know not what they do." They offend thee, not me; they are their own enemies, not mine. Exaggerate as you will the malice and injustice of your foes; their unrelenting violence ; the injury they have done your person, your property or your reputation ; expatiate on their ingratitude, which you have never provoked by the slightest act of unkindness, but from which, on the contrary, many benefits should have screened you. To all your arguments, Jesus hanging on the cross, eloquently replies ; if you refuse to forgive, his example condemns you; you oblige him to revoke his last prayer for you, and to substitute for it, "Father, forgive him not, for he will not forgive."

Meekness is a virtue inculcated with peculiar force in the gospel. Its practice is more difficult than it appears at first sight, for pride and self-love oppose it with great strength, and without an interior spirit, it does not seem likely to be attained in any degree of perfection. Our feelings are

sometimes so deeply wounded; we are addressed
in terms so galling; we are treated with such
marked contempt; we are the object of so much
prejudice and antipathy; we are calumniated so
basely; persecuted so relentlessly, that it requires
very great controul over natural feeling to arrest
the first instinctive impulse of indignation thereby
involuntarily aroused; to guard against its external manifestation; to renounce all resentment;
cordially to wish well to those who do us evil; to
testify the sincerity of that desire on all occasions;
in a word, to pardon them, and pray to God to forgive them too. It is a great point to act with such
circumspection as neither to give cause of complaint, nor attract enmity. To be disliked and
envied for the possession of superior virtue and
sanctity, and to bear the trial calmly, without a
murmur, without an evidence of resentment, is
still more difficult and more rare. But to love
our enemies; to render them every possible service; to reserve for them a peculiar share of attention, kindness, and charity; to be ever ready
to sacrifice comfort and convenience for their
sakes; ever disposed to assist them at our own
expense, exposing even life, if necessary, in their
service; offering ourselves to God as victims, to
obtain for them his mercy: this is the most sublime degree of Christian charity; this is the exalted perfection to which St. John exhorts us in
imitation of Jesus Christ. " In this we have
known the charity of God, because he hath laid
down his life for us; and we ought to lay down

our lives for the brethren." (1 St. John, iii. 16,)
This was the heroism of charity exhibited by St.
Stephen, the first martyr, and millions of succeeding Christians, whose prayers were offered
for the conversion of the Pagans, at the very
moment their hands were reeking with the blood
of their murdered victims. We are not now
placed in circumstances similar to these, yet they
may enter into the future designs of God over us;
our study should be to dispose ourselves for them
by the daily forgiveness of trivial offences.

CHAPTER LXI.

*Christ abandoned by his Father, yet persevering
in immutable submission to his decrees.*

THE abandonment of Christ by his Father may
be said to have commenced in the garden of
olives. From the moment of his entrance there,
he appeared in the eye of God as a criminal laden
with all the iniquities of the human race. How
appalling that weight of crime, and how deserving
of the most terrible maledictions, and most terrific
punishment! The desolation consequent on that
abandonment continued to increase throughout
his passion, until, having reached its last extremity, Jesus exclaimed, " My God, my God, why
hast thou forsaken me ?"—(St. Matt. xxvii. 46,)
revealing by these words the extent of the sadness
of his soul, rather than complaining of its bitter-

ness. The twenty-first Psalm commences by
the expressions now quoted, which the Saviour
here applies to himself, and which evidently refer
to him alone.

We cannot reflect without a shudder on the
nature of that awful dereliction. It was not real
assuredly, for never was Jesus Christ so justly
the cherished object of his Father's complacency
as in the hour when he gave him the strongest
manifestation of his devoted love ; but, although
merely apparent, and exerting no influence over
the inner depths of the soul, it produced an impression agonizing beyond the reach of created
intelligence to conceive. It was in a manner
equal to the pain of reprobation, or that caused
by the loss of God, a torment which is exclusively
the portion of the spirit, and incomparably the
most intolerable of the sufferings of hell. The
severity of this torment in the Man-God was
proportioned to his knowledge and love of his
Father's perfections; and as this knowledge and
love surpassed those of all creatures, his perception of the misery of losing God must have exceeded that of all intelligent beings, supposing
them to know and love God to the utmost extent
of their capability. Hence we may form a conception of the desolation of the soul of Jesus
Christ. That desolation was accompanied, it is
true, with imperturbable peace, because it had no
admission to the interior sanctuary of his spirit,
nevertheless it was inconceivably bitter, receiving
no alleviation from the prospect of future comfort,

which Jesus Christ voluntarily excluded from his
views.

To understand the desolation of Christ, we
must compare it by another standard, that of the
punishment due to the sins of past, present, and
future generations, for which he satisfied the
divine justice not only strictly but superabun-
dantly. Of the frenzy and despair which are
exclusively the portion of the reprobate, he could
have no experimental knowledge, but, with the
exception of these sensations, he felt the bitterness
attendant on the loss of God more acutely than
all the demons and damned together. His capability of enduring so overwhelming a weight of
anguish is to be estimated by the invincible constancy of his love, by the plenitude of the grace
which dwelt in him, and by the omnipotence of
the support granted by the divinity to his sacred
humanity.

How did Jesus Christ act under this his bitter
bereavement? He performed the most heroic
act of virtue of which an incarnate God was
capable, resigning his body and soul to his Father,
that he might dispose of them according to his
will. He freely submitted to the demands of that
inexorable justice which so rigorously asserted its
claims, and he voluntarily breathed his last sigh
in this disposition of entire conformity. " Father,
into thy hands I commend my spirit, and, saying
this, he gave up the ghost."—(St. Luke, xxiii.
46.) Could he better evince his generous confidence than by choosing the moment of his

Father's greatest wrath to commit to his hands
his spirit, desolate, forsaken, and in a manner rejected as it was?

We dare not enlarge on this ineffable mystery
of love, or seek to penetrate the communications
of that moment between the Father and Son.
What revelations could human language make on
a subject, which for eternity will engage the rap-
turous contemplation of saints and angels, but
never can approach within the grasp of created
intellect?

We can now conceive one of the principal
reasons for the union of the divine and human
nature in Jesus Christ. It imparted to his soul
the supernatural fortitude which sustained him
under the desolation of that awful hour, and it
rendered him capable of the unparalleled love
which dictated his expiring act of entire abandonment to the will of heaven. No mere creature,
however perfect and exalted, not even the blessed
Mother of God herself, could have supported so
overwhelming a burden; the grace of the hypostatical union alone could render it endurable, and
any other than a Man-God must have been annihilated by the force of that deluge of sorrow.

It is evident that by accepting and enduring
unto death that one torment alone, Jesus Christ
fully satisfied the justice of God, for it could not
demand, nor could he offer a nobler sacrifice. It
is clear again that God derived sovereign glory
from this the surpassing suffering of his Son, for
his glory is, to be loved for his own sake with a

pure, generous, and disinterested affection, and next in intensity to the infinite love of God for himself, was the love which inspired the Redeemer to commit his soul into the hands of his Father at the moment of his dereliction by him. It is further manifest that through the merits of that one suffering, the original crime, and all the iniquities flowing from it, must have been perfectly expiated, for God is less incensed at the insult offered to his majesty by sin, than he is honoured by the reparation of Christ, whose voluntary obedience, humility, and meekness far surpassed our insubordination, pride, and malice. In virtue of that suffering he merited heaven for us, with all the graces by which it is to be purchased, presenting to God, on the part of men, an offering of such priceless value that the Almighty cannot refuse to grant even an infinite reward in exchange.

The steady constancy and solid peace of so heroic a soul, cannot be supposed to have undergone any diminution under the pressure of the torments invented by human cruelty. What were those exterior sufferings contrasted with the interior wounds inflicted by his Father's hand? If the latter were powerless to disturb his equanimity, so assuredly must have been the former. Perfect abandonment to God is the ground-work of the spiritual life. The soul which has consecrated herself without restriction to her Maker, has thereby acknowledged his sovereign right to dispose of her at his pleasure, and to exact of her

any sacrifice he may think fit. Should she refuse
his demands on any pretext whatever, she resumes
the dominion of herself, and revokes her first
oblation. The soul in which it is his will to
glorify himself in a most excellent manner, he will
treat as he treated his only Son. After having
pre-disposed her, by many trials, for the crowning
act of pure love, the nature of which it is not
given to ordinary mortals to conceive, he will
appear to forsake her, to leave her to herself, her
nothingness, misery, temptation, and supposed
sins, and to surrender her likewise to their attendant penalties. Trials so severe are of rare
occurrence, yet to a privileged few they are
accorded, as is amply exemplified in the lives of
the saints. God conceals under the veil of secrecy
these crucifying operations of his grace; the duty
of the soul whom he subjects to them need not be
pointed out, for the example of Christ sufficiently
reveals it. If with him she lovingly complains,
" My God, my God, why hast thou forsaken
me ? she immediately adds, like him, " Father,
into thy hands I commend my spirit," and then
mystically expires in the embraces of the cross.
To merit that God should demand so perfect an
act of love, from which he often derives more
glory than he receives insult from the sins of
a whole kingdom, and which sometimes induces
him to pour on a vast nation the mercy of which
its iniquities had rendered it undeserving, the soul
must faithfully co-operate with grace, under the
prolonged trials with which she is previously

visited by men, by demons, or even directly by God himself. She stands in need of a courage, a greatness of soul, a heroism of sentiment acquired only by generous submission to a multitude of sacrifices painful to the flesh, or humbling and agonizing to the spirit. If she recoil from any of those sacrifices, she will be incapable of offering the final holocaust; that last act far surpasses the strength of nature, and can be consummated only through the agency of a grace sufficiently powerful to annihilate the life of sense. Let us be faithful, humble, and generous; let us aim at the perfection of confidence in God, and disengagement from personal interest; these dispositions are a necessary preparation for the great sacrifice to which God conducts the soul by gradual steps, and in the end consummates, thereby granting her a favour, compared with which ecstasies, revelations, and supernatural communications are as nought.

CHAPTER LXII.

The Resurrection of Jesus Christ.

THE life of Jesus Christ was one of poverty, obscurity, privation, and contradiction; his passion was the combination of unexampled suffering and ignominy; his death was most agonizing, but in his resurrection a total change of circumstances took place. On the third day from his burial,

his soul was re-united to his body ; he came forth
from the tomb alive and immortal, resplendent
with brightness, and triumphant in the defeat of
death and hell.   He was invested with infinite
happiness, unlimited power, incapacity ever
again to suffer in mind or body, and a blissful
security of everlasting felicity, incomparably
superior to that of the blessed spirits, and inferior
only to the happiness of the Deity.

Whence proceeds this miraculous transformation ?   How strange the transition from the cross
to the right hand of the eternal Father ! from the
tomb to the highest throne in heaven ! from helpless weakness to boundless dominion ! from the
depths of sorrow to ineffable joy ! from the abyss
of humiliation to the pinnacle of glory ! from the
condition of " a worm, and no man, the reproach
of men, and outcast of the people," (Ps. xxi. 7,)
to the dignity of Sovereign of the universe, judge
of the living and the dead, the Word before whom
every knee shall bow in heaven, on earth, and in
hell, and who for eternity shall share the homage
offered to the Godhead !   The mind is perplexed
in endeavouring to reconcile these two extremes,
and yet, one was simply the consequence of the
other.   " Jesus Christ humbled himself," said St.
Paul, " becoming obedient unto death, even to
the death of the cross, for which cause God also
hath exalted him, and hath given him a name
which is above all names ; that in the name of
Jesus every knee should bow, of those that are in
heaven, on earth, and under the earth, and that

every tongue should confess that the Lord Jesus Christ is in the glory of God the Father."—(Phil. ii. 8, et seq.)

Such then is the result of the sufferings and humiliations endured for the love of God, and in conformity with his will. Our generous Master will not be outdone in liberality, and, if he requires great sacrifices of his creatures, it is only to restore them in eternity, more than they have yielded to him in time. It certainly is not possible to offer to God a nobler oblation than that of Jesus Christ; but neither is it possible to God himself to bestow a more munificent recompense than that awarded to Jesus Christ. The sufferings, the humiliations, the sacrifice unto death offered by Christ to his Father, were finite, if we consider them with reference to his nature as man, and derived infinite value only from his personal dignity; whereas the glory, happiness, and immortality restored to him by his Father are infinite; divine magnificence, love, and gratitude, could devise and bestow no richer reward on the God-Man, endowed as he is by union with the Divinity, with a capacity of enjoyment inferior only to the divine immensity. If, as already observed, one object of that union was to enable Jesus Christ as man to offer the greatest sacrifice ever immolated to the Godhead, another was to endue him with faculties of enjoyment, expansive, as the reward destined for that sacrifice was boundless. As far as God is elevated by nature above the incarnate Word, so far does the recom-

pense transcend the sacrifice of Jesus Christ.
Our bounded comprehension cannot fully embrace
these truths; yet it can at least understand that
such must necessarily have been the case, since
the sacrifice of Jesus Christ was offered in his
human nature, while the reward decreed to it
was the admirable invention of God's own power
and love.

Let us look with the eyes of faith on our
Redeemer risen from the dead; let us contemplate him in his renovated existence, and remember that his present glory is the result of previous
suffering and ignominy. The view will encourage
us to embrace with joy the self-denial and subjection inseparable from the interior life; it will
animate us to generosity in the endurance of its
attendant trials; it will stimulate us to offer
ourselves nobly for its sacrifices. Pure love
forbids that the soul should derive any comfort
under her actual trials, from the anticipation of
future reward; but, in adopting her first resolution, this motive must naturally have much
weight with her; it is most efficacious also in
supporting her under exterior trials from men, as
well as under the painful casualties of life. St.
Paul frequently proposed it to the faithful of his
time, encouraging them to suffer with Christ, that
they might consequently deserve to be glorified
with him. We should not lose sight of this
powerful stimulus to endurance, or in any way
weaken its influence, bowing, however, to the
ordinance of God when he sees fit to withhold

it; not dwelling on it then with deliberation, but substituting other more perfect views. Jesus Christ on the cross cast no thought on the glory which awaited him, but even in that last extremity would willingly have renounced it, if such had been his Father's will. Is it not just that the soul he has chosen for his favoured spouse should imitate him in this, when it is his pleasure to elevate her to so perfect a degree of conformity with himself?

Let us apply to ourselves the practical lesson inculcated by the mystery of our Saviour's resurrection, and imbibe from it the solid instruction suggested by the apostle. Conversion from sin to grace is one species of resurrection, and the most essential of all others. As the renewed life of Jesus Christ is permanent, death no longer possessing dominion over him, so should it be with us after our spiritual resurrection. We should guard against sin, which extinguishes the life of the spirit, and carefully avoid those occasions which might expose to destruction our renewed life in God.

Conversion from tepidity and dissipation, to a fervent and interior life, is a resurrection of another kind. And as Jesus Christ after his resurrection belonged no more to this world, appearing on the scene but seldom and briefly, and solely to promote his Father's glory, so, "if we have truly risen with him, we must seek only the things of heaven, where he is seated at the right hand of God; we must mind the things that are above, not those that are upon the earth," (Col. iii. 1, 2, 3,) and study detachment from all terrestrial objects. As an encouragement to constancy in the practice of penance, and a support to our weakness under corporal infirmity, and the prospect of approaching dissolution, with the attendant horrors of the loathsome tomb, we should reflect that the resurrection of Christ is an assured pledge of our own, and that our body, if we have laboured to sanctify it here below, will one day participate in the qualities of the glorified body of Jesus Christ. The fifteenth chapter of the first epistle to the Corinthians, which treats of this subject, is a beautiful and consoling study for the Christian.

The most exalted degrees of perfection do not exclude profitable reflection on the resurrection of Christ, considered as the result and recompense of his sufferings. It would be quite erroneous to suppose so; the subject should, on the contrary, be recurred to as long as it continues to afford food for thought. Extreme suffering has its intervals of alleviation, and those intervals should be employed in treasuring up all possible resources to facilitate the patient endurance of the impend‧ing cross.

CHAPTER LXIII.

Descent of the Holy Ghost.

AT the moment of his resurrection from the dead, Jesus Christ took possession of the glory which awaited him ; he, however, remained on earth for forty days, frequently appearing to his apostles during that period, and conversing familiarly with them.   On the day of his ascension he was visibly elevated from Mount Olivet in their presence, and finally concealed from their view by the interposition of a cloud.   By thus disappearing from among them, he disengaged their hearts from earthly affections, and rectified their erroneous ideas regarding his future reign, clearly proving that his kingdom was not of this world, and that, to merit a share in its glory, they should first transfer their desires and ambition from earth to heaven.

He thus prepared them for the descent of the Holy Ghost, whom they could not receive until first deprived of the sensible presence of Jesus Christ.   " It is expedient to you," said he, " that I go ; for, if I go not, the Paraclete will not come to you, but, if I go, I will send him to you."— (St. John, xvi. 7.)   These words convey a useful lesson to those souls who cherish inordinate attachment to sensible consolations, and indulge immoderate regret at the privation of such favours, and they explain how it is in one sense necessary to resign the possession of Jesus Christ, in order that the interior visit of the Holy Ghost may dispose the heart for more pure and perfect union with him.

We are to observe that it was Jesus Christ himself who sent down the Holy Ghost on his apostles. "As yet," says St. John, "the spirit was not given, because Jesus was not yet glorified."—(St. John, vii. 39.) The connection between these events is worthy of note. It was necessary that Jesus should suffer before entering into his glory; it was necessary also that he should be glorified before he sent down the Holy Ghost. Thus we are indebted to the sufferings and humiliations of our Redeemer for the descent of the Holy Spirit, who is styled *the Gift of God*, by excellence.

In the work of our sanctification the Almighty completely reverses this order. He begins by sending on us his Holy Spirit, who takes possession of the heart, and replenishes it with divine charity—that is, with Himself. The disposition next infused is one first of esteem, and then of love for the cross; to this succeeds the desire of suffering, followed, through the virtue of that same adorable Spirit, by the graces necessary for bearing the trials imposed. After patient and persevering submission to affliction has destroyed the old man with his two principal vices of pride and self-love, the Holy Ghost reigns in peace over the new man, the production of his own grace; he gradually leads his docile disciple to perfection, and, when the appointed measure of sanctity has been attained, the happy soul exchanges this land of exile for the regions of eternal bliss.

It is the visit of God's Holy Spirit which disposes the soul for the interior life. She is unable to understand its meaning until his light reveals it, and more incapable still of esteeming its value, or desiring a share in its treasures, until his grace has inspired those sentiments. What is the interior life? A life based on the doctrine and example of Jesus Christ. That doctrine and example are wholly supernatural. The maxims of Christ are incomprehensible until the spirit of God deigns to develope their meaning; his examples are powerless to influence the conduct or touch the heart, until the same divine spirit imparts to human weakness the aid of a special grace. This fact is exemplified in the history of the apostles. They had spent three whole years in the company of Jesus Christ—they had heard his instructions, witnessed his conduct, and beheld his miracles—he had taken particular pains to form their minds and hearts—he revealed to them all he had himself learned of his Father, yet they retained their primitive ignorance to the end, and made no advance in the knowledge of heavenly things. This was because they had not yet received the Holy Ghost; their thoughts and desires lay grovelling on the earth; their attachment to their master was a purely natural feeling, founded on the hope of temporal advantage, as their conduct during his passion clearly evinced. The Spirit of truth had not yet elevated their views above this transitory scene, and to that cause is the imperfection of their sentiments to be attributed.

After his descent, those same individuals were instantaneously changed into other beings, not externally, but in ideas and feelings. The world lost its attractions for them ; their thoughts were all fixed on heaven; their energies directed to the means of safely reaching that blessed country, and of assisting others in their efforts to attain it too. They ceased to admit any but supernatural objects of their love, hatred, fear, desire, joy, and sadness. The once timid disciples, who had basely abandoned their Lord and Master, now proclaimed his name with intrepid courage, daunted neither by threats nor injuries, and rejoicing at being found worthy to suffer reproach for the name of Jesus. They preached but his cross; they loved but his cross; they lived at peace in the embraces of his cross; they traversed the universe to seek it, and ambitioned no higher reward for their labours than the honour of shedding their blood for the glory of their Redeemer. This marvellous transformation was effected by the Holy Spirit, who in one moment perfected a work not even commenced at the end of three years spent in the school of Jesus Christ.

The conversion of the first Christians of Jerusalem is no less admirable. They were Jews by birth, and men so deeply attached to this world, that they rejected their Messiah only because he disappointed the ambitious views of temporal aggrandizement they had connected with his reign; yet no sooner had the regenerating waters of baptism cleansed their souls; no sooner had the Spirit of God descended into their hearts, than they were suddenly transformed into interior men; men so disengaged from earth that they sold their possessions, placing the produce at the disposal of the apostles, and not even reserving to themselves the right to distribute it among their indigent brethren. Free from the solicitude entailed by worldly cares, and living in community, they unanimously persevered in prayer; the holy eucharist became their daily nourishment, and charity united them in so close a bond that they had but one heart and one soul. The descent of the Holy Ghost produced the same wonderful results on Gentiles and idolaters long plunged in an abyss of vice and corruption. They formed those fervent Churches which have excited the admiration of succeeding generations, and of which the last trace has for many ages vanished from the earth. To them it was that St. Paul addressed those divine epistles, which the degene-rate successors of the primitive faithful can neither understand nor relish, because presenting to their vision the incomprehensible characters of an unknown tongue.

Why were the terms Christian and interior man synonymous at that time in almost every instance, and why is the case nearly reversed now? Was the grace of the Holy Ghost more profusely lavished then than at present? No, assuredly.

Were the previous habits of the Jews and Gentiles better calculated to dispose them for the interior life? No. To what then must the difference be attributed? To this.—No sooner had the light of truth shed its brightness on the understanding of those early Christians—no sooner had its unction touched their hearts, than they at once embraced it with their whole soul; they renounced all interior affections which might oppose its triumphant progress; they trampled on human respect, and all external obstacles to its undivided dominion; they were ready to sacrifice at its shrine wealth, relatives, honour, and life. In these sentiments it was that they became Christians and received the Holy Ghost. Can we wonder at the miraculous effects his coming produced in them?

At the present period children receive the Holy Ghost while scarcely able to comprehend the meaning of being Christians. The most carefully instructed, and most pious among them go through their religious exercises as a mere matter of form. As yet they are, I admit, incapable of aspiring to the interior life, but neither parents, instructors, nor confessors ever consider the necessity of disposing them for it. They are taught their catechism and prayers; they have books to guide them at mass, confession, and communion; much attention is given to impressing them with the necessity of exterior gravity and decorum while engaged in these holy duties, but little or no notice is taken of the interior disposition of the soul, and yet this it is which constitutes the Christian. Meanwhile years pass on; the world in which they become gradually immersed, communicates to them its opinions and prejudices; the cares and pleasures of life engage their hearts; impressions conveyed through the senses assume strength and durability; the latent powers of passion are aroused into action through the medium of the senses; pride and self-love take root and acquire vigour; even those who retain the fear of God and the spirit of devotion, adopt a plan of piety regulated by themselves, not dictated by the Holy Ghost. That plan does not comprise any aspiration after the interior life, of which they neither have, nor wish to have, a practical knowledge. It does not propose the example of Jesus Christ as a rule of conduct; it does not advert to the necessity of following the guidance of his grace; of esteeming and loving what he esteemed and loved, and selected for his own peculiar portion; but it admits the dominion of private judgment, self-will, natural character, humour, and caprice, as long as no manifest sin appears to follow their indulgence. It is, in fine, a plan of piety which excludes self-denial; one quite consistent with the gratification of self-love and natural inclination; one perfectly adapted to the views of those who never aspire to perfection, and are fully satisfied as long as they can flatter themselves with the conviction of not having forfeited grace. Is not this, with very few exceptions, the ordinary disposition of Christians?

Externally their conduct presents nothing particularly reprehensible; they regularly perform their religious exercises; they frequent the sacraments; they daily read a portion of some spiritual work. But, excluding the minutes thus given to God, they live habitually for self; they indulge continual dissipation of mind; their pursuits are all guided by the impulse of human feeling; they know not what it is to enter into their souls, there to listen in silence to the voice of God; on the contrary, they dread to be alone with their own hearts; they involve themselves in a multiplicity of exterior affairs, and turn a deaf ear to the accents which recal them to interior solitude. Is it surprising that Christians such as these never receive the Holy Ghost, or that his descent should fail to produce in them effects similar to those it led to in the primitive Christians?

CHAPTER LXIV.

Eucharistic life of Jesus Christ.

JESUS CHRIST resides permanently in the tabernacle where his body and blood are deposited for the use and the comfort of the faithful. His corporal presence on the altar, is among the most dearly-prized treasures of interior souls, whose delight is to contemplate their Saviour in the dwelling of his love, to visit him in the day and in the night,

to converse with him familiarly, to impart to him
their joys and sorrows, to consult him in their
difficulties, to view him, in a word, under the endearing aspect of a cherished friend. Supremely
happy in thus possessing under the veil of faith,
the eternal Joy of saints and angels, they envy
not the felicity even of heaven's beatified inhabitants. Jesus Christ, on his side, communicates
himself to his loving adorers with equal eagerness
and condescension. As love for man alone retains
him on the altar, his merciful views are in a great
degree frustrated, when he is left alone in his de-
serted temple; he desires to attract visitors to his
sanctuary, he notices those who evince their respect by frequenting it, and he selects the moments
of their approach to lavish on them the choicest
of his favours. No practice is better adapted to
ensure a rapid progress in prayer, than that of
habitually visiting the blessed Sacrament, provided
those precious intervals be spent in pouring out
the natural feelings of the heart, and without
studied methods or formal acts, speaking to Jesus
Christ in the language of love and confidence.
Our divine Redeemer proposes his eucharistic
life in a very particular manner to our imitation,
presenting us therein with an admirable model of
the virtues he chiefly esteems. The most conspicuous of these virtues are, love of obscurity and
humiliation. In the tabernacle, his glory is
shrouded; his abode restricted within the nar-
rowest possible limits: his humanity not only concealed, but in a manner annihilated. His adora-

ble body although present on the altar, is invisible, the sacramental species which veil it from human eyes, conveying to the senses, and almost to the understanding, an impression that it does not and cannot exist beneath them. It is a living body, yet it betrays no evidence of life. It is present in the perfect integrity of its members, yet seems reduced to nearly imperceptible dimensions. How deep the love of obscurity which could have suggested to the Man God to exert his omnipotence for the purpose of rendering himself invisible! Jesus in the eucharist is a model of interior and exterior silence; he is absorbed in communion with his Father, but he does not give expression to his sentiments in words; his actual condition is in itself a prayer. He is an example also of perfect self-renunciation, of entire self-immolation, his life is wholly interior, producing no external act or function. His "Father who seeth in secret," (St. Matt. vi. 4.) is the sole witness of the homage perpetually offered to heaven by that silent victim of consuming love.

O Saviour of the world! "verily art thou a hidden God!" (Is. xlv. 15.) In every condition of thy mortal life, the title applies to thee, but no where more than in the eucharist. Thy study in all places and all ages, has been to conceal from human eyes the dazzling lustre of thy immortal glory, and thy determination is, never while time endures, to renounce the obscurity thou so tenderly cherishest.

How holy, how glorious to God, how confor-

mable to the example of Christ on the altar, is a
life hidden in God; unseen, unnoted, unsus-
pected by men! The hidden saint associates
with his fellow mortals, but receives no mark of
recognition from them. He seems to take a part
in their concerns, but his heart is satiated with an
invisible food, of which they know not the name.
He discharges the temporal trust committed to
him, as if it engrossed his interest, and he has no
other interest than to advance in the knowledge
and love of his Creator. While engaged in necessary conversation with creatures, he converses
interiorly with God by uninterrupted prayer. He
is absorbed in recollection, but so calmly, so naturally, that it escapes the notice even of the most
acute observer. He is annihilated in spirit, and
he betrays no external evidence of his interior
condition. Scarcely a moment of the day passes
unmarked by the practice of virtue, but so cautiously are those heavenly acts screened from human
view, that the eye of God alone beholds them.
He seeks the shade, but without affectation,
avoiding above all other things the ostentation of
openly proclaiming his preference for the hidden
life. O blessed obscurity! unnoticed by men,
and concealed under the semblance of ordinary,
every-day pursuits, how precious art thou in the
sight of God, but how rarely to be found on earth!
The natural impulse of man, so strongly tends to
the love of distinction and pre-eminence, that
even in the holiest persons, that instinctive ambition is not always perfectly subdued. The glory

of God, and the edification and utility of our
neighbour, are often alleged as pretexts to justify
its indulgence, nevertheless it is certain that except in the case of a peculiar vocation, very evidently revealed either by interior inspiration, or
by the duties attached to our state, or by the
commands of superiors, the charcteristic of grace is
love of the obscurity, retirement, and silence which
Jesus prized, and from this disposition must naturally result distaste for the pre-eminence the
world esteems, and extreme caution in concealing
from men the virtues, graces, and favours bestowed by heaven. The soul imbued with such sentiments, would perform a miracle, were miracles
in its power, to avert the observation of creatures,
and render herself invisible like Jesus Christ.
To be known to God, and unknown to men, living
even in the bosom of their own families, as strangers, and persons of no repute, like St. Alexius,—
such is the earnest aspiration of all truly interior
souls.

CHAPTER LXV.

On devotion to the sacred Heart of Jesus.

THE foregoing instructions have no doubt prepared the reader to understand the practical
meaning of devotion to the sacred heart of Jesus;
a devotion, new as to its title, but ancient as
the church itself as to its object, and more correctly understood, as well as more perfectly prac-

tised in the primitive ages of Christianity than it has ever been since.

Our divine Redeemer revealed this devotion to a saint of the last century, it is true, but his intention in doing so, was merely to re-animate the declining fervour of these latter times, and to revive in the faithful of the present day, the spirit of the martyrs and confessors of the three first ages;— a spirit we cannot fail to admire, though unfortunately our ambition does not soar to the desire of participating in it.

By the heart of Jesus is to be understood his interior feelings and dispositions. The heart is the centre of the human system, and the source of those qualities which stamp the character for good or evil, and render it pleasing or displeasing to God. The mutual love and esteem of creatures, depend on the amiability of heart they discern in each other; and so well established is this principle, that the great study of those who are destitute of such amiability, is to feign at least its outward semblance. The heart of Jesus, then signifies his virtues;—his love for his Father and for us, his meekness, his humility. It signifies again, the sentiments which exercised an ascendancy over him throughout his life and during his passion; sentiments of ardent zeal for his Father's glory; of mercy, tenderness and compassion for us, with a lively desire of our happiness, to the attainment of which two ends he sacrificed his life. As in human language, the head is the seat of thought, so the heart is the seat of the feelings, as well as of the passions of joy, sadness, fear and desire. In Jesus Christ, these passions were supernatural, and excited only by the two great motives of God's glory and man's salvation. In this point of view it is, that the sacred heart of Jesus is proposed to the faithful as the object of their study, their love and their imitation. To be solidly devoted to that adorable heart, is to endeavour to discover by the aid of prayer, its dispositions and inclinations; the principles which guided its conclusions; the virtues which formed its habitual practice, and the sources whence flowed its pleasures and pains. It is to cultivate the sentiments which should actuate us in regard to that sacred heart—sentiments of love and gratitude, of regret for sin which caused its sorrows, and of sincere and efficacious desire to glorify it, and to leave nothing undone for the expiation and reparation of past infidelities. It is in fine, to direct our most strenuous efforts to imitate the example of Christ, according to the exhortation of the apostle, "having in us the same mind which was also in Christ Jesus;" " putting on the Lord Jesus Christ," (Phil. ii. 5. Rom. xiii. 14.) speaking, thinking, and acting like him, from the same principles, and for the same ends, so that we may resemble him both interiorly and exteriorly, one being the necessary consequence of the other. This is in abstract the doctrine of the Gospel, and of the apostles, particularly St. Paul. This is the most solid, and the most practical purpose to which the know-

ledge of religion can be applied. This is the
very essence of genuine piety, the most agreeable
to God, and most beneficial to the soul. Viewed
in this light, devotion to the heart of Jesus, may
truly be said to have commenced with the origin
of the Church ; it was in fact the practice of that
devotion which stamped the character of interior
men on each and all of the primitive christians.

If devotion to the heart of Jesus be understood
and developed in the manner now explained, it
must necessarily lead to the formation of an interior spirit, the interior life essentially inculcating
the contemplation, the love, and the imitation of
Jesus Christ. " Lord, to whom shall we go ?"
should we frequently say with St. Peter ; "thou
hast the words of eternal life." (St. John, vi. 69.)
Christ has himself declared, " this is eternal life :
That they may know thee, the only true God,
and Jesus Christ whom thou hast sent." (Ibid.
xvii. 3.) " I am," said he, " the way, and the
truth, and the life. No man cometh to the Father, but by me." (Ibid. xiv. 6.) If we know
the Father, only in as much as we know Jesus
Christ, and if we know Jesus Christ with the
practical knowledge of love and imitation, only in
as far as we can learn to understand the perfections of his sacred heart, is it not evident that a
knowledge of the heart of Jesus leads to a knowledge of the interior life, and eminently comprises
the practice of the virtues peculiarly appended
to it ?

How shall we gain access to the heart of Jesus?

Our own efforts can never procure us admittance to that sacred sanctuary, but if we give our hearts to our Redeemer, unreservedly resigning them to the influence of his divine inspirations, he will lead us into it; he will disclose to us its secrets; he will communicate to us a share of the love which consumes it, and at the same time grant us the virtues inseparable from that love. The best security for gaining the affections of another, is first to surrender our own. Jesus Christ has given us his, and thereby acquired a right to ours. By refusing them, we forfeit our claim to the possession of his heart, and irrevocably close it against us.

You will tell me that you are in the habit of giving your heart to Jesus, but that you do not find yourself in consequence nearer to the possession of his; more recollected, more disposed for prayer, more interior. How do you give your heart to Jesus? Perhaps in words only; perhaps by merely going through the forms laid down in works of piety, adding to the acts suggested by the author, the excitement of your own over-wrought imagination. The gift of the heart must be the spontaneous dictate of the heart itself; the offering must be made with all the uprightness and generosity of which that heart is susceptible; it must be accompanied by a renunciation of self-dominion, and by a disposition of docile submission to the ordinances of Jesus Christ. The solid effects following this donation will give the truest evidence of the sincerity with which it has been offered. Those effects are, never to

revoke the gift by yielding to self-love, sensibility, or natural inclination; to be faithful to
grace, which will continually suggest the necessity of dying to self, that Christ may live in us ;
to bear patiently the mortifications, contradic-
tions, and humiliations arising from intercourse
with creatures; and to renounce all objects that
dissipate the mind, engage the affections, withdraw the thoughts from God, or extinguish the
spirit of prayer.   These are the duties consequent
on the donation of the heart to God. How do we
fulfil them ?

You are animated with devotion to the heart
of Jesus—that is, you would be well pleased that
your meditations on that adorable heart proved a
fertile source of holy emotions and heavenly
affections, exciting you to pious tears, and reple-
nishing your soul with sweetness.   The heart of
Jesus is undoubtedly the deep fountain whence
flow these refreshing waters, but you commit a
fatal mistake in limiting your desires to these
consoling sensations, for this, assuredly is to love
yourself, not the heart of Jesus—this is to seek
in your devotion to your Saviour, a mere sensible
gratification, on which you foolishly base the
erroneous conclusion that your piety is solid,
while it is in truth but a phantom.   Aim at the
substantial reality of this devotion—reform your
heart on the model of the heart of Jesus—copy
the. virtues he presents to your imitation—his
meekness, his humility, his patience, his charity.
Examine how he thought on all subjects, and

strenuously labour to imbibe his sentiments ; incessantly pray to him for strength to acquire them, and deeply regret the dissimilarity between yours and his. This is truly to honour the heart of Jesus, and to enter on the paths of real and interior devotion. Those who deem it objectionable to present the material heart of Jesus to the faithful, as the object of their homage, should consider that, from its natural constitution, the human mind requires the occasional stimulus derivable from the contemplation of sensible objects, and, moreover, that the heart of Jesus, as a corporeal organ, is in itself adorable, because united to the Divinity ; nevertheless, that heart is not in itself the ultimate object proposed to the veneration of Christians—the express intention of the church being that our views should finally rest on the sentiments of the soul of Jesus, of which the heart is the symbol. If these critics were not so thoroughly blinded by unjust prepossession, they would blush at such pitiful cavilling, adapted only to excite the contempt of the well-judging and the horror of the truly pious.

CHAPTER LXVI.

Motives for cultivating an intimate union with the Interior of Jesus.

THE interior faculties of man are, as it were, the

life of his soul—his external qualities being only
the visible manifestation and the dependent consequence of his internal dispositions. This observation
developes the great motive for cultivating intimate
union with the interior of Jesus. The most
minute and precise acquaintance with every particular of his life, including all he was, all he said,
all he did, and all he suffered, does not constitute
the knowledge of Jesus Christ, unless to this be
added a knowledge also of the interior spirit
which animated and directed his words, actions,
and sufferings, and even the actual possession of
that supereminent knowledge becomes at best
useless, unless applied to the regulation of our
opinions, and the guidance of our conduct.

In contemplating the nativity of Christ, how
many confine their attention to its attendant
humiliation, poverty, and privation; to the stable
which sheltered his infant head; the comfortless
crib in which he reposed; the swaddling clothes
which enveloped him, merely uniting their tears
of sympathy with the sighs and sobs of the suffering child. Yet this is but the surface of the
mystery; we must penetrate beyond into its
depths, by reflecting that the young victim of so
many sorrows is the Son of God, the king of
heaven and earth, to whom belong all honour,
riches, and dominion; that the destitution of his
birth was embraced voluntarily to glorify his
Father, and purchase for men the peace of
heaven; that, although weeping as a helpless
child, he is the eternal wisdom, the power of God,

the omnipotent Lord of creation: that he exults
in his sufferings, and already offers himself to his
Father for greater sacrifices. But it will not
suffice to close the subject with considerations
such as these ; we must further apply the mystery
to our individual necessities, saying to ourselves,
" it is for me that Jesus was born under these
circumstances—to correct my pride, to subdue
my independence of mind and feeling, to condemn
my refined self-love; to teach me contempt for
the honours, pleasures, and affluence of the world ;
to inspire me with humility and simplicity, the
preliminary dispositions for the interior life, of
which he offers us so perfect a model in his birth.
What resemblance is there between my present
sentiments and those of my infant Saviour?
between my thoughts and affections and his?
What must I do to become like him ?" Are there
many Christians who thus study the mystery of
Christ's nativity, drawing from it practical conclusions for the reformation of mind and heart ?
If the work were undertaken thus seriously and
effectively, would not the whole aspect of Christianity undergo a transformation? and would not
the intentions of Jesus Christ be accomplished by
this universal effort to copy his interior dispositions? The foregoing observations on his birth,
are applicable to all the other mysteries connected
with him ; to the least of his actions, and to every
point of his doctrine. To consider them with
profit it is essential to investigate their principle,
to examine their meaning, and to apply the instruction they convey to our personal wants.

It does not depend on our own choice to imitate the external circumstances of the life of Christ. God requires this but of few Christians, some of whom he calls to practice the poverty of their Redeemer ; others to imitate his hidden life ; others to share in the laborious duties of his public ministry; others to participate in his humiliations and sufferings. These various arrangements of Divine Providence are necessarily dependent on the various states and conditions of social life. But all, noble and obscure, ignorant and learned, rich and poor, master and servant, are called to imitate the interior of Jesus Christ, and to all is the facility of doing so imparted. Without making any alteration in the external circumstances of our condition, it is in our power to practice humility, either by sincerely despising human distinctions, if we live amidst them, or by patiently submitting to obscurity, if God has cast our lot beneath its shade, never blushing at our lowly rank, never ambitioning a higher, nor envying our superiors in station. It is in our power to detach our hearts from wealth if we possess it ; to look on God as its true proprietor, and ourselves only as its administrators, obliged to employ it according to his intentions, and to render him an account of its disposal; or, if we live in poverty, far from complaining of its inconveniences to support it calmly, and even joyfully, blessing God for the resemblance it establishes between us and his divine Son. It is in our power either to command with meekness and humility, as simply intimating the orders of

heaven, and strictly obliged to imitate Jesus
Christ in the exercise of the authority we hold
from God alone; or with interior and exterior
submission to obey men for the sake of God
whom they represent, avoiding mean servility
and human respect, and acknowledging only
the noble and exalted views of a Christian aspiring to copy him who " came not to be minis-
tered unto, but to minister." (St. Matt. xx. 28.)
All have grace thus to conform to his interior
sentiments: to think and act in their respective
conditions as he would himself have thought and
acted. Therefore, if we do not resemble him,
we are inexcusable, for we cannot doubt either
that he wills we should, or that he gives us the
graces necessary for that end.

According to St. Paul, our predestination
depends on our conformity with Jesus Christ;
"whom] he foreknew he also predestinated to be
made conformable to the image of his Son."
(Rom. viii. 29.) How shall we conform to him
if not in his sentiments? And what is the image
we are required to copy, if not the interior image
of the Son of God, which depicts his virtues in
such glorious colours? We are to transfer to
our own interior a copy of the interior of Jesus,
developing it feature by feature, and endea-
ouring to embody in the likeness the perfection of the original. The more closely we
apply to the study, the better grounded will be
our hopes of occupying a place among the pre-

destined : the more we neglect it, the more reason shall we have to apprehend exclusion from their ranks. Let us deeply weigh this motive, so closely connected with our vital interests. The secret of our predestination is absolutely hidden from us, and yet if there be a point on which, above all others, we must desire even a probability of security, it is assuredly this. One conjecture regarding it lies within our reach, which, if not possessing the force of actual certainty, leaves, however, no room for deception. If God behold in us the image of his Son, our predestination is, beyond a doubt, secure. If humility forbids that we bear testimony to the faithful delineation of that image in ourselves, conscience may at least certify the ardour of our desire, and the earnestness of our efforts to perfect its features. Let us devote all our energies to the imitation of the interior of Jesus, and we shall never experience any well-founded alarm regarding our predestination, occasionally receiving, on the contrary, the most consoling assurances of it, although for our greater good it will not be permitted that such assurances should impart a feeling of permanent security here below.

Our last sentence will be pronounced by Jesus Christ, whom his Father has appointed Judge of the living and the dead. Nothing can be more awful than that judgment which is to decide our lot for an eternity of bliss or misery. What more effectual means of averting its terrors, than so perfectly to copy Jesus Christ that he cannot condemn us without at the same time condemning himself? Let us as far as possible become representatives of Jesus Christ, that he may discern in us his spirit, or at least the first outlines of his virtues; let our interior be a reflection, even though but a faint one, of his, and how can he discard us from his presence—how refuse us his mercy.

"My sheep hear my voice," said Jesus, "and no man shall pluck them out of my hand, or out of the hand of my Father."—(St. John, x. 27, 28, 29.) Can we hear that voice which speaks to the heart; can we be even disposed to listen to, and obey its injunctions, without being interior? What does that voice say, and what do its instructions suggest? Does it not inculcate the practice of the virtues Christ taught us by example, especially those interior virtues which tend to God as to their immediate object, and serve as a foundation to all others? But can we follow Jesus Christ, as it is the peculiar character of his sheep to do, if we neglect to imitate him in the essential point—his interior dispositions? Clearly not. Yet we are not of his sheep, that is, of the elect, unless we hear and follow his voice.

"I am the vine," he says in another passage, "you the branches."—(St. John, xv. 5.) The branches derive life from union with the vine, which communicates to them its own vital juice. The spiritual life of Jesus Christ as man is derived from union with the Divinity, whence his humanity imbibes the spirit of God; that same

spirit must be imparted to us through Jesus Christ,
and render us like him interior and divine, of
course with due proportion.   Our union with
him, and through him with God, is indispensably
necessary to our transformation from terrestrial
into spiritual beings.   " As the branch cannot
bear fruit of itself, unless it abide in the vine, so
neither can we unless we abide in Jesus Christ,
for without him we can do nothing," (St. John,
xv. 4, 5,) as he himself assures us.   What is it to
abide in Jesus Christ, if not to become interior
like him ? and what fruits of grace can the Christian hope to bear for eternal life, if the germ of
those fruits do not spring from the interior of
Jesus itself ?   It will be objected that sanctifying
grace suffices to dispose the Christian for producing such fruits.   But why does Christ bestow
that grace unless to enable us to think and act on
supernatural principles as he did ?   Is not that
grace itself a vivifying principle of the interior
life ?   We abandon it to inaction, and risk its
total loss, unless by leading an interior life, we
in a manner extend and diffuse the life of Jesus
Christ.

To enumerate all the passages in the gospel
which enforce the necessity of imitating the interior of Jesus, would be an endless task.   I shall
quote but one more, taken from the Redeemer's
last solemn prayer before his passion.   After
having prayed in an especial manner for his
apostles, he added, " not for them only do I pray,
but for them also, who, through their word, shall

believe in me."—(St. John, xvii. 20.) These
words personally regard us, who owe our belief
in Jesus Christ to the instructions of the successors of the apostles. What was the object of his
prayer? " That they all may be one, as thou,
Father, in me, and I in thee; that they also
may be one in us." And again, " I in them,
and thou in me; that they may be made perfect in one." (Ibid. 21, 23.) Jesus Christ im-
plores for us the spirit of unity, which is the perfection of charity; he reduces his petitions to this
point, which in fact comprises all else, and he exhibits to us the most perfect model of unity, in that
subsisting between his Father and Himself. Such
unity can evidently exist among Christians, only
in as far as all are actuated by one spirit, the interior spirit imbibed in the heart of Jesus. To
possess similarity of features, paintings must be
copied from the same original. It is remarkable
that interior souls of past ages, and the few who
still retain any pretension to the title, ever have
been, and still are distinguished by the same spirit, the same principles, the same character of devotion, so that two interior persons who meet in
confidential intercourse for the first time, mutually
discern a similarity of sentiment, idea, and inclination, and become entwined in the bonds of a
holy friendship,—the bonds of grace, stronger far
than the ties of nature. The same remark applies
to the writings of interior men, whose doctrine
and manner of expression are uniform. An interior soul will instinctively admire and relish those

writings; they are the echo of her own sentiments, the record of her own experience, and easily distinguished by her from among many spiritual works of a different character. How shall we account for that striking uniformity of sentiment and doctrine among the saints,—a uniformity pervading even the productions of their pen? Simply by the fact that all are animated by one spirit,—the spirit of Jesus Christ, and that every individual among them, more or less participates in the interior dispositions of his divine model. The unity his last prayer invoked upon us, is then the effect and the necessary consequence of our interior conformity with him, and it is consummated, when that conformity becomes as perfect as fidelity to grace can render it. The perfection of unity will, in one sense, be attained in heaven alone, yet it is the will of Jesus Christ that its commencement and its progress should date from the days of our mortality; and that the union subsisting among his followers should evince to the world the truth of his own divine mission.

Jesus Christ gives us his flesh to eat and his blood to drink in the holy Eucharist, only to unite us to his adorable heart, and to instil his interior spirit into our souls. Could he bestow food more spiritual, more supernatural, more adapted to transform us into himself? Do we not frustrate the principal effect of this august sacrament, when we approach it only to enjoy the sweet emotions of transient fervor; when we render it subservient to the gratification of self-love, and bring from the altar no increased desire to

live in Jesus Christ? " I live, now not I ; but
Christ liveth in me :" (Galat. ii. 20.) the true fruit
of communion is attained by the soul which can
in sincerity claim this sentiment as her own. " As
the living Father hath sent me," said our Redeemer, " and as I live by the Father : so he that
eateth me, the same also shall live by me." (St.
John, vi. 58.) How, unless by leading a life of
grace, an interior life, a heavenly life such as Jesus Christ led on earth?

CHAPTER LXVII.

*Advantages resulting from the imitation of the
Interior of Jesus.*

To form an adequate idea of the advantages which
accrue to us from imitating the interior of Jesus
Christ, we must begin by considering the advantages which resulted to Jesus Christ himself from
the possession of his perfections of body and soul.
I do not now allude to the hypostatical union, a
purely gratuitous favour, to which the sacred humanity of Christ had no right or possibility of
right ; for how could a creature merit such a
grace? The infinite value of his merits arose no
doubt from that union, but strictly speaking, those
merits are to be traced to the internal dispositions
he voluntarily cherished, and the deliberate acts
he freely exercised, and those dispositions and
acts it is, which constitute what I term his interior.

By a spontaneous impulse, his will tended to perfect union with God; to the perfection of sanctity; to the exercise of inflamed zeal for the glory of the Deity. United to God as to its sovereign Good, his soul possessed the purest felicity attainable here below, and in every condition of his mortal life, his happiness was unalloyed. To imitate the interior of Jesus, is then to aim at the closest possible participation in the moral union which subsisted between Him and God. To attain this union, the soul must gradually detach her affections from earthly things; she must form in her heart a void, which the spirit of the Lord may replenish; she must apply to recollection and prayer, and devote her attention habitually to God, or to the duties of her state for the glory of God. By these means she attaches herself closely to the sovereign Good, participating more and more perfectly in its beatitude, in proportion as she advances in the imitation of the interior of Jesus.

The soul of Christ was holy, that is, subject to perfect and invariable order; reason dependent on grace, the passions limited to the love of good and hatred of evil, and the tranquillity of the spirit beyond the reach of disturbance from the agency of any cause either internal or external. The peace of his soul being immutable, he enjoyed supreme happiness, for happiness is the necessary attendant of order and peace. The same order, peace, and happiness will be ours, if we labour to sanctify ourselves by forming our interior on that of Jesus Christ.

His soul was inflamed with zeal for the glory
of God; it had no other object, no other interest; self was forgotten, and personal views
over-looked. Experience demonstrates that most
of the sublunary ills we have to encounter,
spring from our inordinate self love, whereas
the sadness and desolation of Jesus could in no
instance be traced to selfish feeling. If after
his example we devote ourselves to the glory
of God, labouring only to promote the divine
interests, abandoning ours unconditionally to
our Creator, neither seeking nor desiring any
happiness but that of fulfilling his will, we
shall never be the fabricators of our own misery,
and the afflictions which arise from extraneous
sources, severely as they may try our feelings,
will never destroy our peace, or undermine our
resignation. Man's greatest suffering invariably
springs from his rebellion against suffering;—in
other words from his self-love; therefore having
once immolated his self-love to the glory of God,
he can never again be unhappy.

Jesus led a poor, obscure, and laborious life,
but it was of his own selection: he loved it in
itself and in its consequences. The will may
deliberately embrace a condition which nature
abhors, and as long as the will rises superior to
nature, that condition instead of entailing a diminution of interior peace, must on the contrary
contribute to its increase, for peace does not
depend on external objects, but on the disposition
of the will regarding them. The privations, the

humiliations, and the weariness attendant on the poor, obscure, and laborious life of Jesus Christ, had no power to disturb his deep-seated bliss. Let us endeavour to imbibe an interior spirit, and neither the pressure of poverty, nor the solicitude inseparable from riches will destroy our equanimity; we shall not be elated by the adulation which hovers round rank, nor depressed by the oblivion inseparable from inferiority : we shall not repine at the toil and dependance incident to mediocrity; still less shall we rejoice at the fatal exemption from restraint, too often considered the privilege of affluence. We shall be indifferent to all conditions in life, because we shall never attach to any in particular ; that happiness which is based on a deeper foundation and fixed in a higher region; if we feel a partiality for any, it will be for those which most closely assimilate us with our divine Model. Is this a trifling advantage of imitating the interior of Jesus ?

Let us now examine the case in its most alarming aspect, and suppose that by seriously undertaking to imitate the interior of Jesus Christ, we expose ourselves like him to envy, contradiction, hatred and calumny; nay, even to persecution, ill-treatment, poverty, infamy and death. The very thought of such sufferings terrifies ordinary Christians, and when it pleases Providence to inflict any of them, how insupportably heavy are they! what lamentations ensue! what murmuring, what rebellion, what frenzy, what blasphemy,

what gloom, what heart breaking, what despair!
The deep abyss of hopeless anguish seems to
yawn at the sufferer's feet; he laments the hour
in which his eyes opened to the light; he calls on
death to break his bonds, and fortunate is it if he
do not actually plunge unsummoned into its arms.
But when a soul has long been exercised in imitating the meekness, the patience, the interior
and exterior silence of Jesus Christ, her peace
will not be ruffled by the storm; she will stand
unshaken, while the tempest rages round her;
she will sincerely forgive her persecutors; she
will cherish no lurking animosity, no angry resentment; far from grieving at her lot, she will consider herself favoured in having occasion to suffer
for Jesus Christ.   Her serenity will astonish the
witnesses of her trials, who must involuntarily bear
testimony to the solidity of that happiness which
the world cannot take away, as it cannot bestow.
Are not these, real and substantial advantages,
even as regards the present life alone?   Does
there exist a Christian so much his own enemy as
not at least to desire this exalted degree of virtue?
How is it to be attained?   By imitating the interior of Christ.   Who shall describe the overflowing consolations which amply indemnify the
soul for all the trials inflicted by the hand of man?
St. Paul testifies that God so comforted him in his
tribulations, that he was able of his superabun-
dance to impart comfort to all who were in distress.   "As the sufferings of Christ abound in
us; so also by Christ doth our comfort abound."

(2 Cor. i. 4, 5.) The disciples of Christ sometimes obtain such perfect conformity with their
divine Master, as to become insatiable of suffering, ever panting for heavier trials, and feeling
that without the cross, life would be insupportable.
Sentiments such as these we admire in a Saint
Francis Xavier, a St. Teresa, a St. Magdalen de
Pazzi, and many others. Why do we not feel a
holy envy of their happiness? Why do we not
dispose ourselves to participate in it? We have
but to labour like these saints to transfer to our
own souls a copy of the interior of Jesus: they
knew no other secret; there is in fact no other.
Shall we say we have no occasion for the exercise
of such dispositions? Alas! who can penetrate
the future? How often has calamity fallen most
heavily on those who least dreamed of its approach?
Our small store of virtue will be quickly exhausted
in the day of trial, because we have never amas-
sed a sufficient provision for emergencies. Let
us prepare for all possible casualties; it will be
too late to lament our neglect of an interior spirit, when the waters of tribulation have closed
over us in their overwhelming weight.

Let us finally suppose that by resolving to
imitate the interior of Jesus Christ, we subject
ourselves to the necessity of participating in the
sorrows of his soul, and, like him, enduring desolation and anguish of spirit. The peace of Christ
was not impaired by trials of this description; he
might have averted, but he preferred to embrace
them; he was willing to drain the chalice pre-

sented by his Father; he was scandalized at St. Peter's eager efforts to deter him from doing so. He could have descended from the cross, as his enemies insolently challenged him to do, but he chose to cling to it until his last sigh. Any condition we love, cannot be the source of unhappiness, however painful in its own nature that condition may be. The imitators of Christ who follow their Saviour even to Calvary; who, like him, are apparently forsaken by God, and expire either really or mystically in that state of awful desolation, are not in reality the objects of compassion they seem to us; they feel no pity for themselves, nor do they seek to excite the sympathy of others, being in fact in the enjoyment of perfect peace. The Almighty will put a term to their sufferings in his own time, but, far from desiring the cessation of their pains, they are well content to endure them even for eternity. This appears inconceivable, yet it is true. It is the imitation of Jesus Christ which exalts his followers to this sublime degree of fortitude, and ensures that neither the malice of men, nor the rage of demons, nor the most severe trials from God, can cast a shadow over their peace or disturb their happiness, which, like Jesus Christ, they place in the accomplishment of their heavenly Father's will.

I have enumerated only the advantages derivable in the present life from the imitation of the interior of Jesus Christ; those connected with the life to come, surpass all that the mind can conceive. The eternal glory and happiness of

the imitators of Jesus Christ are to be measured
by the standard of the glory and happiness which
Jesus Christ himself enjoys; that is, in proportion as they more perfectly resemble him, so
much will they be exalted and glorified above the
rest of the elect.   In God's everlasting kingdom
there are many mansions ; the highest will surely
be for those whose interior dispositions will be
found to bear the closest similarity with those of
their Redeemer.   He himself will distribute the
crowns of his servants, and it is not to be apprehended that he will mistake the relative claims of
the candidates for reward.

CHAPTER LXVIII.

*Falsity of the pretexts alledged as a dispensation
from imitating the interior of Jesus.*

THE interior life of Jesus Christ being a formal
condemnation of our pride and self-love, with all
the vices thence arising, it is not surprising that
corrupt nature should feel a strange repugnance
to embrace that life, nor that it should conjure
up every imaginable pretext of dispensation from
it.   I shall not dwell on all those diversified pretexts, as the detail would exceed my limits, but
confine myself to the most ordinary of them, the
refutation of which includes that of all.

First pretext.—We can be saved without imitating the interior of Jesus Christ.   This argu-

ment, considered in its general bearings, is false,
and plainly contradicted by many passages of the
Gospel, some of which I have already quoted.
How unworthy of a disciple of Jesus Christ is the
assertion, that he can attain everlasting life without walking in the footsteps of his divine Master!
Jesus Christ was sent from heaven as our model,
and twice did the eternal Father command us to
hear him, whose lessons of life all tend without
exception to inculcate the imitation of his interior
dispositions. Again, Jesus Christ is no less our
Physician than our Model, and as the inner
depth of the soul is the true seat of our spiritual
maladies, to that point it is that the requisite
remedies must be applied. We cannot expect
salvation until those diseases be healed, nor can
we hope for a cure unless we eradicate our natural propensities, and substitute for them the
virtues of our Redeemer. The imitation of Jesus
Christ is, then, clearly necessary for salvation;
the assertion can be qualified in one way only—
by adding, that the imitation of Christ, though
indispensable, is requisite but to a certain extent.
But who shall define that extent? It is essential
to discover it, and yet it is not specified by the
Gospel, by St. Paul, or by any of the writers of
the New Testament. In no part of the sacred
volume are boundaries assigned to the obligation
of embodying in our lives and conduct the sentiments of Jesus Christ. Is it from self-love, from
human reason, from corrupt nature, that we are
to take counsel on a matter of such vital conse-

quence? Have they authority to decide so important a question? Have they light to comprehend so intricate a subject? May we not rest assured they will deceive us, as it is manifestly their interest to do? The whole system of Christian morality tends to reform our nature, which sin has vitiated; Jesus Christ came on earth, spoke, acted, lived, suffered, died, and rose—only to accomplish this great object. He waged perpetual war against nature; he preached the renunciation of nature as a necessary preliminary to becoming his disciple; and we shall appeal to nature, as a competent judge of the extent to which that renunciation should be carried! Is it credible that Christians can indulge such thoughts, or express such sentiments? Yet there is no middle course: Jesus Christ or nature must decide the point, and by the decision of one or the other we must be guided.

Again, to assert that salvation is attainable without imitating the interior of Jesus, is manifestly to exclude all view of God's glory. This sentiment evinces a desire of salvation only in as far as connected with our own advantage, and an ungenerous ambition to realize that advantage at the least possible expense to self. But, O Lord, wilt thou save the soul which never felt an emotion of zeal for thy glory? —which served thee for itself alone, actuated rather by the fear of losing its own happiness, than by the hope of possessing thee? Should not thy glory be our first object, and if we lose

sight of this, can we expect to attain the second-
ary end of our own happiness? This I venture
to declare an impossibility. But can we look to
the glory of God as our primary motive, unless
we imitate the interior dispositions of our divine
Model? Was not that glory the main-spring of
his existence? And can it vivify our sentiments
and conduct, unless we are more or less living
copies of our Redeemer?

"Salvation is attainable without the imitation of
the interior of Jesus;" supposing this to be the
case—supposing no risk of perdition to be in-
curred by the neglect of that imitation, how prolonged and how terrible will be the sufferings
awarded in purgatory to the soul which has
regulated her conduct by this principle! Jesus
Christ will admit none into heaven but those who
possess at least the leading features of their
Model. But if with these, you likewise retain
nearly every feature originally traced by the
hand of nature, the avenging flames will penetrate your spirit, to consume and annihilate; you
will be saved only after inexplicable torments,
and, even then, solely in virtue of your resemblance with Jesus Christ. Is it not manifest in-
sanity to run the risk of losing your soul—to
renounce all pretension to the enjoyment of peace
on earth—to ensure yourself prolonged and intense sufferings in the next life, and, as the end
of all, to attain only one of the lowest places in
heaven; whereas, by devoting yourself to the
imitation of Jesus Christ, you would acquire a

moral certainty of salvation—you would altogether avoid, or considerably abridge, the pains of purgatory—you would secure an exalted position in the kingdom of eternal glory, and purchase for yourself, in time, the blessing of interior peace and the abundance of celestial consolation.

Second pretext.—The observance of the commandments of God and the Church, suffices to constitute a good Christian; it is unnecessary to aim at higher perfection, or to submit to the restraints of an interior life, formed on the model of that of Christ. Such is the language of ordinary Christians, who live at ease under this impression. With the observance of these precepts, clergymen combine the obligations appropriate to their state, such as the recital of the divine office, and the discharge of the functions connected with the care of souls. Persons consecrated to God, add to them the solemn vows of religion and the rule appertaining to their peculiar institute. A few words to each may not be misplaced.

The ten commandments of God simply include the obligations previously imposed by the law of nature and suggested by reason itself; the observance of them does not constitute the Christian. By the commandments of the Church, certain external duties are assigned to her children, whose submission to the authority of their holy mother is tested by their fidelity in the discharge of those duties. To be a true Christian, it is farther requisite to believe and practise the doc-

trine of Jesus Christ, which is wholly supernatural, and enforces more exalted perfection
than that exacted by the decalogue. It is necessary to imbibe the spirit of Christ, esteeming and
loving what he judged worthy of esteem and
love—despising and rejecting what he deemed
deserving of contempt and aversion. It is not
possible, as I have already observed, to assign
precise limits to the dominion his Spirit should
exercise over ours, but that it must acquire some
degree of ascendancy is beyond question; a
Christian merits his title only as far as he is animated by that spirit. The life of a Christian is
a life of grace; the principle of that life must,
then, necessarily be interior; it must emanate
from Jesus Christ. The tendency of grace is to
inspire the desire of imitating Christ, and the
more faithful we are to its voice, the further will
it lead us in that imitation. Clergymen are the
ministers and representatives of the Redeemer;
they are consecrated to the service of the altar,
the administration of the sacraments, and the
instruction and edification of the faithful; therefore, they contract the obligation of a peculiar
resemblance to Jesus Christ. If they overlook
or neglect this obligation — if they discharge
their functions without an interior spirit—if
they are satisfied with exemption from the
grosser vices and fail in the practice of the
sublimity of Christian virtue, they prove themselves unworthy of their exalted character, and
although they may not openly sully it in the eyes

of men, they assuredly dishonour it in the eyes of heaven.

The object of the Religious in renouncing the world, consecrating his being to God, and subjecting himself for life to the observance of a particular rule, is only that he may become more like to Jesus Christ—that he may be under the happy necessity of imitating his divine Model—that his facilities for that imitation may be increased, and the obstacles which surround it with difficulties removed. Every order embraces the imitation of the interior of Jesus as its chief end, and although each may propose to itself a different feature of his life—some, for example, his solitude, silence, and fast in the desert—others his active exertions for the glory of God, and the spiritual good of men—all, nevertheless, ultimately tend to the same object, which is, to transform their members into faithful copies of the divine Original. A religious person who loses sight of this end, who neglects to labour for it with all his strength, referring to it his pious exercises, his active occupations, and the observance of his rule, cannot flatter himself with possessing the spirit of his institute or fulfilling its object.

Third pretext.—All are not called to imitate the interior life of Jesus Christ. Reverse the remark, and say, rather, that all *are* called, each according to his condition and the measure of grace bestowed, but that, unhappily, few correspond with the heavenly invitation. To every

Christian, without one exception, Jesus Christ
is proposed as a Model; therefore, on every
Christian devolves the obligation of imitating
Jesus Christ. Are not all called to love God with
their whole mind, and heart, and strength? Did
not Jesus Christ love God thus? His love surpassed, it is true, the highest degree ours can
ever attain; nevertheless, ours must be of the
same character as his, and must possess the same
qualities. No feeling is more closely intertwined
with our innermost souls than that of love; and
the peculiar tendency of divine love, is to rule
over the affections and to render them subservient to itself, as to their principle and their
end. Again, all are called to love their neighbour as themselves, for the love of God, and
Christ formally commanded his disciples to love
one another as He loved them. The interior of
Jesus was wholly absorbed by the love of God
and man; now, as this virtue comprises in abstract
the two great precepts of the law, which we are
unquestionably bound to observe, it manifestly
follows, that, to discharge this evident obligation,
we must conform our interior sentiments to those
of Jesus Christ.

If these arguments can be established, you
will say, all Christians are obliged to be saints.
Yes, they assuredly are obliged to endeavour to
become so. This truth was considered so self-
evident in the primitive church, that the Apostles, in their letters to the first Christians, invariably addressed them by the title of saints. If

the ideas of men have undergone a revolution since that period, the doctrine of Christ has certainly preserved its character of immutability. A saint is nothing more than a perfect Christian; and, without voluntarily degenerating from his high dignity, it is plain that no Christian can deliberately live in a state of imperfection.

CHAPTER LXIX.

The only admittance to the interior of Jesus is through the practice of self-denial.

To acquire a knowledge of the interior of Jesus, the lights of human reason must be renounced; to relish its perfections, self-will must be sacrificed; to imbibe its virtues, the continual practice of universal self-denial must be embraced.

In contemplating the perfections of the interior of Jesus, we must ever bear in mind that human feeling had no existence in him, but that his whole being was under the controul, and at the disposal of the Word, who attributed and referred all its acts to himself; so that the soul, although perfectly free, was but a simple instrument, either active, to execute the commands of the Word, or passive, to concur in his operations; having no power to act from the impulse of its own will; no liberty to reflect on its condition, to seek its interests, or to appropriate its perfections. It is absolutely necessary to descend to the depths of the moral annihilation of Jesus Christ, before we can rise to the contemplation of the lofty edifice of virtue erected by the hand of God on that solid foundation.

Now it is impossible, by the aid only of human reason, that is of the faculty which naturally guides the judgments and decisions of man, to penetrate the deep abyss of such annihilation; to conceive a rational nature divested of the spirit of self-appropriation and the love of personal interest, yet retaining perfect freedom in its operations, and at the same time renouncing both the power and the will to call those operations its own. Reason, left to its own unaided strength, cannot comprehend the mystery; guided by faith it believes and submits. But it requires the assistance of a special light, to catch even a glimpse of the moral results produced by this mystery on the soul of Jesus Christ, and that special light is granted only to those, who renouncing their own wisdom, humbly draw near to the interior of Jesus, and beseech him to introduce them by his grace into that sacred sanctuary. An equally powerful grace, and an equal renunciation of the lights of human wisdom are requisite to elevate the human mind to the consideration of the sublime virtues infused as a habit into a soul whose self-annihilation prepared it to receive and contain all the gifts and treasures of heaven. Reason aided by ordinary grace, cannot fix a steady gaze on the dazzling flames of love which consumed the souls of some privileged saints; neither can it comprehend the sacrifices

which that love demanded of its happy victims—
still less can it concentrate within its narrow
limits the ever-expanding fire of charity which
glowed in the heart of the blessed Virgin Mary.
How, then, could it fathom the depths of the
love of Jesus for his Father? Humility and self-
denial are the only medium through which it
can receive that divine knowledge which sheds
the light of heaven on the soul, and absorbs its
faculties in a species of fascination. The same
remark applies to the love of Jesus for men—
particularly for his enemies; to his meekness,
patience, humility, and other virtues. Human
reason, far from fully understanding, cannot
even acquire a superficial insight into them. A
supernatural knowledge of the perfection of those
virtues, is imparted to it, only in proportion to its
humble conviction of incapacity to attain such
knowledge by any investigations of its own. Hence
it is that those treatises which enter somewhat
deeply into the interior virtues of Jesus are so
little understood, and that the Gospel itself and
the epistles of St. Paul are but a dead letter to
the generality of readers. Because their meaning is deep, it can be penetrated only by the aid
of Divine light; a light which must be implored
with humility and received with gratitude. God
never discloses the mysteries of the interior of
Jesus to a soul inflated with self-sufficient reliance on its own strength.

To know the interior of Jesus, avails little, if
the knowledge be not accompanied by solid love

of its perfections. But how completely opposed
to the love of that Divine interior are our natural
inclinations, tending as they do rather to horror
and aversion, than admiration and esteem. The
fulfilment of our obligation on this point especially, demands the sacrifice of self-will. Where
is the individual, who, with a view to please God,
selects from choice, and prefers poverty to riches,
obscurity to splendour, the dependence and subjection of a laborious life to the liberty of following the pursuits dictated by caprice or mis-
spending time in total idleness. Even among the
most pious, are there many who love retreat, recollection, interior solitude, and habitual communion with God ? Many who adhere to their Creator for his own sake, who sacrifice their personal
interests to those of Jesus Christ, who retrench
all views and reflections suggested by self-love,
who forbid themselves even a self-complacent
glance—who disengage their hearts from the
consolations of heaven, who never appropriate
the virtues they possess, and willingly submit to
the extreme of spiritual destitution! How many
are there who love their neighbour so well as to
renounce life for his sake, to suffer patiently the
trials he occasions, to pardon the injuries he
inflicts, and to pray for his salvation at the very
moment he gives the strongest demonstration of
his hatred and ill-will ? Even among Christian
heroes, of whom the world can now so seldom
boast, where are those who understand the intrinsic value of that suffering which combines

corporal agony and mental humiliation ?—who
love the extreme of contempt and opprobrium ?
—who would gladly undergo the death of Jesus
Christ, hanging like him on the cross, forsaken
by heaven, and abandoned to the rage of men
and demons ?   Nature recoils in terror from the
vision ; the will shrinks in alarm from the mere
thought of such complicated horrors.   There is
not a virtue of Jesus Christ which we do not feel
an instinctive reluctance to embrace in practice ;
to expect to relish those interior virtues, without
the previous sacrifice of the most deeply-seated
inclinations and aversions of nature, is, therefore,
chimerical ; self-love, that fatal tendency, which
resides yet more in the heart than in the mind,
must be immolated, before the Spirit of Jesus
can be substituted for ours.   The distance is
great, again, between the knowledge and love of
the interior of Jesus and its imitation.   After
receiving the most sublime light, and experiencing
the most heroic sentiments at prayer and communion, how strong the opposition, how great
the weakness, how powerful the temptation to
retract, which the soul experiences, when the
opportunity occurs of reducing those sentiments
to practice !   She begins the work—then inter-
rupts it ; then resumes—to discontinue it once
again.   Nothing is done, until a strong resolution has been formed to adopt the practice of
universal and perpetual self-renunciation.   This
absolute and entire self-renunciation cannot of
course be attained at once, but the soul must aspire

to it, co-operating with grace to the utmost of her power. She must continually and vigorously struggle against nature; she must allow her heavenly Father to accomplish in her what of herself she could not do ; she must submit to his crucifying and annihilating operations until nature shall expire, if she wish to retrace in herself a faithful copy of the great Original presented to her contemplation on Mount Calvary.

The observations I proposed to myself on the interior of Jesus are now closed; they comprise but little ;—nothing by comparison with what might be said on such a subject. But let us turn to good account the light vouchsafed us, and we shall receive stronger in proportion to our progress. The increase of heavenly light, and our advancement in perfection keeping mutual pace, our fidelity, courage, and generosity will gradually elevate us to the conformity God desires to establish between us and his only Son. Amen.

THE INTERIOR OF MARY.

SECOND PART.

CHAPTER I.

Of the immaculate Conception of the Blessed Virgin Mary.

THE Word of God having from eternity predestined Mary for his mother, it cannot be doubted that he endowed her soul at its creation with the most exalted prerogatives, and enriched her with graces proportioned to her destined dignity, the highest to which a mere creature could be elevated. It is the general belief of the Church, though not an article of faith, that the Blessed Virgin alone, of all the children of Adam, was exempt from original sin and its consequences—that in her conception she was gifted with sanctifying grace, and with a holiness which rendered her an object of complacency to the Most High. It is also probable that she possessed the use of reason long before the age when it is usually developed—perhaps at her birth, or even at the moment when her soul and body were united. It is but just to suppose that nothing within the power of the Word to accomplish in favour of his future mother, was left undone ; nor need we fear to carry our credulity on this subject beyond due limits.

This point established, it cannot be doubted that, at the moment of her conception, the sanctity of Mary surpassed that of men and angels— that she was then able to glorify God more perfectly than all united creatures—that she had no inclination to evil, but a disposition, on the contrary to the highest supernatural virtue, as far as its practice was compatible with her age and circumstances—that, without being impeccable by nature (the attribute of God alone) she was so by grace, never once during her life committing a deliberate imperfection. At her birth she possessed an enlightened understanding, an upright will, strictly conformable to the will of God ; a more perfect liberty than that of the angels, or of Adam in his innocence—a liberty which, far from abusing, she was, on the contrary, to employ, and actually did employ, in the most excellent manner. She was exempt from ignorance and concupiscence, the two great sources whence originate the sins and sorrows of the human race. Her passions were ever under control, ever in order, ever in accordance with the dictates of reason and grace. Her flesh, destined to become one day the flesh of the Man-God, was gifted with eminent purity and sanctity. She received an extraordinary degree of sanctifying grace, with actual graces of a superior order, for the regulation of her thoughts, affections, and conduct. She had no evil tendency or vicious habit to contend against inwardly ; no temptation to combat outwardly. She had an extreme horror of the very shadow of sin—an inclination, a desire, an inexpressible facility for the practice of every virtue. Continual union with God, absolute devotion to his will, inviolable fidelity to grace, total forgetfulness of self, ineffable purity of intention, which referred all, without exception or reserve, to the greater glory of God, and excluded all selfish views of personal merit and reward,—such was the groundwork of the interior of Mary.

It is an article of faith, that the rich gifts lavished on that interior at its first formation continued to multiply with time, and that the extent and rapidity of its increase in sanctity was proportioned to the original degree of its perfection. What a height must that perfection have attained as her mortal career advanced ! What at the end of her existence !

" How," you will say, " am I to imitate so perfect a model ? I should for this end have received graces similar to those bestowed on Mary." It surely must be possible to imitate Mary, since the Gospel proposes to you an infinitely more perfect model in the person of Jesus Christ, on our conformity with whom depends our predestination. Are we authorized to dispense ourselves from that imitation because we have not received the grace of the hypostatical union, like Christ? God requires us to copy the perfection of Jesus and Mary only in proportion to the degree of grace conferred on us. Mary was sanctified, not by the privilege of her immaculate conception, nor by the eminent degree of sanctifying grace communicated to her, but by her free act of devotion to God on attaining the use of reason—by her irrevocable perseverance in that first oblation—by her inviolable fidelity to actual grace. Can you not devote yourself to God like her, even though less perfectly? Can you not endeavour to persevere in that devotion like her, condemning and regretting your weakness as often as you revoke that first free offering? Can you not faithfully cooperate with grace, and lament even your least infidelities? By adopting this line of conduct, you will prove yourself a true imitator of Mary. If God bestowed on her more abundant graces, he required of her a greater amount of perfection in return; and she, on her part, accomplished the measure of sanctity exacted. Be generous, like her, in proportion to the value of the talents you have received; sincerely and earnestly desire to correspond with the liberality of your Creator; humble yourself at the view of your faults, and repair them by a renewal of loving confidence in

God; this is all he asks of you. It is evident
that the models proposed to our imitation by the
Almighty must be unexceptionably perfect, or
they would otherwise be unworthy of his majesty.
But, perfect as they are, they are not the less
adapted to our imitation, because the all-powerful
aid of heaven will be amply provided to supply
for our inherent weakness. If God refused that
aid, he would be unjust, and we should have
reason to complain; but nothing is wanting on
His part, and we can blame only our own pusillanimity for our little progress in virtue. Let
us study those points of Mary's example in which
it is imitable, and, aided by her powerful media-
tion, let us earnestly labour to become like her.

CHAPTER II.

Presentation of Mary in the Temple.

An ancient tradition, commemorated by the
Church in a particular festival, informs us that in
her early infancy, Mary was presented in the
temple by her parents, and there consecrated to
the service of God, as little Samuel had been many
ages before.

What were the dispositions of Mary in that
renewed consecration, and what the sentiments
with which God inspired her? We cannot doubt
that her dispositions and sentiments were as
perfect as was consistent with her age, and the

degree of grace bestowed on her, or that on so important an occasion, she received an accession of grace, which became the fertile seed of additional fruits of sanctity. Concealed from the eyes of men by the shade of the sanctuary, absorbed in God, and engrossed by the ceremonies of his worship, she made daily and gigantic strides in the interior life, and unconsciously disposed herself for her destined dignity. The designs of God were unknown to her, but she faithfully obeyed his inspirations, studying to attain a more intimate union with him, and to acquire a deeper knowledge of her own nothingness; aspiring only to be known to God, and a stranger to all beside.

Life of obscurity, silence, recollection, and retreat—life unnoted by any eye save those of God's angels—life concealed from the observation of creatures, and even from the view of the soul herself, how precious art thou in the sight of heaven! Men know not thy value; they are incapable of estimating thy worth. Ill regulated piety is ever ready to come forward, under the specious pretext of edifying; true piety aims as far as possible at concealment; if it seeks the light, it is only from necessity, as far as the glory of God and the good of others require, and its mission being accomplished, it vanishes without delay from the scene.

Mary was a treasure of sanctity, hidden within the inclosure of the temple, even from the companions who dwelt beneath the same roof. She never spoke of herself; she made no display of her interior sentiments. Simple and unaffected; never attracting notice by singularity in her external practices, she exteriorly led a common life, while interiorly endowed with the sublimity of sanctity; and she had no aim but to conceal her spiritual prerogatives within the depths of her own soul, and to avert the observing gaze of creatures. She no doubt diffused around the sweet odour of her good example, and edified the more, in proportion as she was the less intent on doing so. But piercing must have been the eye which could detect her real pretensions; how, indeed, could others discover a secret yet unknown to herself?

If God should call you to the religious state, let your entrance into the cloister be to you, what Mary's presentation in the temple was to her. Give yourself to God as she did, and devote your life exclusively to prayer and mortification. But let your interior be sealed like that of Mary; reveal it only as far as may be necessary to those appointed to guide you. Aspire only to a simple, common life; avoid observation; refrain from all but unavoidable intercourse with the world you have forsaken; forget this earth and its concerns; desire to be known to God, and blotted out from the memory of creatures. Be impressed like Mary, with the sense of your nothingness; never think with deliberation of yourself, and seek, but without affectation, to divert the attention of others also from your concerns.

CHAPTER III.

Mary's vow of Virginity.

It is not known at what age the Blessed Virgin consecrated her virginity to God; but it is certain that the act was very particularly inspired by the Holy Ghost, and the engagement preceded by a full and perfect comprehension of the consequences it entailed.

The history of her people offered no example of such a vow, the Jews invariably engaging in the married state, without the exception even of the tribe of Levi, destined for the service of the temple; of the priests, or the high priest himself. Jephtha's daughter, condemned by her father's rash vow to an early death, mourned only her misfortune in dying a virgin, and asked permission, before her sacrifice should be consummated, to retire to the solitude of the mountains, and there, in the society of her companions, to bewail her virginity. Sterility was commonly considered a disgrace by the Jewish women, who especially ambitioned the honours of maternity. By her vow, Mary acted in open opposition to the deeply seated prepossessions of her people, and voluntarily attached to herself a species of stigma.

The sacrifice of the Blessed Virgin is not to be estimated by her renunciation of the pleasures and advantages connected with the married state. Being emancipated from the concupiscence of the flesh, her vow perfectly harmonized with her natural inclinations. Disengaged from earth, she felt no desire to contract a worldly alliance ; happy in possessing the Lord for her portion, she knew no ambition for the dignity, the comforts, or the resources conferred by matrimony, and she willingly embraced the solitary, lonely, hidden, and dependent life, recognized to be the virgin's peculiar inheritance.

In pronouncing her vow, she offered to heaven a sacrifice of quite a different character. She knew that the Messiah was to spring from the tribe of Judah, to which she herself belonged ; she knew that he was to be of the family of David, which was also hers. Several prophecies concurred in referring the coming of Christ to the precise period in which she lived. Both Jews and Gentiles so confidently expected him, that when St. John the Baptist appeared, the Jews sent to inquire if he were not the Messiah, and the Samaritan woman said to Jesus himself, " I know that the Messiah cometh, (who is called Christ) therefore, when he is come he will tell us all things."—(St. John, iv. 25.) It seemed, however, to have escaped mens' minds that the Saviour was to be born of a virgin mother, and the prediction announcing the miraculous fact was altogether overlooked. Therefore, in devoting herself to a life of continence, Mary seemingly renounced every rational hope of giving birth to the Redeemer ; she renounced it with a distinct perception of the results entailed by her voluntary act; she renounced it from a motive of profound humility, and while considering herself absolutely unworthy of the surpassing honour, she was equally incapable of an emotion of jealousy in regard to the yet unrevealed object of God's greater favour.

Such were the sentiments which the Almighty himself instilled into her heart; such the interior and exterior self-renunciation by which he prepared her to be the mother of his Son. How different are the views of God from ours! to attain its ends, his supreme wisdom adopts means which appear of a directly opposite tendency. Who could have imagined that the state of virginity which the Jews despised and rejected, would have been actually prescribed by God himself as an indispensable appendage to the mother of his only Son? Who would have believed that the renunciation of that dignity was an essential preliminary to the enjoyment of it?

In rendering virginity fruitful in the person of Mary, the Almighty performed a singular miracle never to be renewed. But the prerogative of spiritual maternity he daily confers on the virgins consecrated to his service, who can merit the favour only by imitating the dispositions of the Blessed Virgin; by never aspiring to it; by unhesitatingly admitting their unworthiness of it; by so far renouncing it, as to limit their zeal to their own perfection, and never undertaking to advance that of others, unless manifestly obliged to do so. Time will reveal the designs of God over souls so humble, so unpretending, so faithful in cultivating the virtue of interior solitude; he will infallibly employ them to extend his empire, and promote the sanctification of many. Let us totally lose sight of ourselves, never attaching importance to our weak efforts, or fancying that we are capable of accomplishing anything great. God delights to work on nothing; from that deep foundation it is that he raises the creations of his power. We should be full of zeal for God's glory, and at the same time convinced of our incapacity to promote it. Let us sink into the abyss of our worthlessness; let us take shelter under the deep shade of our lowliness; let us tranquilly wait until the Almighty shall see fit to render our active exertions instrumental to his glory. For this purpose he will make use of means quite opposed to those we might naturally expect. Next to Jesus Christ, no one ever contributed to the glory of God in the same degree as the Blessed Virgin Mary, and yet the sole object to which her thoughts deliberately tended, was her own annihilation. Her humility seemed to oppose an obstacle to the designs of God, but it was on the contrary, that humility precisely, which facilitated the accomplishment of his all merciful views.

CHAPTER IV.

Her Marriage with St. Joseph.

THE consecration of virginity to God, being at that time altogether unexampled, Mary's vow remained a secret between heaven and herself. It is not likely that she communicated it even to her parents, supposing them to have been still alive, for, although most pious, they were probably too deeply imbued with the prejudices of their people, to have given it sanction. The Almighty intending to conceal for a time the miraculous conception and birth of Jesus Christ, and for this end to veil the mystery under the solemn rites of marriage, inspired Joseph, who like Mary was of the tribe of Juda and family of David, to propose an alliance with her. To this request her parents acceded, and before the embassy of the Angel Gabriel, Mary and Joseph had been affianced, perhaps married.

The holy virgin now found herself necessitated to reveal her vow to Joseph, and before consenting to become his spouse, she exacted a promise from him to respect its privileges. Joseph on his side devoted himself to a life of continence, and thus the chaste union of these two saintly beings presented to the eyes of heaven's angels the novel and delightful spectacle of virginity combined with marriage.

But although Joseph was *a just man,* and

although Mary had ample reason to rely on his promise, it surely required the perfection of confidence in God, and of abandonment to divine providence, thus to depend on the faith of a mortal; to maintain with him the free, familiar intercourse supposed by the conjugal union; to acknowledge his authority as her spouse, and at the same time to banish all apprehension concerning the observance of her vow. She had hitherto abstained most cautiously from intercourse with men, and now by a strange contrast, she united herself to Joseph in the strictest bands, choosing him for her spouse, and adopting him as the guardian of her chastity. He certainly realized her expectations in their fullest extent,— but to understand the perfection of her abandonment to God under circumstances so critical in their own nature, and entailing results of so much importance to her future prospects, it would be necessary also to comprehend the depth of her love of purity, and the ardour of her desire to maintain its unsullied integrity. While vigilantly guarding this, her best prized treasure, she was obliged for the sake of appearances, externally to maintain the relations of a spouse in regard to St. Joseph, and to preserve an intimate, familiar, cordial, and holy union with her saintly protector,—a great trial, of her virtue no doubt, —and one destined as a preparation for the revelation of God's high designs. In contracting an engagement apparently incompatible with her previous pledge to heaven, she was guided by divine inspiration, and by the wishes of her parents, who, ignorant of her vow, exercised their legitimate authority in the disposal of her lot in life.   Placing her hopes of protection in the Lord, she discarded all solicitude regarding the means he might employ to ensure the fulfilment of her vow, and thus freed from suspicion and doubt concerning Joseph, she resigned her fate into his hands with the same confidence as she would have committed herself to the guardianship of an angel.

What lesson do we here learn from the example of Mary?   Not to reason on the manifest will of God ; not to apprehend the perils to which he himself exposes us ; fearlessly to confide to him our dearest interests, and firmly to believe that he will guard them more cautiously than we could ourselves.   The interior life is a life of faith and of abandonment to Providence , it is not liable to the rules of human wisdom ; it is wholly under the dominion of grace, therefore grace, subject to the direction of obedience, must be our only guide.   Had Mary followed the dictates of her own judgment, or the impulse of her own will, she would not have consented to espouse St. Joseph ; had she listened to the suggestions of human reason, she would have supposed that consent to involve an infraction of her vow.   She could easily have justified herself for refusing compliance ; the strongest arguments apparently sanctioned her doing. so ; and having no power to foresee the future, neither could she trace the yet invisible connection of those circumstances which were afterwards to clear up the mystery. Yet, as the event proved, had she refused her consent, she would have opposed the will of God ; but while the event is not only impervious to the view, but beyond the reach even of imagination, it certainly cannot serve as a rule of conduct ; in such a case we must seek another rule, the infallible rule of absolute abandonment to the will of God, and of the total sacrifice of reason to faith. The whole tenor of Mary's life evinces that she was invariably guided by that divine faith which is stronger than human reason, and more enlightened than human wisdom.

CHAPTER V.

Embassy of the Angel Gabriel.

MARY lived in retirement at Nazareth, a small town of Galilee, the poorest and most obscure district of Judea. She was indebted for her support to the industry of Joseph, a poor carpenter, and she passed her time in the discharge of her humble domestic duties. God had preordained these circumstances from eternity, selecting that remote town, that poor workshop, that lowly dwelling, as the theatre of his most stupendous miracles. The period appointed for the manifestation of his power and mercy having arrived, he deputed, not an angel of an inferior grade, but a bright and glorious archangel, to announce to the holy recluse of Nazareth, that he had chosen her for the mother of the world's Redeemer. A promise had been made to David that the Messiah should spring from his race, and to realize that promise, the Almighty waited until the posterity of the holy king had sunk into the despised ranks of the suffering poor. An obscure tradesman of Judea was elected the reputed father of God's only Son, the spouse of that tradesman his mother! What then is to become of the magnificent descriptions traced by prophets' pens of the splendours of the Messiah's reign? O man! how grovelling are thy views, contrasted with the mighty thoughts of God's eternal mind! The glory of the Messiah's reign is to spring from far other sources than thou supposest! He will be great before God, and for this end he must be contemptible in the eyes of mortals; his parents must be persons of no repute with the world, and yet more humble in heart, than they are abject in their external condition.

To Mary then, in her poor home at Nazareth, the angel Gabriel appeared, and revealed his commission in the following terms : " Hail, full of grace, the Lord is with thee : blessed art thou among women," a style of address bespeaking the respectful homage of a subject to his queen. Among the many communications of angels with men recorded in Scripture, not one commences with the word " Hail." It was reserved for Mary, whose humility was a shield against the vanity likely to ensue in any other case. The expressions which followed were still more calculated to inspire vain glory. *Full of grace.* An angel speaks on the part of God, and utters none but the words dictated by the Spirit of God ; Mary was therefore not only authorized, but even obliged to consider herself full of grace, since eternal Truth had certified the fact. But the increase of her humility kept pace with the magnificence of the eulogies lavished on her, and, without allowing herself a thought on the salutation of the angel, she interiorly acknowledged her intrinsic nothingness, and recognized the operations of divine grace in her soul.

The Lord is with thee. The same words had once been spoken to Gedeon, but, as addressed to Mary, they contained a deeper meaning, applicable to herself alone. The Lord is, and ever has been, with thee by the plenitude of his grace, and soon he will be with thee by his corporal presence, assuming human flesh in thy chaste womb.

Blessed art thou among women. Other women before thee have been blessed, but none ever were or shall be blessed like thee ; thou art blessed because of thy immaculate sanctity ; thou art blessed because consecrated to the Lord by vow, and thou art about to be supremely blessed in becoming the mother of thy Creator, and at the same time retaining the privileges of a spotless virgin. Humility inspired thee to renounce this super-eminent dignity, and that humility it is which God has determined to crown with a diadem of unparalleled splendour. Other women have esteemed it an evidence of merit, and an act of piety, to aspire to the honour of the divine maternity, but, by deeming thyself unworthy of it, thou hast deserved to be preferred before all. The special benediction of the Most High has descended on thee, because thou wert so deeply penetrated with the conviction of thy nothingness. Mary was disturbed at the words of the heavenly messenger; she could scarcely attribute such expressions to an angel, nor could she suppose them to be addressed to herself. Her perplexity arose only from the low estimate she had formed of her own merits. She apprehended illusion; she feared the snares of the devil; she distrusted a salutation couched in so commendatory a strain; she became suspicious of circumstances that tended to exalt her in her own esteem, and her humility took alarm to an extent which it required an angel's word to re-assure.

How pleasing to God was Mary's distrust of a salutation which she considered totally inapplicable to her! He permitted that she should be addressed in these flattering terms because he knew her to be incapable of attributing the angel's praises to her own deserts, and he would have dictated one more guarded, had he foreseen any cause of apprehension for her humility. There is undoubtedly no stronger temptation to vanity than that which springs from the commmendations bestowed by the God of truth himself.

The soul must hear that commendation, she must believe it, and yet she must indulge no self-complacency, but refer all the glory to God alone. Would virtue less heroic than Mary's have withstood the trial? The triumph of her humility was, that it acquired increased stability in proportion to the violence of the shock it seemed to receive.

We should never desire a share in the extraordinary graces granted to the saints, or in the testimony on some occasions given by heaven to their virtue. Let us rather imitate Mary, who never anticipated the angel's message, and who would have rendered herself unworthy of the favour had she been capable of ambitioning it. Such privileges are dangerous or not, according to the disposition of heart in which they are received. It is infinitely better never to enjoy them than to pervert them into a source of vanity; the only security against the danger is to renounce not only the desire, but even the very thought of them. It would be a vain and fatal illusion, to imagine that supernatural favours had been granted as the reward of our ambitious desires. We should never deviate from the beaten path of our own accord, and if it please the Almighty to direct our steps into another way, we may be persuaded that only humility like that of Mary, will guide us safely through its intricacies.

CHAPTER VI.

Declaration of the mystery of the Incarnation.

THE angel re-assured the perplexed and timid virgin by the consoling words : " Fear not, Mary, for thou hast found grace with God." (St. Luke, i. 30.)　He it is who has sent me to thee, and dictated my words of peace and benediction. Thou hast found favour with him ; thou art more pleasing in his sight than any other created being ; he has selected thee as the co-operatrix in the greatest of his designs—the reparation of his glory, and the salvation of the universe. "Behold thou shalt conceive in thy womb, and shalt bring forth a son, and thou shalt call his name Jesus. He shall be great, and shall be called the Son of the Most High, and the Lord God shall give unto him the throne of David his father : and he shall reign in the house of Jacob for ever." (Ibid. 31, 32.)　How magnificent a promise, and how calculated to elate any heart less humble, less annihilated than that of Mary !　She shall have a son named Jesus, or the Saviour, who shall be great, absolutely, essentially, and incomparably ; great beyond all created dignity, because the son of the Most High !　This son, the descendant of David, shall be placed by the hand of the Lord on the throne of his illustrious ancestors—not the material throne which has fallen to rise no more, but a spiritual throne, of which David's was but the figure. He shall reign for ever over the true children of Jacob, that is, over God's faithful servants, to whom he shall be a master, a lawgiver, and a model; his reign of grace shall know no end; after having commenced on earth it shall endure eternally in heaven. Such was the meaning of the angel's words, which Mary at the time understood as far as was consistent with the obscurity of faith to which her soul was still subject. It is not probable that the sense of the promise was then as fully developed for her, as it is for us, now that the veil is withdrawn and the mystery revealed. God dispenses his heavenly light with wonderful economy, always leaving ample room for the exercise of faith. Mary herself, although more enlightened than any other mortal concerning the destiny of Jesus Christ, understood it fully only after the prophecies had been entirely accomplished in his person. Of this fact the gospel furnishes more than one instance.

Mary was less struck by the mysterious sublimity of the great events announced to her, than by the apparent impossibility of reconciling the fulfilment of the angel's promises, with the observance of her vow. She was informed of her high destiny as mother of God, and she had solemnly consecrated her virginity to heaven. "How shall this be done," she asked, "because I know not man?" (Ibid. 34.). Without in the least distrusting the infinite power of God, she simply represented the apparent impediment to his designs offered by her vow, inquiring how she was to fulfil her resolution of observing it inviolate, and at the same time give birth to the Redeemer.

We cannot too often advert to the fact, that the thoughts and words of Mary were ever supernatural in their principle, and most especially so on this occasion. The disposition she manifested to the angel, was precisely that produced by the grace of God himself. Every feeling she cherished at that moment, every word she uttered, was inspired by the Holy Ghost, and while the angel unfolded her sublime destiny, the Spirit of God taught her to restrain her solicitude to the preservation of the purity she so dearly prized. Hence we may conclude that in the estimation of heaven, the love and practice of any virtue, even that which regards only the purity of man's material portion, are of greater value than the most exalted supernatural favours. Like Mary, let us esteem the smallest act of virtue beyond all the gifts of heaven, because it is not those gifts, but the virtues, which subdue nature, that give glory to God, and sanctify the soul. God does not bestow his gifts, that for instance of prayer, merely to enrich us with spiritual treasures considered in themselves, but that such gifts may facilitate the practice of Christian perfection, which consists in self-denial, forgetfulness of personal interest, and total death to nature. Prayer which does not produce these results, however sublime and exalted it may appear, is in reality of no avail, and will tend only to our condemnation. If Mary had suffered herself to be so dazzled by her destined dignity, as to lose sight of the apparent necessity it involved of transgressing her vow, God would beyond a doubt have rejected her. The words both of Mary and the angel had been previously prepared, foreseen, and arranged in God's eternal counsels, and had she deviated in the slightest degree from the prescribed order, she would have caused the failure of the most celebrated embassy ever known on earth.

CHAPTER VII.

Declaration of the accomplishment of the Mystery.

" THE Holy Ghost shall come upon thee, and the power of the Most High shall overshadow thee." (St. Luke, i. 35.) By these consoling words, the angel allayed Mary's anxiety concerning the preservation of the precious virtue she cherished more highly, than the dignity of Mother of God. Thou shalt conceive by the operation of the Holy Ghost; the Most High will display in thy favour the prodigies of his omnipotence; he will infringe an inviolable law of nature, miraculously to form in thee the flesh to which the Word shall be united. This great work shall be the production of the adorable Trinity, each of the Divine persons concurring in its accomplish-

ment. Ineffable mystery! holy secret! impervious to all but God, and unintelligible even to
the spirit of light sent from heaven to disclose it!
It exceeded the limits of Mary's comprehension;
therefore, to believe it, required the strongest
effort of her faith. She inquired how the mysterious promise could be realized; the explanation
was given, but in terms too abstruse, too sublime,
to be fully understood. Reason could not penetrate the clouds which darkened round it; but it
could, and it did, submit its lights to the supreme
wisdom of Him, who can easily command resources beyond the comprehension of his weak
creatures.

"And therefore," added the angel, "the Holy
which shall be born of thee shall be called the
Son of God." (Ibid.) The body formed by the
operation of the Holy Ghost in thy chaste womb,
and of thy purest blood, shall be sanctified even
with the holiness of the Son of God, to whom it
shall be united. That flesh shall be truly styled
the flesh of the Son of God. The union of a
human soul thereto, will not produce a separate
individual; but these two substances, inseparably
united to the Word, will form but one person
with him : so that his soul will be the soul of the
Word—his body the body of the Word incarnate.
It was fitting that the flesh destined for the
earthly tabernacle of the Son of God, should be
formed in the womb of a virgin, and by the operation of the Holy Ghost.

To render more palpable the facility with

which the Lord of power could accomplish so great a miracle, the angel added, " Behold thy cousin, Elizabeth; she hath conceived a son in her old'age ; and this is the sixth month with her that is called barren. Because no word shall be impossible with God." (Ibid. 36, 37.) It is God who speaks to thee by my lips ; God, who declares that thou shalt become a mother, without ceasing to be a virgin. He is sovereign truth and infinite power. The laws of nature, first established by his decree, are subject to his all-controlling will ; he can reverse them at pleasure. Hesitate not then to believe His word.

When God has any extraordinary design on a soul, although it may not enter into his wise arrangements fully to develop its nature, or clearly to manifest the means by which it shall be accomplished, he yet explains himself so far as to establish a firm conviction of his boundless power and to remove all grounds of anxious apprehension. He requires of that favoured soul, a compliance based on motives at once intelligible and incomprehensible to her ; incomprehensible, because human reason cannot penetrate the deep secrets, buried in the bosom of God ; intelligible, because she has in the veracity and omnipotence of the Almighty, clear and manifest reasons for submitting. We should never permit ourselves curiously to anticipate the trials to which God may subject our fidelity, and the means he will provide for the accomplishment of those sacrifices. These are matters surpassing our comprehension ; could we understand them, they would cease to provide an exercise for our faith, and, consequently, an occasion of merit. We should rely implicitly on the word of God, and having been once assured by those who hold his place that he has really spoken, we should unhesitatingly believe, even against the clearest evidence of sense and reason.

CHAPTER VIII.

Consent of Mary.

RE-ASSURED on the point which had most excited her uneasiness, and trusting to the words of the angel, although she could not understand them, Mary no longer hesitated to give her consent. " Behold the handmaid of the Lord," said she; " be it done to me according to thy word." (St. Luke, i. 38.)

Several important reflections here suggest themselves. First, the Almighty expressly demanded the consent of the Blessed Virgin Mary to become the mother of God, deputing an angel to ask that consent in his name—an evidence of the tender consideration with which he treats his creatures, when he destines them to concur in the accomplishment of such designs as deviate from the ordinary course of events. Before executing those designs, he proposes them to the acceptance of his servants, and condescendingly listens to

the reasons they may have to allege in opposition.   He solicits, but does not extort, their
consent, desiring that it should be the free ema-
nation of an unshackled will.   The dignity of
mother of God was a singular favour, an incomparable privilege, an unexampled distinction,
never again to be renewed.   But the exalted title
involved equally important obligations.   It required that Mary should give to God, in the same
proportion as she had received from him ; that
she should aspire to the most heroic sanctity ;
that she should unreservedly immolate herself to
the will of God, and absolutely die to her own ;
that she should submit to the most severe trials ;
that she should share the sufferings of her Son,
and thus co-operate with him in the redemption
of the human race.   She was too deeply versed
in the spiritual meaning of the prophecies, not
to know that the Messiah was to be " a man of
sorrows," (Is. liii. 3,) and a victim of woe.
While she listened to the angel's communication,
a general view and impression of these facts were
no doubt imparted to her mind; perhaps the
celestial messenger may have unfolded to her
more of her future lot, than in her humility she
has seen fit to disclose.   It is quite probable that
she anticipated the consequences of the consent
she was about to pronounce, and foresaw that, as
the mother of the world's Redeemer, she should
share more largely than any other being in his
cross ; her consent would otherwise have been
far less meritorious than it was.   Her first act,

on consenting to become the mother of Jesus, was to immolate herself as a holocaust to God's glory ; just as the first act of her divine Son, on assuming human nature, was to offer himself as a victim to his Father's will.

Secondly, in accepting the title proposed to her by the angel, Mary stood in need of a greater fund of heroism, generosity, and courage, than at first sight appears ; this the foregoing reflections clearly prove. In the dignity of mother of God, we discern only a supernatural favour, which exalts its happy possessor above men and angels ; and, viewed under this aspect, we do not understand that it could have cost Mary an effort to accept it ; we imagine, on the contrary, that she should have grasped the proffered honour with joyful eagerness. But because we judge of supernatural favours by the standard of human feeling, we are liable to grievous errors. That dignity was in truth a burden, and a heavy one ; the weighty crosses destined for Mary were all dependent on it, as the overwhelming cross prepared for her divine Son, was a consequence of the union of the Word with the sacred humanity. As, by its union with the Word, that sacred humanity was in a manner annihilated, and made a victim of divine wrath for the sins of men ; so, by her union with Jesus as his mother, Mary was likewise reduced to a species of annihilation—that union involving the total destruction of nature, preceded by a martyrdom inferior only to that of her Son. Hence we may infer the heroism with which she pronounced the fiat, on which depended the reparation of God's glory and the salvation of the human race.

A third reflection arising from this mystery, and very strongly urged by the holy Fathers, regards Mary's profound humility. An angel saluted her Mother of God, and, at the very moment of accepting the title, she styled herself his handmaid. The wonderful privilege which was to give her authority over an incarnate God, she accepted solely through submission and obedience, impressed at that moment, even more deeply than before, with a sense of her unworthiness. While exercising the prerogatives of a mother, Mary will ever remember that she is a servant—and the servant, too, of the very Being on whom she imposes her commands. The higher her exaltation, the more profound will be her humility. Such is the effect of heavenly favours, when they are received and employed according to the intentions of the Donor. Those favours invariably demand the practice of sublime virtue, particularly of humility. The more God exalts us, the more should we humble ourselves. It is not supernatural favours which unite the soul to God, but her fidelity in cherishing the recollection of her nothingness amidst those favours. O, humility! who understands thy value? who prefers thee before all treasures? who endeavours to reap from every occurrence of life the precious fruit of self-abjection? Such a soul is great in the sight of God, and, beside this, there is no true greatness. Next to Jesus Christ, Mary furnishes the most striking example of the virtue. How glorious was the dignity of Jesus Christ, and how absolute the annihilation of which that dignity was the measure! How exalted the prerogatives of his mother, and how deep the humility her singular privileges produced!

CHAPTER IX.

Accomplishment of the Mystery of the Incarnation.

As soon as Mary had given her consent, the angel departed, and with this circumstance the evangelist closes his narrative, drawing a veil over the ineffable mystery at that moment accomplished in the Blessed Virgin. The Holy Ghost came upon her, and formed the body of the Man-God in her chaste womb, and of her purest blood. At its creation, that diminutive body was complete and perfect in all its parts, and, with his soul, was immediately and inseparably united to the person of the Word. St. Luke makes no allusion to this subject, his gospel having been dictated by the Blessed Virgin, who buried in secrecy the prodigies then wrought within her. Doubtless, it would have surpassed her power to expound a mystery at once incomprehensible and inexplicable. But she could at

least have described the divine ecstasy in which
her soul was plunged—the heavenly delights
with which her heart overflowed. Yet she preferred to conceal the wondrous secret; and when
the supernatural visitation had passed away, she
did not permit herself to recal it, even by a
thought.

Since the Spirit of God and her own humility
both concurred in suggesting to Mary the expe-
diency of silence on this subject, our duty is to
respect and imitate that silence. What, indeed,
could human lips explain of so deep a mystery!
and would not any attempt at such details bear
the colouring of imagination, not the stamp of
truth. St. Paul says, that, in his translation to
the third heaven, he heard mysterious words,
not given to man to speak. Sublime as were
the revelations granted to the apostle, they certainly bore no comparison with the wonders
wrought through the ineffable union of the holy
Spirit with the Blessed Virgin. Let us learn
from her example, first, to conceal the extraordinary graces it may please God to grant us,
communicating them even to our spiritual di-
rectors merely as a necessary preservative against
illusion. Secondly, not to investigate curiously
the effects produced by the sensible operations
of grace, and to banish all reflections on the
subject. The tendency of self-love is, unfortunately to indulge such reflections, which inevitably produce temptations to vain-glory. The
soul should be a mere channel to receive those

graces and allow them an unimpeded flow, making no effort, either of will or understanding, to
arrest them on their way. Thirdly, not to scan
with too eager an eye the communications of
the saints with God; not to dwell too long on
those passages of their lives which treat of such
subjects, and, above all, to avoid the works of
injudicious, although pious authors, who profess
to explain truths far removed above the reach of
mortal understanding. Observe the admirable
caution of the Scripture in treating of such matters; it merely states necessary facts, and leaves
no room for the exercise of vain curiosity. Let
us not attempt to dive into the secrets of God;
he reserves the revelation of them for the next
life, because he knows it would be both useless
and dangerous in this. It was not those graces
which sanctified God's servants; and our only
anxiety should be to discover the means by which
they attained the holiness we revere in them.
On this point, more than any other, we should
practise that "wisdom unto sobriety" recommended by St. Paul, (Rom. xii. 3.) Many spiritual works inculcate a false, or at best a
dubious, doctrine. Among these, all such as
enter too deeply into the mysteries of prayer,
hold a conspicuous rank. They should be distrusted; far from elevating and enlightening the
mind, they merely create abstract and confused
ideas, founded on no solid principle; they puff
up the soul, and exhaust the fountain of piety.
Devout females are fond of books of this descrip-

tion, which unfortunately tend only to excite their imaginations, to bewilder their minds, and to supply them with a mystic jargon, which they habitually adopt without understanding.   The worst feature of the evil is, that, applying to their own individual cases the maxims laid down in these works, they create for themselves an imaginary state of spiritual existence, and fancy they are gifted with a clear insight into the actual condition of their souls.   It is incredible to what profit the enemy converts this fatal ambition for the reputation of spiritual science.   Avoid the defect, and take example from Mary in this, as in all else.   No one on earth was ever so thoroughly versed in the knowledge of divine truths —a knowledge derived, not from books, but from personal experience; compared with her, the most learned doctors, the most enlightened saints, the apostles of Christ themselves, were ignorant.   Yet no one was ever more reserved in displaying the treasures of her wisdom; and from her reserve, we learn a more profound and instructive lesson, than she would have conveyed by the most sublime revelations on her interior condition.

CHAPTER X.

Reflections on the Divine Maternity.

MARY is now about to enter on a new state, more holy and perfect than any by which it has been preceded. The angel has hailed her *full of grace ;* she possesses within herself the author of grace, and not for a passing moment merely, since for nine months he will repose in her womb. While she imparts nourishment from her own substance to the body of her Son, and while that adorable body constitutes but one with her own, her Son spiritually nourishes her by the influence of his Divinity. He is to the soul of his mother, what she is to his body, communicating to her his divine substance, if the expression be admissible, in exchange for the corporal substance he derives from her. How close a union ! There is none more intimate in the order of nature, than that of a mother with the child of her womb. All the dispositions and impressions of that mother are communicated to her child; whatever affects one, affects the other by sympathy, for physically they are but one. Neither can there be a more intimate union in the order of grace than that of Mary with Jesus. The dispositions and sentiments of the Son are communicated to the soul of the mother ; he imparts to her a share in every affection of his heart, every impression of his spirit, and morally speaking

they form but one. Mary was already habituated
to the practice of interior recollection, but how
different the recollection in which she was now
absorbed, a recollection of which she had not previously even an idea! She constantly enjoyed the
presence of God, but how imperfectly in comparison with the present privilege, which authorized
her to say, "God is really within me, he is more
intimately present to me than I am to myself, and
as my life is his, so his life is also mine."
Hitherto she prayed habitually, but now, it is
Jesus Christ himself who prays in and with her,
so that her prayer is one with the prayer of the
Word incarnate. She has no need to transport
her thoughts and affections beyond their own
sphere, in order to find her God, for she possesses him in herself. Union with him has become in one sense her natural condition, the
same divine Being who reposes from eternity in
the bosom of the Father, dwelling in time in her
chaste womb. This last remark includes all that
can be said of the interior of Mary, and nothing
remains but to confess it incomprehensible.

In what besides does the Word of God instruct his blessed Mother during the period of his
abode in her womb? He enlightens her to discover more clearly than ever the majesty of the
Creator and the nothingness of the creature.
He imparts to her thoughts and sentiments of humility, which she did not, and could not previously
know. He teaches her, that if the Deity can be
worthily honoured only by the humiliations of a

God made man, our most perfect homage can
have no intrinsic value in his sight, or even deserve acceptance for its own sake. What a lesson!
And by whom was that lesson ever more perfectly understood, than by the Mother of Him who
was made flesh to restore to his Father the glory
due to him? From that moment, Mary thought not
of glorifying God by her own homage, but, penetrated with the knowledge of her incapacity, she
glorified him now only through his Son. "I can
do nothing," said she, "I am nothing; I have
nothing to offer thee of myself O my God! but I
have the Son whom thou hast given me; and
through him, I adore thee, and I thank thee for
all thy benefits. Do not look on me, for I am
unworthy to meet thine eye, and to be admitted
to thy presence; but look on thy Son, who is
mine, as well as thine. He has annihilated himself in acknowledgment of thy sovereign dominion,
and far from considering his present humiliation
excessive, he would stoop yet lower if it were
possible. Alas! what can I do but unite the
nothingness of my nature to his voluntary annihilation, and intreat thee to receive the homage of
the Mother through that of the Son?"

As soon as Mary became Mother of God, she disappeared altogether from her own eyes. Her finite
nature was engulfed in the immensity of the self-
existing Being she possessed in her womb, and as
a drop of water is lost in the wide expanse of the
ocean, so was she absorbed in the abyss of the
Divinity. Thus, to repeat a remark of frequent

recurrence in these pages : an increase of humility is ever the result of the spiritual exaltation which God confers.

O incomparable humility! I know thee not, and unless the strong, clear light of heaven reveals thee to my view, I never shall know thee. If any thing can impress me with esteem for this great virtue, it must be the knowledge that the Mother of God herself cherished and practised it, and that even to her, it was of indispensable necessity. How humble she must have been to merit the title of Mother of God, and how much must her humility have increased after that glorious appellation had been conferred! How unjust we are, how deserving of contempt, when we aspire to be anything great! how culpable when we convert the gifts of God into an occasion of vanity; when we appropriate them, or consider their possession an evidence of superior sanctity! This is totally to subvert order, to oppose the designs of God, and to insult him most sensibly. To pervert into a source of vanity, the gifts destined to produce an increase of humility, is to imitate the pride of the infernal spirits themselves. O incarnate Word! through the intercession of thy holy Mother, I beseech thee to employ the omnipotence of thy grace, in crushing and annihilating my pride and self-love! Spare me not I beseech thee, but pluck up those vices from the very root, for I shall never be anything before thee, while I am of importance in my own eyes. If thou foreseest that I shall arrogantly glory in thy gifts, withhold or withdraw them, for I am willing to be spiritually destitute, provided I be but humble!

CHAPTER XI.

Mary's visit to Saint Elizabeth.

MARY having learned from the angel that St. Elizabeth was likely soon to become a mother, resolved, under the inspiration of divine charity, to pay her an immediate visit of congratulation, and to render her the services due from a relative under such circumstances. Jesus, in suggesting this idea to his mother, had in view the higher object of sanc‑ tifying his precursor John, and remotely preparing him to discharge the peculiar functions attached to that office. He did not reveal this object to Mary, who was unacquainted with the particulars of the late events connected with Elizabeth, and quite ignorant of the destiny of John, but he made use of this visit to bring about its accomplishment. "In those days," says the evangelist, and immediately after the angel's apparition, "Mary rising up, went into the hill country with haste into a city of Judea." (St. Luke, i. 39.) This city was at a great distance from Nazareth, and quite at the opposite extremity of Judea; the journey was therefore long and fatiguing to a young person only fifteen or sixteen years of age.

The history of this journey is fruitful in useful reflections. Mary, although the inferior of Eliza-

beth in point of age, was as Mother of God immeasurably her superior in dignity; had she been
capable of deciding this question at the tribunal
of human feeling, she would have concluded herself dispensed from visiting her cousin, and obliged at most, to offer her congratulations and trans-
mit her inquiries through the medium of a third
person. But such are not the notions of humility.
That a visit to Elizabeth could be in the least degree derogotary to her own dignity, did not even
occur to the mind of Mary; on the contrary, the
courteous act appeared to her an imperative duty,
and she was eager to depart on her mission of
love.

Having been apprised of Elizabeth's condition
by an angel, and not by herself, Mary might
reasonably have supposed that her cousin would
not impute her absence to neglect; this one argument would in fact have been considered conclusive by any one but herself; but when charity and
humility have acquired an ascendancy such as they
exercised over Mary, the arguments prompted by
human feeling are silenced at once and for ever.
She was not deterred from visiting Elizabeth, because indebted to a heavenly revelation for her
knowledge of her state; she did not take umbrage
at her cousin's omitting to inform her of the favour God had done her; she did not say, "Elizabeth ought to have apprised me of her situation,
if she expected that I should visit her," but without hesitation, she prepared to congratulate her
in person on her joyful prospect of miraculously

becoming a mother, firmly determined to refrain from the slightest allusion to her own happiness.

Mary's alacrity teaches us to sacrifice retreat, silence, prayer, and pious exercises, for the fulfilment of certain duties imperatively demanded by the claims of relationship or the forms of civility. If her piety had been ill-regulated, how many plausible reasons she could have alleged to dispense with this visit, and to justify herself for remaining alone with God in the solitude of Nazareth? Grace does not authorize the neglect of any duty to our neighbour, not even of the attentions prescribed by the forms of politeness, and to omit duties of this description under the pretext of devotion, is totally to misapply, as well as to misunderstand piety. If, on these unavoidable occasions, we follow the example of Mary, our virtue will suffer no detriment; but, like her, we should carefully guard against dissipation, and avoid unnecessary intercourse with the world. Mary forgot herself to think of her cousin, but she did not forget God, and amidst the exterior distractions inseparable from a long journey, she never for a moment lost sight of his holy presence.

When duties of this nature are discharged from a pure motive; when our intercourse with men is animated in its most minute details by an upright intention, the Almighty frequently renders ordinary conversation subservient to designs far above those to which of its own nature it seems to tend; those designs he conceals until the moment marked out for their completion. The principal result attached in the views of God to Mary's visit was the sanctification of the precursor of Jesus. She was ignorant of the fact, yet unconsciously concurred in fulfilling the will of heaven. This visit was the means appointed for the realization of a momentous design ; had the visit been omitted through Mary's neglect, she would have been responsible for the failure of the great design. This truth is one of much practical importance. Circumstances apparently insignificant, are often connected with others of vital consequence to the spiritual interests of our fellow- creatures. This connection is concealed from us, but we may and should presume on its existence, and should therefore be careful never to omit a duty even of civility, since on that mere form, serious results may depend. For example, we receive or pay a visit, which seems nothing more than a matter of ceremony ; perhaps in the all-wise arrangement of God, great spiritual profit is to accrue to our neighbour from that visit. An accidental observation will pave the way for a confidential communication ; grace will exercise its softening influence on the heart, and precious will be the fruits of salvation produced by a seemingly inadequate cause. How many conversions may be traced to interviews of this description, commenced with no serious intention ? how many souls have entered by this door into the way of perfection ! St. Francis of Sales did more good by familiar conversation, than by his sermons and controversial discourses. Let us carefully observe the forms prescribed by the usages of society, and that from a pure motive, and under the guidance of divine grace, so that our thoughts and words being directed by heavenly inspiration, God may derive glory from our efforts.

CHAPTER XII.

Interview of Mary and Elizabeth.

" Mary," says St. Luke, " entered into the house of Zachary, and saluted Elizabeth. And it came to pass, that, when Elizabeth heard the salutation of Mary, the infant leaped in her womb. And Elizabeth was filled with the Holy Ghost, and she cried out with a loud voice, and said: ' blessed art thou among women, and blessed is the fruit of thy womb.' " (i. 40, 42.)

How many wonders wrought by the meeting of the two holy relatives, and the mere salutation of Mary ! Jesus Christ was in reality the sole agent in accomplishing those prodigies, Mary being only his instrument ; yet he totally refrained from manifesting his divine action. While the voice of Mary sounded in the ears of Elizabeth, the voice of Jesus gently whispered to the heart of John. While the presence of Mary imparted heavenly peace to the spirit of her cousin, the presence of Jesus purified the soul of John from original sin, enriched it with grace, enlightened it to know and adore the Redeemer whose way he was destined to prepare, and replenished it with such overflowing joy, that the happy infant bounded with exultation in his mother's womb. At the same moment Elizabeth was herself filled with the Holy Ghost, and the cause of her child's miraculous exultation was revealed to her. By the light of faith, she discovered the dignity of Mary, as mother of the divine Infant from whose mere presence emanated the miracles effected in herself. In a holy transport she declared Mary to be blessed above all women, because of her twofold privilege of virginity and divine mater‑ nity ; and the fruit of her womb she proclaimed supremely blessed because of its union with the Word. Elizabeth derived from John the clear knowledge granted her of the mystery of the incarnation, and John had in turn received the heavenly communication from Jesus. Once more, how important were the results consequent on a visit of mere courtesy !

Great must have been Mary's surprise when she found that the Holy Ghost had revealed to her cousin the wondrous secret, over which she herself had resolved to draw a veil ! But knowing that the Almighty was at liberty to manifest it at his own pleasure, she adored the depths of the designs she was unable to fathom. Being igno‑ rant of the spiritual communication between Jesus and John, she knew not that Elizabeth was indebted to her son for the supernatural informa‑

tion she possessed. "Whence," pursued Elizabeth, "is this to me, that the mother of my Lord
should come to me?" (Ibid. 43.) Thus clearly
and emphatically declaring her belief in the divine
maternity of Mary. The unaffected surprise, and
deep sense of unworthiness, which accompanied
the words, proved that they had been dictated by
the spirit of God himself, and thus, through the
lips of her cousin, Mary received a certain con--
firmation of the reality of the favours bestowed
on herself. She did not ask that confirmation,
she did not seek it, and God granted it at the
moment it was least expected.

What a fund of instruction this circumstance
unfolds to souls whom God leads by extraordinary
ways! Doubt, and distrust of their interior condition, not uncommonly succeed to perfect confidence; this alternation of feeling is to be traced
either to the gradual decline of an impression at
first strong, or to the enemy's malicious efforts to
disturb their peace, or to the agitation they themselves create by anxiously dwelling on the vicissitudes they experience. They should not importune
heaven to guarantee the security of their state,
but, on the contrary, humbly and calmly trust
like Mary, that the certitude will be granted if
necessary. God will not forsake such souls in
the hour of their need, but will very clearly prove
to themselves and others that their interior condition is the work of his grace. Until it is his
will to speak, the obscurity of faith should be
their refuge, and the judgment of their spiritual

guides their anchor. They should not at all times seek assurances which the wisdom of God reserves for peculiar seasons, and which, given at any other period of their career, would serve but to retard their progress. They have to accomplish no less a work than that of entire death to self, and this they certainly could never effect had they a permanent security concerning their actual state. Mary never asked a favour of the kind, and yet, as the gospel amply testifies, her faith was more severely tried than that of any other of God's servants.

Elizabeth doubtless understood the mysterious cause of her son's exultation in her womb, since on that circumstance she founded Mary's claim to the title of "mother of her Lord." As if to account for applying to her that appellation, she added the remark, "as soon as the voice of thy salutation sounded in my ears, the infant in my womb leaped for joy."—(Ibid. 44.) The source of this miraculous joy she knew to be the presence of the Son of God, who, from his mother's womb, exercised his divine influence on the soul of his yet unborn precursor.

"And blessed art thou that thou hast believed," continued Elizabeth, "because those things shall be accomplished that were spoken to thee by the Lord." (Ibid. 45.) On what does she principally congratulate the holy virgin? On her faith. She believed the two wonderful predictions of the angel, first, that she should be the mother of the Son of God according to the flesh, and next, that

in giving birth to Jesus Christ, through the operation of the Holy Ghost, she should retain the
privileges of inviolate virginity. Silencing the
suggestions of reason, she bent its powers beneath
the dominion of faith, and without asking an
explanation of a subject which surpassed her
comprehension, she blindly submitted to the
authority of God.

Faith is in truth the great principle of all
spiritual blessings. This observation refers not
merely to that faith which is common to all
Christians, but to that peculiarly strong faith
necessary to those souls whom grace especially
directs. A high degree of the virtue is requisite,
blindly to believe the revelation of God's designs,
and courageously to refrain from desponding
doubts when the confident security which accom-
panies the actual revelation has passed away.
Neither does it demand a less lively faith to persevere in believing, when the means employed by
the Almighty for the execution of his work,
appear contrary to the end proposed ; when
seemingly insurmountable obstacles arise in all
directions, and events assume an aspect quite
opposite to that with which the words of God
appeared originally to invest them.

The predictions of the angel concerning the
prerogatives of the Messiah are well worthy of
attention. " He shall be called the Son of the
Most High, and the Lord God shall give unto
him the throne of David his father, and he shall
reign in the house of Jacob for ever." Let us

compare the angel's promises with the actual
circumstances of the life of Christ; the destitution
of his obscure birth at Bethlehem; the poverty
of his hidden life of thirty years, spent in the
workshop of a poor tradesman; the privations of
his public career, during which he lived on alms,
and had no spot whereon to rest his head; the
sufferings entailed by the envy and hatred of his
persecutors, who calumniated his doctrine, denied
his miracles, combined to seize his person, and
finally awarded him the death of a blasphemer,
because he had declared himself the Son of God;
the humiliations heaped on him as a mock king;
the contempt evinced in the universal preference
of the malefactor Barabbas; in fine, the ignominy of the cross.   How is he to substantiate his
claim to the promised throne of David?   How
is he to realize an endless reign over the house of
Jacob?   Does not the life of Jesus present a
manifest contradiction of the angel's splendid promises?   How strong must have been the faith on
which rested Mary's confident expectation of their
realization at a future period—the period following her son's triumphant resurrection from the
dead, when they were fulfilled in a spiritual sense
infinitely more exalted, and more worthy of their
divine author, than that apparently implied by
the words of the angel.

CHAPTER XIII.

Explanation of the Canticle of the Blessed Virgin.

MARY replied to Elizabeth in a canticle, which may be styled the ecstasy of her humility. Its subject is twofold,—God and herself. Of God, she speaks, to proclaim his praises; of herself, to publish her nothingness. " My soul," she exclaimed, "doth magnify the Lord: and my spirit hath rejoiced in God, my Saviour," (St. Luke, i. 46, 47.) Who can describe, who can understand, the sentiments which warmed the heart of Mary while her lips pronounced these words? It is not within the reach of human capacity to explain the divine ecstasy which at that moment transported the soul of the favoured virgin beyond itself, or the perfection of the spiritual disengagement which gave all glory to God alone, and reserved absolutely nothing for self. God bestowed on her a degree of glory immeasurably surpassing that ever granted to a mortal. Mary received that glory only to restore it in its integrity to the Giver, and no creature in return ever glorified God so perfectly as she did. What a triumph to the Almighty, if so strong an expression be admissible, to see that the supereminent privileges of this thrice-favoured soul were converted only into a new incentive to praise his mercy! How pleasing to know that she had absolutely forgotten herself to think of him; that her existence was absorbed in his immensity—her faculties engulfed in his perfections. Her soul overflowed with celestial joy, but not on account of her personal exaltation, sublime as it was. All her thoughts were directed to God, the Author of her happiness, who had taken flesh in her womb, to effect her salvation and that of the human race. So completely did she banish the remembrance of her own interests, to fix her view on those of God, that even the attainment of heaven's bliss appeared to her desirable, not so much for her personal advantage, as on account of the glory thence resulting to God. Do we thus refer to God all the benefits we receive from him, and do we esteem perfection itself only for the sake of the glory it gives to our Creator? How few are influenced by sentiments so pure! The generality of Christians, even the holiest, have no idea of thus refining their views, the common practice of men being to appropriate the favours of heaven, and to desire sanctity, not for the glory of God as its primary motive and principal end, but as a personal acquisition. To advert to that glory, requires a premeditated effort, the spontaneous impulses of nature ever tending to self. O, fatal self-love! how universal is thy dominion! how widely diffused the influence of thy deadly poison! how daring thy efforts to encroach even on the love due to God himself, and, as far as thou canst, to enhance thine own glory by detracting from his! O, Mary, obtain for us light to see the dreadful deformity of this vice, courage to combat it, and generosity to submit to those crucifying operations of divine love which tend to its destruction !

Why is the Blessed Virgin transported with holy joy? "Because the Lord hath regarded the humility of his handmaid," (Ib. 48.) In herself she was nothing, and never could have been anything; God has looked on her, and to that divine glance she owes all she is. Although elevated to the rank of mother of God, she does not lose sight of her lowliness; she does not forget that she is *his handmaid*, but assumes this as her distinctive title. With what complacency, O Lord, must thou have looked on her who, while exalted to the pinnacle of unparalleled dignity, still cherished the memory of her no-thingness! Alas! it is because we indulge vanity amidst innumerable causes of humiliation, that God does not look on us. He knows, that were he to do so, the favour would serve only to increase our self-sufficiency. What a contrast between us and Mary !

"Because he hath regarded the humility of his handmaid, from henceforth all generations shall call me blessed," (Ibid.) To that merciful look I am indebted for all my prerogatives; but for it, I should be nothing. Considered in myself, the qualities I possess, far from entitling me to esteem, deserve the utmost contempt. Considered in the transformation effected by the look which God has cast on me, a look directed

solely by his gratuitous mercy, I can lay claim
to the glorious appellation of *blessed* through all
future ages, even to the end of time. I shall eternally praise for the favour the Divine Being who
has deigned to look on me, and I shall faithfully
restore all the honour paid me to God, its great
source, who alone is worthy to be praised in me.
Such are the sentiments of the beatified saints,
who entered into possession of the joys of heaven
only when their souls had been purified from the
last lingering remnant of self-love. While yet
an inhabitant of earth, Mary possessed them in
the utmost purity and perfection; and in this
point above all others we should study her
example.

"He that is mighty hath done great things to
me: and holy is his name," (Ibid, 49.) Mary
does not detract, through false humility, from
the great favours God has done her. She recog-
nizes them to be great—so great, that in comparison all the other works of his power and love
are nothing. But to what does she attribute
them? To his omnipotence, which knows no
difficulty in the execution of its designs—which
can trample at pleasure on 'the laws of nature,
and accomplish vast enterprises by a word. What
consequences does she deduce from the fact?
That *the name of God is holy;* that the works
of God all tend to promote the glory of that
name, as their sole object; and that to honour
it should be the single end of the thoughts, feelings, and actions of the creature. After having

thus referred and restored all to God, what does Mary retain for herself? Nothing. She desires nothing, she aims at nothing, but that all may join with her in proclaiming the wondrous manifestations of God's power and praising his adorable name. But the more she forgets herself, the more will God exalt her, for he knows that the honour paid to Mary will revert to himself, and that in her possession his glory will be secure. Let us seek only to promote the glory of God, and he will allow us to share it, without himself forfeiting any portion of it. The glory of Mary is unparalleled, because her humility was also unexampled. The Almighty seeks to place his gifts at safe interest, and he knows them to be secure only in the possession of the humble—a lesson strongly enforced by the example of the Blessed Virgin Mary.

" His mercy is from generation unto generation, to them that fear him," (Ibid, 50.) By those who fear God, the Scripture understands those who love him, and who, through love, refrain from offending him. Now, nothing more deeply wounds the heart of God than to rob him of that glory of which he is infinitely jealous. This is a crime he does not overlook, but invariably punishes. And how? By the subtraction of his mercies—the greatest misfortune that can befall a soul. He lavishes them with profusion on those who are inflamed with zeal for his glory, and apprehensive of depriving him of the least degree of it. Let us endeavour to imbibe that

salutary fear. Pride and vanity are our favourite
vices. Being in themselves detestable and sovereignly unjust, they have recourse to disguise,
that they may altogether elude our observation,
or so completely blind our judgment, that it
actually learns at last to justify them. Let us
often say with St. Philip Neri, " Distrust me,
O Lord, for I am a robber, who seek to deprive
thee of thy glory."

" He hath shewed might in his arm : he hath
scattered the proud in the conceit of their heart,"
(Ibid, 51.)   The expression, " the arm of God,"
as employed both in the Old and New Testament, signifies Jesus Christ.   By that arm, his
Word, he drew forth the world from nothing ;
by that same arm, the Word made flesh, he produced his wondrous creations in the spiritual
order.   How did that mighty arm chiefly display
its power?   By dispersing and punishing the
proud, who had impiously conspired to rob the
Most High of his glory.   These he humbled—
these he crushed, creating for their especial chastisement the torments of hell, where their eternal
punishment will be to restore to God the honour
they had vainly attempted to wrest from him.

" He hath put down the mighty from their
seat, and hath exalted the humble.   He hath
filled the hungry with good things : and the rich
he hath sent empty away," (Ibid, 52, 53.)   Such
is the plan of God's providence.   He humbles
the mighty, whom their high prerogatives inflate
with pride, raising the humble to their vacant

ranks. If not always guided by this rule in the present life, he never fails to act on it in the next. The highest places in heaven are for the humble ; the deepest dungeons in hell for the proud. Let us hunger and thirst after justice, and, recognizing our extreme weakness, let us recur to the aid of Him who will replenish our souls with heavenly food. If we abound even in spiritual treasures, and, by appropriating, pervert them into the food of pride, God will withdraw them; he will cast us from his presence, and consign us to the last extreme of indigence. Such is the lesson inculcated by the words, and forcibly illustrated by the example of Mary. Never shall we detest and shun pride as it deserves to be hated and avoided ; never, either, shall we adequately esteem or sufficiently pursue the practice of humility.

"He hath received Israel, his servant, being mindful of his mercy. As he spoke to our fathers, to Abraham, and to his seed for ever," (Ibid, 54, 55.) The real promises made to Abraham, his posterity, and those whom St. Paul terms the Israel of God, were of a spiritual nature, and destined to receive their fulfilment only in the coming of Christ. The hour of his descent on earth has dawned : he has taken flesh in the womb of Mary, and, even before his birth, He, the father of the true Israelites—He, whose day Abraham had desired to see, exulting to behold it even in spirit, pours benedictions on his holy precursor. Figures are about to cease ; Abraham will no longer be styled the Father of the Israelites, according to the flesh; but he will be considered the father of the faithful of all nations, and, with this posterity, will form the chosen people of the Redeemer. Mary, on this occasion, speaks the language of prophecy, and points out the accomplishment in her own person of the great promises made by God at the beginning of time, and since then renewed from age to age. Let us intreat her to explain to us herself the signification of her admirable canticle, and, above all, to inspire our hearts with a share in the sentiments in which it was uttered.

CHAPTER XIV.

Mary's return to Nazareth.

" MARY," as St. Luke tells us, " abode with Elizabeth about three months : and she returned to her own house," (St. Luke, i. 56.) She probably remained until after the birth of St. John the Baptist, leaving her cousin only when her services were of no further use to her; she was therefore present when Zachary, having miraculously recovered his speech, announced to men, in a sublime canticle, the accomplishment of the Incarnation, and the future dignity of the Redeemer's precursor. She listened, while the holy patriarch recounted the vision with which he had been favoured in the temple, and described the punishment which had followed his incredulity. Thus she learned the gradual progress of events, and, by a peculiar disposition of Providence, received from Zachary an unsolicited confirmation of the security of her state.

If Elizabeth derived such precious advantages from her first interview with Mary, what fruits must she not have reaped from her holy cousin's sojourn of three months beneath her roof? Mary had no other object in view in her visit, than to pay Elizabeth the attentions dictated by charity and kindness; but being full of grace, and possessing within herself the Author of all grace, her conduct, her words, her very presence, were to her saintly relative a fertile source of spiritual blessings. A new degree of sanctity was imparted to Elizabeth by her intercourse with Mary, and additional graces conferred on St. John through the secret action of Christ, who then laid the foundation of his precursor's future holiness. Although she interrupted for a time the retreat with which habit had familiarized her, and established an external communication with creatures, Mary abated nothing of her recollection—lost nothing of her union with God. She may have devoted less time to prayer than was her custom in her seclusion at Nazareth; she may have communed less with God, and more with her neighbour; but her habitual prayer was never discontinued—her conversation was either of God or it tended to God. She edified St. Elizabeth and her other associates by her amiable, tender charity to her cousin—by her modesty, her affability, her angelic demeanour; so that her visit, while it added lustre to her own perfection, contributed at the same time to the sanctity of all who enjoyed her company.

From Mary's example, we learn many excellent lessons for the regulation of our external intercourse with creatures. First, not to seek society too eagerly, but to wait until God himself leads us into it, interpreting as a manifestation of his will on this point, the duties prescribed by courtesy and politeness. Like Mary, to select seclusion from preference, yet willingly to abandon it at the call of necessity or the suggestion of grace. Secondly, as far as possible, to seek our associates among the pious, from whom we may receive, and to whom we may mutually impart, edification. Not to lament as lost the time devoted to our fellow-creatures from a good motive; yet, on the other hand, not to extend visits of courtesy a moment after it has become evident that they can benefit neither ourselves nor our acquaintances. Thirdly, to guard against the dangers of dissipation, never recurring to the society of creatures as a pastime, or a refuge against ourselves. How often we fly to the company of others, because weary of our own! Visits of this kind cannot fail to undermine the spirit of interior recollection. The heart which enjoys the sweets of union with its Creator, willingly foregoes the conversation of creatures, and communicates with them only through necessity or charity. Fourthly, not to prolong visits even of charity beyond a reasonable time. Mary returned home immediately after the birth of St. John the Baptist; it would not have been kind to depart before that event; it would not have been right to remain after it. As she looked to Elizabeth's comfort, not her own convenience, she terminated her visit when her services had ceased to be necessary to her cousin. Let us imitate her in this, withdrawing as soon as the immediate object of a visit or a conference has been attained. By observing these rules, we shall never suffer spiritual detriment from conversing with our neighbour, those conversations tending, on the contrary, through God's grace, to the sanctification both of our fellow-creatures and ourselves.

CHAPTER XV.

Suspicions of Joseph, and silence of Mary.

WHEN Mary returned from her visit to St. Elizabeth, nearly four months had elapsed since the incarnation of the Son of God. Her condition could not escape the immediate notice of St. Joseph, and, ignorant as he was of recent events, terrible must consequently have been his suspicions. This trial of Mary's fortitude, the prelude of many a sorrow to come, was to be traced to her unborn Son, as to its primary cause. Joseph was deeply impressed with her exalted virtue;

L 3

he knew that she had made a vow of virginity, and espoused him only on condition of his mutually observing continence—so that no tie should bind them but that of a brother and sister. He had ratified the engagement; he was conscious of having observed it to the letter; therefore, no alternative remained but to suppose her criminal. How heart-rending must have been the strong, presumptive evidence against her whom he loved with an affection so deep and holy! How agonizing the conflict of mind and heart, while undecided what opinion to form and what course to pursue! How oppressive the anxiety produced by these torturing doubts!

Respect for Mary sealed his lips, it is true; nevertheless, the agitation of his troubled heart betrayed itself; and too well did the holy Virgin know that she was herself the innocent cause of his anguish. How severe a trial to each, and how intense their mutual sufferings during its continuance! A trial so painful in its own nature was aggravated in the present instance by the particular sanctity of those concerned. Joseph betrayed by a spouse whom he had believed the perfection of purity! Mary suspected of crime, because selected by heaven to be the mother of God! "How dark the stain which has sullied the holiest union ever consummated on earth!" Such was the reflection of Joseph. "How unjust a suspicion! How gross an insult to the Spirit of God, whose power has done great things in me!"—Such might have been that of Mary.

One word from her lips, one allusion to the
angel's embassy, would have sufficed to justify
her, to calm Joseph's agitation, and to transform
injurious suspicion into deep veneration. He
would no doubt have given credit to the recital,
especially if it had embraced a detail of recent
events in the family of Zachary. But she maintained an inviolable silence; her secret was the
secret of God, and she resolved to observe it at
the expense even of reputation and life. Joseph
had it in his power to defame her; he was authorized and even commanded by the law to declare
her guilt to the priests, and death was the terrible
penalty awarded to the crime of which appearances seemed to convict her.

The Divine honour being visibly compromised
in that of Mary, it would appear that for its
defence she should have adopted those measures
which she refused to take for her own justification. So would any one but herself have thought;
but, although urged to speak by many powerful
reasons affecting her own character, the peace of
Joseph, and the glory even of God himself, she
uttered not one word which could serve as a clue
to the truth. Assuredly it was not natural feeling which dictated this line of conduct; on the
contrary, her dearest personal interests lost all
power to influence her decisions; she abandoned
them to God, knowing that, if such were his will,
he could easily manifest the wonders he had
wrought in her. Humility had placed a seal on
her lips, and no human motive could induce her
to remove it.

It frequently happens that the supernatural favours imparted to interior souls become for them an occasion of calumny and persecution. How should they act under such circumstances? The temptation to justify themselves is strong; one word would suffice to turn the tide of opinion in their favour; all possible motives seem to concur in urging the propriety of pronouncing that powerful word. It seems only just to undeceive their neighbour, to dissipate his prejudices, to avert a cause of many faults, which he will assuredly deplore when the truth has sooner or later been made manifest. It is just, also, to defend the cause of God, and to guard against the danger of converting his favours into an occasion of scandal. Something seems likewise due to their own reputation, virtue, piety, and public edification, all demanding that it be provided for. O, how futile are such pretexts, the offspring of self-love! How plainly unmasked and strongly condemned by Mary's example! Imitate her silence, and wait patiently until God shall himself justify you by manifesting his own work. Should you not rejoice when his favours become an occasion of self-sacrifice and interior death? They can produce no effect so glorious to God and so advantageous to yourself as this. If you adopt no measures for your justification, humiliation and suffering will no doubt ensue; but should not humiliation and suffering be the object of your holy desires?

St. Francis of Sales, being accused of writing

a letter derogatory to his character as a bishop, and exposing him to the imputation of vile hypocrisy, merely observed, that his writing had been well imitated, but that the letter was not his. He took no steps to discover the author of the calumny, " for," said he, " God knows the degree of reputation necessary to the success of my ministry, and I desire no more." He retained his peace, and never permitted himself even a desire of justification, although the circumstance had attracted much attention in France, in Savoy, and wherever it was divulged. The author of the imposture publicly confessed his guilt many years after. Opportunities like this of practising humility, seldom occur ; yet, in trifles, we are perpetually liable, particularly in communities, to unjust suspicions and imputations. How meritorious, to bear these trivial humiliations in silence, and without an attempt at exculpation! This practice is undoubtedly very repugnant to self-love, but then, the great occupation of our lives should be to subdue self-love.

CHAPTER XVI.

Mary justified by God himself.

MARY's deep sympathy in Joseph's feelings was powerless to disturb her interior peace ; and although she hoped that God would vindicate her innocence, she did not permit herself a voluntary desire to that effect. Joseph, being a just man, refrained not only from treating her with personal harshness, but even from availing, as he might have done, of the severity of the law. Her eminent virtue, clearly manifest even amidst the most unfavourable appearances, seemed to him a sufficient justification for omitting to see its rigorous ordinances enforced. He could not yet divest himself of profound respect for his angelic spouse; and God, who directed his feelings and proved his virtue, decreed that he should avoid the measures which, under similar circumstances, any one else would have adopted. He would not tarnish her fame, yet he could not continue to associate with her, which would have been tacitly to approve, or at least to connive at, supposed guilt. He therefore resolved to put her away, secretly and silently—a plan the most consistent with his ideas of rectitude, and with his anxiety to screen her reputation.

He was on the eve of executing this project, when God, who never abandons his servants in the hour of need, yet delays his succour until their virtue has been sufficiently tried, dispelled his well-founded anxiety, and changed his sadness into joy the most intense he had ever known. "While he thought on these things, behold the angel of the Lord appeared to him in his sleep, saying : Joseph, son of David, fear not to take unto thee Mary thy wife, for that which is conceived in her is of the Holy Ghost, and she shall bring forth a son : and thou shalt call his name Jesus,

for he shall save his people from their sins."—
(St. Matt. i. 20, 21.)

Thus was the great mystery revealed to Joseph,
God decreeing that the value of the precious
favour should be enhanced by the severity of the
preceding trials which had purchased it. What a
weight of misery was removed from his heart!
What an honour to find himself the spouse not
merely of a virgin, but of a virgin mother of God!
How profound the gratitude which filled his soul!
How inexplicable the sentiments in which he
passed the remainder of that happy night! No
sooner had he risen than "he did as the Lord
had commanded him, and," with renewed faith,
"took unto him his wife," (Ibid, 24.) The Scripture admits into its concise narratives none but
essential facts, and therefore does not specify that
Joseph communicated his dream to Mary, yet the
circumstance may be fairly inferred; his own
anxiety having been removed by the angel's words,
it is only natural to suppose that he was eager to
relieve the distress of Mary, who suffered even
more severely than himself, from sympathy in the
sorrows she could not alleviate. How lively were
the transports of pure and heavenly joy which
succeeded the poignant anguish unintentionally
inflicted on each other by these two saintly beings!
Joseph now looked on his virgin spouse with
other eyes, and he loved, admired, and revered
her more than ever. Mary's previous impressions
of Joseph's virtue were confirmed, and their

already intimate union was cemented by circumstances naturally calculated to dissolve it.

O God! how admirable is thy conduct towards
thy saints! Thy hand dispenses to them painful
trials, followed by sweet consolations, and those
trials and consolations tend equally to thy glory
and their sanctification. They have but to submit to thy operations, to confide in thy goodness,
and their hopes will not be confounded, for thou
never failest amply to indemnify thy servants for
the sufferings endured for thee. If Joseph had
questioned Mary, if Mary had revealed her secret,
and thus removed or anticipated Joseph's suspicions, their virtue would not have been so con-
spicuously manifested, God would not have been
glorified, nor they themselves rewarded.

Let us study the practical lesson taught by
this example; let us patiently endure trial while
it lasts, never seeking, by word or act, to avert
or abridge it, for we should thus deprive ourselves
of great merit, as well as of the heavenly comfort destined to succeed in God's own time.

There can be no question that Joseph respected
even more profoundly than before, the purity of
her who was chosen to be the spouse of the Holy
Ghost, and the mother of the God-man. The
gospel expressly certifies the fact, yet even independently of its testimony, no suspicion to the
contrary could for a moment find admittance to
our minds. Nevertheless, from that period they
maintained a more cordial and familiar intimacy

than ever. The mutual love of Mary and Joseph was a secret too delicate to admit of the scrutiny of earthly-minded mortals ; it was known to the angels only, and, far from encroaching on the incomparable purity of the saintly spouses, it served but to increase its heavenly lustre.

CHAPTER XVII.

Departure of Mary and Joseph for Bethlehem.

JOSEPH and Mary dwelt at Nazareth, and, in the natural order of events, in that town it was that Mary should have brought forth her son. But it had been predicted that the Messiah should be born at Bethlehem, the city of David, in the land of Judea, and it was necessary that God should provide for the accomplishment of the prophecy. He did not intimate his orders to Mary and Joseph through the ministry of an angel, as he could so easily have done, but he made use for this end of means quite natural, and, to all appearance, totally unconnected with the intended issue. The emperor Augustus, under whose sovereign sway Judea was then included, having resolved to number his subjects, in order to regulate the rate of taxation, a decree was published, ordaining that every family should repair to the district whence its ancestors had sprung, there to be enrolled. " And Joseph went up from Galilee, out of the city of Nazareth, into Judea, to the city of David, which is called Bethlehem ; because he was of the house and family of David, to be enrolled with Mary his espoused wife, who was with child."—(St. Luke, ii. 4, 5.)

How admirable are the ways of Providence, which executes its decrees by means apparently disproportioned to the end! What connection between the political edict of a pagan emperor, and the temporal birth of the Son of God? Yet, in the views of heaven, that edict was the means destined to bring about the birth of the Messiah at Bethlehem. The occurrence seemed the work of chance, and it had, on the contrary, been pre-ordained from eternity. In obeying the order of an idolatrous prince, Mary obeyed the command of God, although unconsciously, for it is probable she was not aware that the Messiah was to be born at Bethlehem.

Two lessons are here offered for our instruction. First, not to look on human events as the results of chance, but to believe that it is God who arranges them for the accomplishment of certain designs to be unfolded at a future time. He conceals his designs, that we may learn to execute his will with blind submission. We should not deviate from the arrangements of Providence, even in matters which appear of no moment, nor should we imagine that God leaves us at liberty to follow our own inclinations on these points. Between the various events of life, and our salvation and perfection, there is a link, of which we are unconscious, discovering it only after the event has manifested the connection. We often imagine that external circumstances, such, for example, as the residence we select, the society we frequent, and the projects we form, can have no material influence over our spiritual interests. But we mistake, as we should infallibly discover, if we were careful to examine the consequences produced by those external circumstances. A glance at the events of our past life, a reflection on the unexpected results, either for good or evil, entailed by those events, will serve to convince us of this important truth. We should submit unconditionally, even in temporal matters, to the authority of those appointed to direct us. If we are free to dispose of our own lot, we should adopt no resolution without having first consulted God. He has measured and regulated our steps, which will lead us to a happy or a miserable eternity, according as we follow his guidance, or swerve from it. But are we to have no control over our own position? None; and so much the better, for when we have totally abandoned it to God, he will assuredly dispose of it for our greater advantage.

We are taught, secondly, to refrain from the presumptuous expectation that God will accomplish his designs over us by extraordinary means. Nature loves to deviate from the common order, and thus to gratify spiritual vanity; God, on the contrary, desires to subject us to that fixed order— he subjected Mary and Joseph to it—except in cases of urgent necessity. Are we superior to them, or better entitled to God's extraordinary favours?

Another important lesson is here enforced by the example of Mary. She was on the eve of giving birth to the Son of God; she was very poor: at Nazareth, she was almost destitute of the comforts indispensable in her critical situation, and now, in addition, she was compelled to undertake a distressing journey in the winter season, and to seek an asylum among strangers, exposed to the risk of wanting actual necessaries both for herself and her infant. Still she did not complain, she did not murmur at the rigorous dispensation of Providence, or rebel against the human ordinance which so seriously inconvenienced her. She asked no mitigation of the sentence, no delay; she did not urge the consideration due to her child as a plea of exemption; she did not repine at a lot so little in accordance with that to be expected by the mother of God. No such thoughts occurred to her; she knew that God would provide for all emergencies, and she resolved to go where his will called, trusting to his goodness, submitting to affliction for his love, and blessing his name in all occurrences. In these sentiments she departed confidently and calmly, accompanied by Joseph, her spouse, her protector, and her guardian.

CHAPTER XVIII.

Birth of Jesus at Bethlehem.

THE history of Christ's nativity, as narrated in the gospel, is short and simple, yet, in its connection with the holy virgin to whom these pages principally refer, it is fruitful in instruction. "And it came to pass, that when they were at Bethlehem her days were accomplished that she should be delivered. And she brought forth her first-born son, and wrapped him up in swaddling clothes, and laid him in a manger," originally destined for the use of cattle, "because there was no room for them in the inn."—(St. Luke, ii. 6, 7.)

In the silence of night, in the coldest season of the year, in a stable exposed to the inclemency of the weather, and destitute even of absolute necessaries, the Saviour of men came miraculously into the world, without violating the integrity of his virgin mother. How wonderful in the views of faith is that humble birth, and how well did Mary appreciate the circumstances which ennobled it!

Her first act on beholding her divine infant, was to adore him profoundly as her God, to embrace him tenderly as her son, to envelope his delicate frame in swaddling clothes, to shelter him as far as she could from the cold air, and to lay him on a little straw in a crib.

O how severely was Mary's faith now tried; her son is the Son of God, and he is born in a stable, in the last extreme of destitution, his birth witnessed only by herself and St. Joseph, and unknown to the world beside. "Eternal Father, canst thou recognize in this crib the Almighty Being whom from eternity thou hast begotten in

the splendours of the saints? Holy Spirit! is
this He to whom thou hast miraculously imparted
human flesh?   The angel told me he should
be great, yet never before was the birth of an
infant attended with so much poverty and humiliation.   O my God! how different are thy ideas
from ours!   Reason is bewildered in considering
this mystery; it can but submit, and silently
adore.   A God suffers; a God weeps; the Omnipotent feels the helpless weakness of infancy;
he cannot assist himself by a movement; he
cannot express his feelings otherwise than by
inarticulate cries.   He is the eternal wisdom, and
he cannot speak; in fine, he is in no way distinguished externally from ordinary children." Reflections such as these must have engrossed the
mind of Mary, and filled it with inexplicable
wonder.   Vainly should we endeavour to understand her thoughts and feelings at that moment;
her peace, her joy, her adoration, her annihilation, and, at the same time, her ardent, tender
love, her deep maternal solicitude!   She is a
creature, and the mother of her Creator; how
opposite the sentiments which these two appel-
lations suppose!

   With this event commenced the sensible consolations lavished on Mary during the early
infancy of her divine son.   How intense was her
happiness when she clasped him in her arms;
when she pressed him to her heart; when she
tenderly embraced him; when she fed him with
her substance!   How much more profound her

felicity when Jesus looked on her in his love, when he rewarded her with one of his heavenly smiles ; when his little hands caressed her ; when his infant arms encircled her ! The caresses of Jesus were not the result of mere instinct, as in the case of ordinary children ; they were dictated by reason and grace, inspired and commanded by the Divinity ; they were the caresses of a God--man, and by their own virtue instilled ineffable sweetness into the heart of his mother. With what perfect disengagement she received those mute expressions of his love, never appropriating, but referring them unreservedly to their author.

All the motives which can excite the love of Jesus Christ in the human soul combined their influence over Mary, and subjected her undivided heart to her infant son. She loved him as her God, and her peculiar Saviour ; she loved him as her son, her only son, the son exclusively her own ; the son who loved her in return with a singular affection. She did not fear to exceed in her love, for he was infinitely and sovereignly amiable. That love was in every sense supernatural and divine ; nothing arrested its progress, retarded its action, or divided its ardour. She indulged it freely and securely, and could she in justice have reproached herself on any point, it would have been with a deficiency in her love ; but such a reproach would have been unfounded, since she loved with all the capacity of her heart, and according to the full measure of the grace conferred on her; these reflections may enable us partially to conceive the torrents of delight, the overflowing joy, which inundated the soul of Mary. But vast is the interval between understanding a truth, and feeling its influence; experience, which we shall never have, could alone enable us to appreciate the sentiments of the mother of Jesus. Let us dive no deeper into these holy secrets, for the joys, the sorrows, all the sensations of the heart of Mary, far exceed our comprehension.

If her love for Jesus Christ was the source of her happiness, it was likewise that of her griefs; every pang of the suffering infant wounded the heart of the tender mother. Her anxiety kept pace with the ardour of her affection; the two feelings seemed to divide her soul in equal proportion, but neither her joys nor her anguish disturbed the firmly established peace of her soul, or created any anxious reference to her own interest. She was not elated by consolation, nor dejected by trial; she neither desired and clung to the one, nor dreaded and shunned the other.

What practical lesson shall we derive from this example, if not to love Jesus Christ for his own sake; to combine a holy disengagement from his divine consolations, with the profound esteem they merit, and, like Mary, to endure in the spirit of self-immolation, the trials to which his love may subject us.

CHAPTER XIX.

Adoration of the Shepherds.

THE very night of the Redeemer's birth the angel of God announced the great event to some shepherds in the vicinity, who kept watch over their flocks, telling them that a Saviour was born to them, whom they should recognize by the swaddling clothes in which he was enveloped, and the manger on which he reposed. How strange a sign, and how calculated to try the faith of those simple-minded beings! But such is the invariable plan of divine Providence, whose arrangements are ever incompatible with the views of human prudence. At the same moment they heard the melody of a multitude of heavenly spirits, who sang " Glory to God in the highest, and on earth peace to men of good will."—(St. Luke, ii. 14.) If the view of the Saviour's destitution was well calculated to weaken the faith of the shepherds, the splendour which environed the heavenly messenger, and the words of benediction which fell from his lips, were equally adapted to animate its vivacity.

No sooner had the celestial vision disappeared than the shepherds said one to another, " Let us go over to Bethlehem, and let us see this word that is come to pass, which the Lord hath showed to us. And they came with haste, and they found Mary and Joseph, and the infant lying in the manger," (Ibid, 15, 16,) thus clearly ascertaining the truth of the angel's announcement. They no doubt communicated to Mary and Joseph the glorious tidings sent them from heaven, at the same time offering their heartfelt homage to Jesus Christ, and testifying to Mary their respectful love. From finding her in perfect health, they must have concluded, as a natural inference, that the birth of her mysterious infant was in itself a miracle.

While the shepherds adored their Saviour, and narrated the prodigies they had witnessed, how was Mary interiorly occupied? Her heart was filled with admiration at witnessing the manifestation of God's only Son to men, whom angels led to the forsaken crib, there to glorify him by their prostrate homage. It glowed with gratitude for the favour personally granted to herself, whom the shepherds recognized and honoured as the mother of the Redeemer. She marvelled to find that the poor, the simple, and the untaught, were the first selected by God, and summoned even by his own angels, to know, to love, and to adore his Son. Bethlehem was near Jerusalem, yet, not to Herod and his courtiers, not to the priests and doctors of the law, not to the great, the rich, and the learned of the capital, but to the poor ignorant inhabitants of a rural district, was the momentous intelligence first conveyed. How much more clearly than ever did she now understand that poverty of spirit, humility, and simplicity, are alone great in the estimation of

God ! When she witnessed these striking proofs of his predilection for the poor, how did she bless him that she too was poor, and the spouse of one destitute as herself!

The gospel does not describe the kind reception given by Mary to the shepherds, nor her interview with them, nor the modest ingenuousness with which she answered their inquiries, neither does it mention their cordial offer of the trivial services in their power to render, nor her gratitude for that slight assistance, so valuable in the extreme poverty against which she was unable to provide now that her divine infant required her undivided care. But it is easy to supply the omission, and to imagine what passed between Mary, Joseph, and the shepherds, in an interview especially arranged by God, immediately directed by grace, and referring solely to the Author of grace, who had already begun to display the riches of his mercy as the Saviour of men.

The gospel takes no note of these interesting and affecting details, yet it expressly observes that " Mary kept all these words, pondering them in her heart."—(Ibid, 19.) Not one escaped her, for she saw that each was inspired by God, and she carefully treasured them as the subject of future meditation, and the precious nourishment of her soul. Value for the communications of heaven, whether conveyed interiorly or exteriorly, and fidelity in turning all to good account, are among Mary's characteristic features. Always

on the watch to seize and profit of the treasure,
no grace was ever lost in her hands. On the
present occasion none failed to fructify in the
hearts of Mary, Joseph, or the shepherds, for all,
and most especially Mary's, were well disposed.

Every particular of this event furnishes important and profound instruction. We all need the
mercy of a Saviour, and all anxiously desire to
find one. By what sign shall we recognize him ?
By his infancy, that is, the spiritual infancy which
Jesus so highly valued, and which he preached
and practised throughout his life. The shepherds
whom he first summoned to his crib were of these
happy children, and Mary, the most simple,
humble, ingenuous and docile of human beings, also
occupied a conspicuous position among them.

If we consider heavenly things in the spirit
of infantine simplicity, we shall understand them,
we shall relish them, we shall practise them with
love.   Spiritual infancy introduces the soul to the
practice of every virtue ; in possessing this, she
likewise possesses all others in an eminent degree,
but without being aware of it, and consequently
without being exposed to the danger of vanity.

The second sign by which the Saviour is to be
identified is the swaddling clothes in which he is
wrapped.   An infant thus attired is the very per-
sonification of weakness.   It cannot use its limbs,
but is incapable of movement or resistance.
Jesus, the eternal wisdom, voluntarily submitted
to this state of abject dependence to teach us that
before we can hope to advance in the interior

life, we must subject our will to spiritual bondage. How weak that will is in the practice of virtue! how strong, on the contrary, in the pursuit of evil! Unless its natural impulses be restrained, it will infallibly convert them into engines of self-destruction, and, in its blindness, it will counteract the designs of heaven. That God may rule over it without opposition, it must be made captive in the salutary bonds of obedience. As the limbs of the divine infant were swathed by his blessed mother, so must the soul be reduced to subjection by her spiritual guide, submitting to his conduct as unresistingly as Jesus yielded to the will of Mary. By the practice of obedience she will infallibly make a rapid progress in perfection.

The comfortless crib is the last sign by which the Saviour desires to be known,—a sign of humility, poverty, and mortification. We cannot choose our original condition in life, but at least we can esteem and cherish what Jesus selected for himself, knowing that his choice could be no other than a wise one. We should endeavour to love whatever lowers us in the estimation of men; we should confine our ambition within the limits of our station, never aiming at earthly distinction. We should love poverty, and embrace its practice as far as can be done without affectation or sin- gularity. We shall be poor in the eyes of God, even amidst abundance, if our hearts are disen- gaged from riches; if we freely dispense them to our indigent fellow-creatures; if, far from despising the poor, we feel a holy envy for their condition, as the most conformable to the doctrine and example of Jesus Christ. We should esteem exterior mortification, and never yield to sensuality and effeminacy ; we should inure the flesh to suffering, by secretly subjecting it to privations. The love of honours, riches, and plea‐ sure has at all times been, and ever will be, the efficient cause of man's perdition. The contempt of the transitory advantages flowing from these three sources has ensured, and will ensure, the salvation of multitudes of Christians. That con‐ tempt alone does not constitute sanctity, but it introduces the soul into the path of holiness, and removes the principal obstacles which obstruct the way of perfection.

CHAPTER XX.

Adoration of the Sages.

It was not by the shepherds alone that Mary had the consolation of seeing her divine Son recognized and adored. He who had come to save both Jews and Gentiles, received the homage first of the Jews, in the person of the shepherds, and then of the Gentiles, in that of the Magi. These wise men beheld an extraordinary star in the East, and an interior revelation having at the same time enlightened them as to its myste‐ rious signification, they generously resolved to quit their country, and, under the guidance of the strange meteor, to travel into Judea, there to adore the newly-born King of the Jews. They applied to Herod for information concerning his birth place, and on learning from the Scribes and Pharisees that the prophets had indicated Bethlehem as the privileged spot, they set out for that town, again conducted by the star, which had disappeared at their entrance into Jerusalem. It rested over the stable in which lay the divine object of their search, and, entering it, they found the child and his mother; and, prostrating themselves before him, they offered him gold, frankincense, and myrrh.

It is very probable that they disclosed their personal history to Mary, and informed her how God had spoken to their hearts through the agency of the star; they no doubt also testified the veneration due to her as the mother of the Saviour. Their respectful homage excited in her no feeling of self-complacency; she received the evidences of their respect with perfect disinterestedness, referring them to her Son, with whom she identified herself and in whom she existed. The prevailing feeling of her soul at that moment was gratitude to God for manifesting his Incarnate Word to the idolatrous nations of the earth, and, through him, undermining the empire of the false deities destined for utter extinction. How happy it made her, to see her Divine infant adored by the great and the learned, who on their return would loudly proclaim his name in their own land! She rejoiced for his sake, not for her own; and if she displayed nore simplicity in the visit of the shepherds, her equals in rank, she exhibited greater humility in that of the Sages, whose homage would have mortified her, had she not seen and adored the will of God in that, as in all events of life.

Attentions are most flattering, and, consequently most dangerous, when emanating from persons of rank; but to Mary the marked respect of the holy kings could be productive of no evil results, for, far from being elated at their recognition of her eminent dignity, she only sank the more deeply in her own estimation. In the veneration of the Magi for herself, she traced the operation of grace, and that she might oppose no obstacle to its divine action, she permitted the free expression of their sentiments, rejoicing at the glory given by them to God, and valuing that redounding to herself, only on account of its connection with the honour of the Most High. What purity of intention is requisite thus perfectly to identify the glory of God with that rendered to ourselves! It is great humility to shun the applause and distinction often attached to the favours of heaven; but it is greater humility still to receive without appropriating those evidences of respect and esteem, and to refer the glory of them to God alone. It is not too much to assert that Mary's admirable virtue was to the

Sages a conclusive proof of the divinity of her Son; and they departed with the impression that only the mother of God could combine humility so profound with a dignity so exalted.

CHAPTER XXI.

The Circumcision.

" AND after eight days were accomplished, that the child should be circumcised; his name was called Jesus, which was called by the angel, before he was conceived in the womb," (St. Luke ii. 21.) We shall at present consider the circumcision of Jesus Christ merely in its connection with Mary, setting aside for the moment its reference to her divine Son.

She saw the adorable Infant subjected, by the decree of his heavenly Father and the free act of his own will, to a rigorous and an humbling law, which was not made for him. She saw that by submitting to that law, the all-holy God recognized his claim to the punishment due to sin, and bound himself to observe the ordinances of the Mosaic dispensation. She had an indistinct perception that it was by the effusion of his blood he would accomplish the deliverance of his people, as predicted to Joseph; she felt that in his circumcision he was already offering its first fruits to his eternal Father, and that the present painful ceremony was but the prelude to a future and a most agonizing sacrifice.

How deep was the anguish of that sorrowing and tender mother, while following the progress of the knife which gashed the flesh of her Son— while listening to his infant cries, and watching the tears as they trickled from his eyes, and the blood as it gushed from his veins! The sufferings, natural on such an occasion to any mother, were immeasurably aggravated in the present case. The knife which mangled the flesh of Jesus, equally wounded the heart of Mary, who was no less sensible to the keen incision than the divine Infant himself.

Yet with what perfect resignation the holy Virgin endured the trial, adoring the decrees of the eternal Father, participating in the sentiments of her Son, and offering her anguish in union with his blood as a satisfaction to God's justice and a reparation of his outraged glory. Foreseeing the afflictions which cast an anticipated reflection over the remainder of her existence, she submissively accepted the personal sorrows entailed by the sufferings of Jesus, and generously united her sacrifice to his. Her life was to be a perpetual exercise of faith; therefore she was not permitted clearly to understand the object of that first effusion of her Son's blood; but as suffering was likewise to be her habitual portion, a strong presentiment of her future trials was imparted to her.

If she comprehended the sublimity of the

adorable name of Jesus, if she foresaw that, through the merits of that name of salvation, God would extend pardon to guilty man—that it would one day receive universal homage, every knee in heaven, on earth, and in hell, bending at the sound, she also understood the obligations it entailed both on her divine Infant and on herself. She felt that Jesus was destined for a man of sorrows and a victim of humiliation, and she knew that the mother of Jesus must inevitably share the lot of her Son. She knew that if the venerable title of mother of God was to exalt her above angels, it was first to degrade her beneath all creatures. Such were the thoughts and sentiments which occupied the heart of Mary throughout the painful operation, and during the period which elapsed before the wound was healed.

"If we suffer with him," says St. Paul, " we shall be also glorified with him," (Rom. viii. 17.) The more perfectly we belong to God, the more closely we are united to him, the more surely we may expect to suffer. He will undoubtedly require of us that circumcision of heart which may truly be styled a protracted and agonizing martyrdom ; but the love of Jesus, union with Jesus, the desire of resembling Jesus and his holy mother, will alleviate the pains of that martyrdom—will inspire esteem for it—will strengthen us to prefer its bitterness, not only to the false joys of earth, but even to the solid consolations of heaven.

CHAPTER XXII.

The Purification.

On the fortieth day after the nativity of Christ, Mary, ever punctual in the observance of the law, repaired to the temple, there to be purified, to present to the Lord his own possession, her first-born Son, and to offer for his ransom a pair of turtle-doves or pigeons. Every Jewish mother observed the same forms on similar occasions, but Mary fulfilled the ordinance with a perfection peculiar to herself. She was in fact dispensed from the law of purification, having given birth to her Son without detriment to her virginity; yet she submitted to the ceremony, and thus assimilated herself in public estimation with ordinary mothers, carefully concealing the secret of her miraculous virginity, and never betraying her privileges even by a word. How striking an example of humility! Like Mary, we should conceal God's favours under the veil of external conformity to ordinary usages; and in this view we should cheerfully submit to certain observances from which we might lawfully claim exemption. The favours of heaven are great, no doubt; but greater still is the humility which endeavours to hide them. Were we exalted above the seraphim, our desires should not soar beyond the reputation of ordinary Christians, and never should we deliberately seek the marked esteem of our intimate associates. We must endeavour to be holy, and even as holy as we can be; we must edify our neighbour by word and act; but we should ever remember that the only sure road to sanctity is fidelity in concealing the gifts of heaven and avoiding singularity.

Mary offered her Son to God as a treasure which already belonged to him, and which she had received only to restore. She united her offering to the oblation which Jesus Christ at that moment made of himself to his heavenly Father, and the same spirit of self-immolation influenced and vivified the sacrifice of both. The Son distinctly understood the consequences entailed by his act of consecration; the mother foresaw them but vaguely, yet, both as regarded her Son and herself, she unconditionally submitted to the yet unrevealed designs of God. In offering Jesus, she not only offered herself, but what was infinitely dearer to her than self; and the oblation, both in its reference to him and to her, was perfectly unreserved; it was offered in the fulness of her heart—in the plenitude of generosity and love; it embraced the most minute details of God's will, both as already manifested and as still concealed.

In the law of grace, man belongs to God on far stronger titles than did the first-born under the law of Moses. Our primary duty, the first obligatory use of our reason and liberty, is, to offer ourselves to him, that he may dispose of us at pleasure, that he may exercise his sovereign

dominion over us, and accomplish in us his holy
will. Oh! if we were once thoroughly convinced
of this great truth,—that we belong to ourselves
in nothing—that we have nothing of our own—
that we exist for God, and not for ourselves,
with what fervour we should consecrate our
being to him! with what love we should serve
him! with what disinterestedness we should
labour to promote his glory! with what generosity we should offer him every sacrifice he
exacts, knowing that in bestowing his gifts he
does not relinquish his original claim to them,
and esteeming ourselves happy in being allowed
to restore them! God evinced his infinite liberality towards Mary, in giving her his Son;
Mary restored to God all she possessed, in consecrating that Son to his glory; she sacrificed to
his love all things here below, and thus merited
to recover all in heaven, where, through her
adorable Son, she dispenses the treasures of the
Divinity. When God recals his favours, it is
not because he regrets his liberality, but because
he desires, first, to detach us from his gifts, and
then to restore them with interest. It was thus
he acted towards Jesus and Mary, and so will he
also act to us, if we imitate their generosity.

In pursuance with the ordinance of the law,
Mary presented for the ransom of Jesus a pair of
pigeons or doves, the offering appointed for the
poor. God looked not to the value of her gift,
but to the love of her heart; and many a precious donation laid at his feet by the affluent,

found less acceptance in his sight, because offered with different dispositions. What value can God attach to our gifts, if they be not the oblation of love? And when they are, what does it signify to him whether we bestow little or much? Love can refuse nothing to God; it gives all it has, or is at least always disposed to give whatever God requires. If it has nothing, it gives itself, and this gift abundantly supplies the deficiency of all others. Mary understood this well, and therefore did not deplore the poverty which could give but little to God; the little she had, she offered with love so ardent, that no donation ever equalled or could equal hers in value. How far does God esteem the earthly possessions and splendid prospects renounced for his sake? Only in proportion to the love which has inspired that renunciation. The apostles gave up only their boats and nets; yet, in renouncing a crown, monarchs have given less, if their donation was less generously bestowed. Men consider only the external sacrifice which meets the eye; God, on the contrary, looks but to that of the heart, which, whether it be a poor or a valuable one, it is in our own power alone to bestow.

CHAPTER XXIII.

Meeting of Jesus and Mary with Simeon.

" There was a man in Jerusalem," says St. Luke, " named Simeon, and this man was just and devout, waiting for the consolation of Israel ; and the Holy Ghost was in him. And he had received an answer from the Holy Ghost, that he should not see death, before he had seen the Christ of the Lord. And he came by the Spirit into the temple, and when his parents brought in the child Jesus, to do for him according to the custom of the law. He also took him into his arms, and blessed God, and said, Now thou dost dismiss thy servant, O Lord, according to thy word, in peace. Because my eyes have seen thy salvation, which thou hast prepared before the face of all people ; a light to the revelation of the Gentiles and the glory of thy people, Israel. And his father and mother were wondering at those things, which were spoken concerning him." (St. Luke, ii. 25—33.) Thus, new and stronger light continually breaks in on the mind of Mary, disclosing to her more clearly the destiny of her Son, and confirming the reality of her own super-eminent privileges. So it likewise happens to the soul on her first introduction into the paths of sublime perfection, God then granting her multiplied proofs of his paternal protection, and removing all doubt of his designs both from the favoured object of his love and from her spiritual director, and thereby fortifying the faith which is destined for future severe trials. We are here once again to observe, that Mary did not ask the security which was invariably granted when least expected.

Simeon was led by the Holy Spirit into the temple, at the moment when Jesus entered it, and receiving the divine Infant into his arms, he profoundly adored and tenderly caressed him. Then, in a transport of holy joy, he besought God to put a term to his earthly pilgrimage, now that his eyes had beheld the Redeemer of men, the light of nations, and the glory of Israel. Mary listened to his words as if they had been addressed by God to herself in person; she considered them with profound respect and deep attention, treasuring them as the future food of her soul, and never losing the memory of a single expression which bore reference to her Son. She saw with ardent gratitude the gradual increase of heavenly light, her interview with Elizabeth, with the shepherds, with the wise men, and with Simeon—all contributing to strengthen her confidence; and both she and Joseph were filled with admiration at the wonderful revelations they heard concerning the infant Jesus.

Not inferior is the astonishment of the soul to whom God has manifested his peculiar designs, when she finds that many persons are, as it were, raised up by him expressly to confirm her faith in the original revelation granted her. The more she refrains from anxious doubts and perplexing investigations, the more fully will she be re-assured, and that in the manner she least expects.

What are we to conclude hence? That we should trust to God, firmly and blindly, believing that he will refuse us no necessary evidence of the security of our state. He does not permit us to refer to our own judgment for conclusive argu-ments on the matter; such a step would only lead to error and illusion, for divine things can never be subjected to the interpretation of human reason. But he requires that, his designs being once revealed, we should tranquilly and confi-dently expect from himself alone the confirma-tion we require. He will infallibly grant it, not to the eager desires of impetuous nature, but to the humble confidence which calmly trusts in him, and never permits itself to anticipate the dawning of supernatural light. He does not prodi-gally lavish those evidences of security, but dis-penses them with wise economy, sufficiently re-moving the soul's anxious apprehensions, yet not fully withdrawing the veil which impedes the clear light of heaven. He raises it gradually, but never entirely, until his designs have been perfectly accomplished. In pursuing this plan, the Almighty consults both his own glory and our real advantage. Were he to unfold all his designs at once, we should be overwhelmed by the anticipation of coming trial; again, being acquainted beforehand with the destined issue of those trials, we should lose the merit of blind submission to God's guidance ; and, lastly, the sacrifices offered with a clear foresight of their results, would be productive of no solid glory to him.

Next to the destiny of Jesus Christ, that of the Blessed Virgin was the most exalted ever allotted to a human being ; yet she never curiously investigated its details ; she never swerved from the path of faith ; she profited of the lights bestowed, but did not eagerly desire them, quite satisfied to dwell amidst darkness, if such were the will of God. To imitate her example in this respect, is not easy; we shall accomplish the difficult task only by the persevering practice of death to self.

CHAPTER XXIV.

Predictions of Simeon regarding Jesus and Mary.

" AND Simeon blessed them, and said to Mary his mother : Behold this child is set for the fall, and for the resurrection of many in Israel, and for a sign which shall be contradicted. And thy own soul a sword shall pierce, that out of many hearts thoughts may be revealed." (St. Luke, ii. 34, 35.)

The portion of this prophecy which relates to Jesus Christ, is among the most profound of any on record; it announces, that not only during his mortal life, but even to the end of time, the God-man shall be a cause of salvation to some; of perdition to others; and that he shall be a sign exposed to contradiction, in order that the secret thoughts of hearts may be revealed. Mary, to whom these words were addressed, partially understood that her adorable Son was to offer to the eyes of men a combination of majesty and abjection; of power and weakness; of glory and ignominy; of light and obscurity, which should attract some, and repel others; which should try the faith of his followers, and by trying, should confirm it; which should alienate the incredulous, and lead to their destruction; which should display in bright colours, the rectitude of the former, and the malice of the latter. She understood that her Son was destined to be contradicted by men, and rejected by the great body of that nation which had so long sighed for him as its deliverer; that he was more or less to experience similar treatment from all other nations, and that among the future professors of his religion, a multitude of infidels, heretics, libertines, and bad christians should both in word and action oppose his doctrine and example; in a word that a universal and unceasing war should be waged against him.

This gloomy perspective was not perhaps unfolded clearly to Mary at that moment, yet it was displayed sufficiently to convince her that severe suffering awaited her Son, and consequently herself, as identified with him. Nothing could be more explicit or more decided than the prophecy of Simeon,—" And thy own soul a sword shall pierce." (St. Luke, ii. 35.) What sword if not that which inflicted a death wound on her Son and her God? That sword was to penetrate, not her flesh, but her soul; it was a spiritual weapon destined to rend the heart of the mother, while it gashed the sacred body of the Son. It was not merely to touch the surface of the heart of Mary, but to transpierce its depths, and neither the exterior torments of the martyrs, nor the interior agonies of the saints could bear comparison with those the surpassing griefs of the Queen of sorrows.

In what sentiments did Mary receive this prediction of coming woe? With love, with peace, with entire conformity to the will of God, and perfect union with the future sufferings of her Son. This was the first prediction of the kind ever addressed to her, and one too, for which she could scarcely have been prepared after the angel's recent announcement of the Saviour's glorious prerogatives. God never reveals his views at once, but from time to time he discloses designs, which although they seem contradictory at first, will be ultimately reconciled by his supreme wisdom. Mary, who carefully treasured in her inmost heart, and deeply meditated on every communication she received regarding her Son, must certainly have observed the apparent inconsistency between the words of the angel Gabriel and those

of Simeon.   Yet she was not the less convinced
that both were dictated by the Spirit of God, and
she firmly believed, without seeking to reconcile
them, confident that the divine promises would
all be fulfilled in time.

Three lesssons are here conveyed by the example of the holy Virgin, for the instruction of interior souls. First, that their sufferings are closely
connected with, and dependent on those of Jesus,
the head of the predestined, who honours them
with a share in his cross, solely because they
belong to him in a peculiar manner.   The
heart of Mary was pierced by the keen-edged
sword of sorrow, only because she was the mother of Jesus, and certain chosen souls are likewise privileged to feel its sharp incisions, because
they have the happiness to be his specially favoured spouses ; consequently they should never separate their sufferings from those of their Saviour,
but view them as one with his.   No consideration
is more calculated to inspire fortitude and submission, than this,—' Jesus suffers in me; Jesus suffers with me; Jesus afflicts me only because I am
his own, and because he desires to unite me more
perfectly to himself.'

Secondly, Mary teaches her imitators to accept
with peace, love, and conformity like her own, the
trials ordained by God ; not to be alarmed at the
terrific perspective, but firmly to believe that
strength will be granted in proportion to their
wants ; not to lose courage, not to listen to the
suggestions of imagination, nor to impair their

spiritual strength by anxiously anticipating the hour of affliction.

Thirdly, not to seek to reconcile the heavenly revelation of one period, with that of another. These revelations sometimes appear contradictory, as in the instance of God's command to Abraham, to immolate Isaac, in whom were centred the solemn and reiterated promises of heaven; but in this apparent contradiction consists the trial, and consequently the merit of our faith. Let us believe divine revelations, without attempting to reconcile them, for this is the work of God, not ours. Let us humbly close our eyes, until the destined issue has been made apparent, and then like Abraham and Mary, we shall behold the accomplishment of the heavenly predictions.

CHAPTER XXV.

The flight into Egypt.

HEROD, having learned the birth of the king of the Jews from the wise men, was filled with apprehension for the security of his crown, and resolved to deprive his infant competitor of life. When on the eve of executing this dark project, " an angel of the Lord appeared in sleep to Joseph, saying : Arise, and take the child and his mother, and flee into Egypt ; and be there until I shall tell thee. For it will come to pass that Herod will seek the child to destroy him. Who arose, and took the child and his mother by night, and retired into Egypt; and he was there until the death of Herod." (St. Matt. ii. 13, 14.) The angel delivered the commands of God to Joseph, as head of the holy family. It would seem more natural that the orders of heaven should have been intimated to Mary, yet she felt not the remotest approach to jealousy, at the preference shown her holy spouse. In one sense she was more worthy the honour than Joseph; the divine child was hers; her interest in its preservation must have been deeper; she would have felt a greater security if the word of the Lord had been addressed to herself; at any rate, could not the angel have delivered his message jointly to her and Joseph? Reflections such as these might have arisen in an imperfect soul, yet alive to the impressions of self-love, but over Mary, they had no influence. She thus teaches us to refrain from them, and respectfully to receive the orders of heaven, by whatever means they may be intimated, were it even by persons endowed with grace inferior to our own. Mary looked on Joseph as her superior, and in this point of view she considered him better entitled than herself to receive the immediate intimation of God's will, which was to be afterwards manifested to her through him. Our superiors are the channel through which God makes his will known to us, and we should esteem this a more secure medium for its manifestation, than would be the immediate revelation of God himself, since even that direct revelation should ultimately be referred to the judgment of our spiritual guides.

But how severe this new trial of Mary's faith! Men seek the life of her Son, the Son of the most High, and it is necessary to provide for his safety, as for that of a defenceless child! Has not God power to shield him from Herod's hatred otherwise than by flight? Is not the heart of that wicked prince in the hand of the most High? Is not his life at God's mercy? Why must the adorable Infant, in whose favour heaven is to lavish its miracles, encounter the risks and inconveniencies of a precipitate flight into a strange land? Must not thoughts like these have obtruded themselves on the mind of Mary? Was it natural to expect after the magnificent promises of the angel, that her Son should be exposed at his very birth to perish beneath the murderous weapon of a tyrant?

Again, where are they to seek an asylum in a land of strangers? How are they to subsist there? Mary is poor, her only resource is in the industry of Joseph, and how will he pursue his trade in Egypt, peopled as it is by idolaters who abhor the adorers of the true God? To what extremities shall they not be reduced in their dreary banishment? How long is their exile to last? This the angel has not specified, leaving the matter involved in uncertainty. What a trial to such a mother as Mary,—Mary the mother of such a Son as Jesus!

If the holy Virgin had been less influenced by

abandonment to God's will, and confidence in his
paternal providence, she would have had ample
grounds of anxiety and alarm.   But she indulged
no voluntary uneasiness about her own lot or that
of her Son.   Natural tenderness no doubt asserted
its claims, but her virtue was in no wise impaired
by the trial of her feelings.   With prompt obedience to God's will, she quitted her home amidst
the darkness of night, bearing her divine treasure
in her arms.   What had she to fear for Jesus ;—
what for herself in the company of Jesus?   If we
have faith like that of Mary, we shall dread neither men nor demons while Jesus is with us. We
may have to suffer in his cause, but if we love
him, to suffer for his sake will be our glory and
our joy.

It is very probable, that loving Mary and Joseph with a singular love, and understanding the
heroism of the virtue he had himself infused into
them, the Almighty averted from them none of
the inconveniences attached to their distressing
journey, and their sojourn in Egypt.   Neither
can it be doubted that he at the same time granted
them all the graces necessary for worthily enduring their trials.   They remained in Egypt until
after Herod's death, when an angel again appeared to Joseph while he slept, commanding him to
take the child and his mother and return into the
land of Israel, for those who sought the infant's
life were no more.   Joseph executed the order,
but fearful of going into Judea, where Arche-
laus had succeeded his father, and having once

more received an intimation of heaven's will in a dream, he retired into Galilee.

We are here to observe how carefully Mary and Joseph refrained from acting on the impulse of their own will and judgment, and how punctually they submitted in all things to the guidance of God. They received an order to flee into Egypt; against this they might have imagined themselves entitled to remonstrate, not so much that it involved inconvenience to themselves, as that it threatened danger to their divine charge. Yet they departed silently and instantaneously, not waiting even for the dawn of day. Their residence in Egypt must for every reason have been extremely disagreeable, still they took no measures to abridge it, not even praying to God to shorten the period of their exile, but calmly awaiting the order of the angel, and retiring into Galilee for greater security, only on receiving a specific intimation of heaven's will to that effect. Having once subjected herself to the guidance of God, the soul must seek her security in obedience alone. The Almighty will provide for her interests, and infallibly make known his will to her, were he for this end to employ the ministry of an angel. She will promote the glory of her Creator, and ensure her own peace, only by the practice of blind obedience. She must not take a step of herself; she must neither anticipate the future, nor adopt precautionary measures against it, but tranquilly await the ordinance of God, who never fails to come to the aid of his servants in due time, and who regulates the duration of their trials according to his own sovereign pleasure.

CHAPTER XXVI.

Jesus lost and found in the temple.

AFTER their return to Nazareth, Mary and Joseph repaired every year to Jerusalem, to celebrate the feast of the Passover, and when Jesus was twelve years old, they brought him also to the festival. "And having fulfilled the days, when they returned, the child Jesus remained in Jerusalem; and his parents knew it not. And thinking that he was in the company, they came a day's journey, and sought him among their kinsfolks and acquaintance. And not finding him, they returned into Jerusalem seeking him. And it came to pass, that after three days they found him in the temple sitting in the midst of the doctors, hearing them and asking them questions. And all that heard him were astonished at his wisdom and his answers. And seeing him they wondered." (St. Luke, ii. 43—48.)

The hitherto obedient child, now quitted his parents unperceived; allowed them to depart on their homeward way, and remained in Jerusalem without their knowledge, although well aware of the alarm that step would occasion, particularly to his tender mother. At the close of the first day's journey, they sought him among their relatives and acquaintances, and not finding him, retraced their steps to Jerusalem. Who could describe the agitation of Mary at that moment? "Why," she exclaimed, " has he forsaken me without a previous word of warning? What have I done to him? What cause of complaint have I given him?"

Interior souls, Jesus frequently withdraws from you, without preparing you for his departure. He deprives you, like Mary, of his sensible presence. You deplore your loss; you tremble lest you may have entailed it through your own fault; you examine the recesses of your hearts; you investigate your most trivial failings. But your terrors are unfounded; Jesus has not forsaken you in reality; his divinity is ever with you. He conceals himself, only to give you an opportunity of displaying the ardour of your love, as well as to purify and spiritualize that love. He was the unseen witness of his holy mother's agitation, and he rejoiced in the strong evidences of her tender, devoted attachment, and deep affliction at his loss. Interior souls, He likewise beholds your anguish, and the more intense it is, the more glory it gives him, provided it be calm and resigned like that of Mary, and that it be indeed the absence of Jesus, not the loss of his consolations you bewail.

Jesus delights to be sought with earnestness, such as that which guided the efforts of his holy mother to recover him. She pursued him with untiring ardour; she enquired for him in every direction, perpetually exclaiming, " What has become of my treasure, my joy, my all; the Divine Object, dearer far than life?" Great was the glory which Jesus derived from these demonstrations of her solicitude! The soul which seeks the Lord as Mary sought him, has not lost him in reality, but will yet enjoy his presence more perfectly than ever. How admirable are the inventions of divine love! If its sweets were always felt, they would become familiar and lose their value. To appreciate them as they deserve, it is necessary that their sensible impression be occasionally withdrawn, and the soul left to herself, her coldness, aridity and distraction. She never loves more truly, than when in those hours of desolation, she vigorously and diligently seeks the apparently lost treasure of love. She then redoubles her supplications, her recollection, her fidelity; she loses sight of every thing but the celestial object of her pursuit; all else wearies and disgusts her. "You," she says, "are not He whom I love, and for whom alone my heart sighs." Let us seek Jesus as Mary sought him, and assuredly we shall not long delay to find him.

Where did Mary find her Son and Saviour? Was it among her relations and acquaintances? No. Was it amidst the society of Jerusalem? No, but in the Temple, the house of God. Let us not seek Jesus amidst the ties of flesh and blood, we shall not find him there. Let us not seek him amidst the tumult and cares of the world, for his dwelling is far removed from the noisy scene. We shall find him in his temple; in the holy ta-

bernacle where he perpetually resides, awaiting
our approach. His glory is hidden beneath the
sacramental veils, but the eye of faith can discern
him. There we are ever sure to meet him, for
there he cannot escape us. Let us then go to the
temple in the day of aridity and interior desolation, and let us so frequently take shelter beneath
its shade, that vanquished by our pious importu-
nity, he may at length disclose to us the vision of
his beauty.

How is he occupied in the temple? Externally,
he maintains an inviolable silence, yet from that
throne of his love, he gives us many admirable
lessons, secretly interrogating the heart, and
breathing into it his divine instructions. Those
who understand the heavenly art of listening to
his voice, derive from their visits to his altar, the
only necessary species of knowledge—the science
of the saints, imparted in the temple to the docile
spirit by Him from whom all wisdom flows. Dispensing with the medium of books, let us apply
directly to himself for the information we require.
Let us listen in profound silence to his divine
words, one of which communicates a greater abundance of supernatural light, than could be derived
from long and repeated meditations. What can
books and reflection avail, unless they be the channels to convey the lessons of Jesus?

When his mother had at length found him,
she said, " Son, why hast thou done so to us ?
behold, thy father and I have sought thee sorrowing." (Ibid. 48.) The reproach was dictated

by maternal tenderness, and it was worthy of the mother of Jesus; far from offending, it gratified her divine Son. A holy familiarity with Jesus sanctions privileges, which fear and respect prohibit. His faithful friends sometimes inquire with a holy freedom into the motives of his ordinances in their regard; they represent to him with humble simplicity the pain he inflicts, and, far from being displeased, he delights in such evidences of their confidence. God is not like man, who must be accosted with ceremony and circumspection. He loves the boldness inspired by simplicity, and the language of affection, which addresses him almost as an equal, pleases him better than the measured accents of cold respect. But that familiar language, those gentle reproaches, are permitted only to the parents, the brethren, the sisters, the spouses of Jesus Christ; that is, according to his own explanation, to those who do the will of his heavenly Father. On this, even more than on her title of his mother, was founded Mary's right to treat her Son with a holy familiarity.

But as on the present occasion she listened only to the voice of maternal love, and perhaps considered Jesus Christ too exclusively in his human nature, he, who desired to elevate her to the contemplation of his divinity, and early to impress her with the sublimity of the functions assigned him by his Father, replied to her observation, " How is it that you sought me? did you not know that I must be about my Father's

business ?" (Ibid. 49.) As if he had said : You
should exalt your views beyond my human nature ; you should rise to the consideration of my
Father, who reigns in heaven ; you should remember the glorious mission he has confided to
me on earth, as well as my obligation to fulfil
its duties, preferring them to my affection for
you, which, legitimate though it be, must ever
be subordinate to that I owe Him. He accompanied the words with a tone of gravity and an
air of majesty which, in a child of his age, must
necessarily have convinced the spectators he was
something superhuman. While addressing his
reputed father, according to the flesh, he insinuated to the doctors of the law then present that
he had another Father, whose interests were
dearer to him than his own. He thus publicly,
though covertly, declared himself the Messiah,
and this reply, combined with his previous manifestation of wondrous wisdom, must have given
rise to serious thoughts regarding him. By his
reply to Mary, he also wished to prepare her
early for their separation at a future day, when
during his public career he should in a manner
appear to forget and renounce her.

The Evangelist remarks that neither she nor
Joseph understood his answer, manifestly proving
that, by the Divine dispensation, their faith was
yet mingled with much obscurity, and the nature
of Christ's mission on earth unfolded to them
only by slow degrees. Mary received the words
of her Son with suitable reverence ; she inte-

riorly acknowledged her inability to comprehend
them, and generously silenced the suggestions of
a mother's love.   How pure the soul must be,
how perfectly disengaged from earth, to know
Jesus well, and to love him with undivided affection !   The ties of flesh and blood are as nothing
before him, and must be sacrificed when his will
demands the oblation.   Yet he does not require
that we absolutely renounce the love of parents
and relatives ; on the contrary, he purifies, enno-
bles, and sanctifies the feeling, by exacting that
we love our friends in him, for him, and with
subordination to the love of himself. Great were
the trials of Mary's maternal feelings, the strongest and deepest that ever throbbed in the heart
of a mortal.   Jesus Christ taught her betimes to
disengage herself from him, and in recompense
of that detachment he exalted her to the sublime
purity of his love.   What an example for parents
and children !   If impressed with the sentiments
of Christians, both should firmly believe that the
solidity of their mutual affection depends on
their efforts to spiritualize its emotions, and gradually to purify it from the dross of human feeling, substituting the sentiments which grace inspires.   It would be absurd to imagine that God,
the great Author of nature, should so far contradict himself, as to employ the operations of grace
in destroying the affections originally implanted
by his own hand in the hearts of parents and
children ; but that affection may exceed just
limits, and the Almighty demands that it be

properly regulated ; it may encroach on the love
due to God, and it ought, on the contrary, to be
subordinate thereto. In its origin it is a purely
natural instinct ; cultivated by the Christian, it
should be transformed into a supernatural emotion.

CHAPTER XXVII.

Jesus subject to Mary and Joseph.

JESUS accompanied his parents on their return
home from Jerusalem ; "and he went down
with them, and came to Nazareth : and was subject to them." (St. Luke, ii. 51.) These few
words comprise the history of the life of Christ
from the age of twelve till that of thirty. He
lived at Nazareth in poverty and obscurity,
assisting Joseph in his trade, as far as was compatible with his strength, and submitting unconditionally to the controul of his blessed mother
and reputed father.

Let us enter that humble dwelling so singular-
ly marked with heaven's blessing, and let us inquire into the private history of that privileged
family, the holiest, with whose presence the earth
ever had been or could be honoured. It numbered
but three members :—the Son of God, the mother
of God, and St. Joseph, the spouse of the one and
supposed father of the other. Their poverty was
so great that they sometimes failed even in the
absolute necessaries, beyond which they at no

time aspired ; but amidst their many wants and
privations, they were perfectly contented, blessing
the name of the Lord, and desiring no greater
abundance than it pleased him to give. They
lived in utter seclusion, neither knowing, nor
wishing to be known by men. The inhabitants
of Nazareth had no suspicion that the Word of
God dwelt amidst them in human form ; they
were equally unconscious of the dignity and miraculous privileges of Mary his virgin mother.
The holy family were no doubt considered pious,
exemplary, remarkable for punctuality in the observance of the law, and invariably edifying in
their demeanour : yet their piety produced no external difference between them and their fellow-
creatures ; their real dignity could never have
been inferred from their exterior deportment ;
they furnished no clue to the divine secret buried
within their bosoms, and it is evident from the
Gospel, that the nearest relatives of Mary were
quite ignorant of the great mystery of the Incarnation. Mary and Joseph waited calmly until it
should be God's will to reveal the truth ; until it
should please Jesus to manifest himself to the
world.

How profound the peace, how uninterrupted
the recollection, how perfect the union of that
holy family ! How intimate and unceasing the
interior communication between Jesus and Mary,
between Mary and Joseph ! Jesus profusely
lavished on his mother that heavenly grace of
which he was the source, and she in turn imparted

of her abundance to St. Joseph, so that almost without speaking, they maintained an uninterrupted interchange of sentiment. Jesus was the beginning, the end, the divine centre of the affections of Mary and Joseph. How great must have been their progress in perfection during that long period in which they enjoyed the presence of Jesus, without the absence even of a moment! Who could describe their heavenly conversations, all undoubtedly referring to God, his benefits, his love for his people, his great mercy to the human race. Even amidst laborious toil and domestic cares, their minds were engaged in contemplation, and their hearts inflamed with the purest love. Jesus conveyed to them his divine instructions without affectation, without pretension; insinuating them almost imperceptibly; ever displaying the respect of a submissive child, and but seldom emitting a ray from the divine sun of wisdom which shed its splendours on his soul. Mary and Joseph treasured each of his precious words, recurring to them frequently, as the subject of their reflections, and the food of their hearts.

Yet, notwithstanding the interior homage they constantly paid his Divinity, they maintained and externally exercised the authority he had been pleased to give them over his person. *He was subject to them.* They imposed their orders on him, but with what consideration, what moderation, what meekness, what humility; what an overpowering sense of the infinite distance be-

tween him and them ; what admiration of the love
of abjection, which could induce a God to obey
his own creatures! Jesus obeyed, with a view to
fulfil the will of his Father, whom he greatly
glorified by his submission. Joseph and Mary
commanded him, as holding in his regard the
place of God, and as exercising the dominion of
the eternal Father over Him who had annihilated
himself for that Father's love. The obedience of
Jesus was a virtue altogether singular, unparalleled, and far beyond the reach of our feeble
encomiums. But what must have been the death
to self, the sublimity of grace of his parents, to
dispose them to command Jesus in a manner
worthy to meet his divine approbation! How
glorious a spectacle to the eternal Father and his
holy angels! How deep, how bewildering a
subject of contemplation to the human mind!

Mary appears especially admirable when commanding her Son, not precisely because he is the
Son of God, but because in commanding him, she
practised the most admirable virtues ; because
she commanded him only through submission to
the decree of God himself; because her humility
and self-annihilation increased with the necessity
for commanding him ; because she followed the
impulse of grace, and perfectly died to nature in
the exercise of an authority, which she never
appropriated, but referred without reserve to
God.

Let us silently admire, and as far as possible
imitate, the example here presented to us. To

give God glory, a Being great as he is, annihilated himself so far as to submit to creatures drawn from the dust—creatures who before him are, as if they existed not. And shall I, a nothing, feel repugnance to obey my fellow-creatures whom God has invested with his authority? Shall my pride rebel, and my will refuse to bend? Ah! can any degree of pride resist the example of the obedient Jesus, particularly when we reflect, that it was for our benefit alone that example was displayed!

If Jesus teaches me how to obey, Mary teaches me how to command, and the latter lesson is perhaps the more difficult of the two. I should ever remember that I possess no right to command, further than that which God gives me; that it is not my own authority I exercise, but the authority of God; that in the exercise of that authority I should be influenced neither by caprice nor self-love; but by divine grace; by the spirit of meekness, of charity, of consideration for the feelings of my inferiors; in fine, of humility, which is never more necessary than in the exercise of authority. It is beyond comparison more advantageous to obey than to command, and we shall command in the proper spirit, only in as far as we have learned to obey, but either to command or to obey as we should, presupposes all virtues, particularly humility.

CHAPTER XXVIII.

Life of Mary at Nazareth.

LET us not depart too hastily from the dwelling of the holy family at Nazareth, where so many examples replete with instruction are presented for our consideration. Mary there led an obscure, hidden, and laborious life, and a life at the same time surpassed in sanctity only by that of her divine Son. The ordinary duties which it comprised, she embraced with a love of esteem, preferring their security to the perils of singularity and distinction. She had been the favoured object of heavenly revelations and stupendous miracles; but now the day of prodigies had passed, and she rejoiced to repose once more beneath the shade of common life. Angels were no longer deputed to reveal God's will to her; nor were a Zachary, an Elizabeth, or a Simeon, again raised up to disclose her exalted destiny. The most humble domestic duties now limited her sphere of action. Her prayer was as simple as it was sublime; she was utterly unconscious of the operations of her soul during its progress, and never allowed herself to advert to them. The sweets of interior recollection, the sensible impression of God's holy presence, were withdrawn. Her prayer, while unceasing, was wholly confined to the secret temple of her heart, and attracted no human observation. Her familiar

associates noticed nothing striking about her—
nothing which could lead them to suppose her a
person of more than ordinary piety. If Mary
had been capable of an emotion of self-complacency, it would have arisen from the contemplation of her position as an undistinguished
member of the nameless crowd. Whether our
lot be cast in the world or in religion, we should
deeply esteem a common life, and most carefully
avoid singularity. We should study to purify
our hearts, that they may be worthy to meet the
eye of God, who penetrates their depths ; as for
the exterior, beyond which man's scrutiny cannot
reach, it should be edifying, but in no way remarkable.

Secondly, the life of Mary was hidden and
obscure. Devoted to the care of her simple
household, she left that humble home only when
summoned forth by necessity or charity. Persons
of her condition are not expected, she was aware,
to appear in public—not entitled to admission
among the circles of fashion. The poor village
of Nazareth could boast, it is true, of none but
inferior society, yet even from that she in a great
measure abstained. The few visits she paid were
inspired by grace, and dictated by courtesy.
They were never unnecessarily prolonged ; they
embraced no topics of conversation but such as
were calculated to edify ; curiosity, detraction,
and idle news were carefully excluded ; and her
duty to her neighbour once fulfilled, she returned
with alacrity to her lowly home. She never spoke

of her personal concerns, or those of her divine Son, but cautiously concealed her high prerogatives, and loved to rank in public estimation only as an ordinary woman. O, how difficult it is perfectly to screen the extraordinary favours of heaven, not permitting even a ray of the glory within to reflect its brightness without. How admirable, that the simple and uniform tenor of Mary's existence should have effectually hidden from men the rich fund of her interior sanctity! What unceasing vigilance it requires to imitate her in this, particularly at the commencement of the spiritual life, when imaginary zeal for the progress of others leads to many a confidential disclosure of the secrets of grace! Such communications are manifestly suggested by self-love, spiritual vanity, or, at best, indiscretion; and few are sufficiently on their guard against these subtle and dangerous enemies.

Lastly, the life of Mary was laborious. We must not suppose that she was perpetually absorbed in prayer, or that she passed whole hours in inactive contemplation. She was an enemy to the piety, or, more correctly speaking, the indolent self-indulgence of many females, who devote their time exclusively to prayer, because they erroneously imagine that the possession of wealth entails a dispensation from useful occupation. She had no leisure for prayer of this description, for she had to prepare the frugal repasts of Jesus and Joseph, and to regulate without assistance the domestic concerns of their poor establishment.

But amidst her almost uninterrupted exterior avocations, she lost neither her peace of soul nor the remembrance of God's presence ; and she invariably reserved her leisure moments for prayer. Let us love labour as she did; it is the great pillar of the interior life, for, by engaging the mind profitably, it excludes idle thoughts and vain speculations. It is useful in the season of heavenly consolation, acting as a counterpoise to the sensible comfort which the soul might be tempted immoderately to enjoy. It is profitable in the day of aridity, diverting her attention from the temptations and trials which beset her, and thus insensibly supporting her courage. In fine, it is beneficial, and even indispensable, under every vicissitude of the spiritual career.

The life of Mary was the most saintly, the most pleasing to God, which this earth ever witnessed. Of this we can have no doubt, when we seriously reflect on Mary's peculiar gifts. But if we confine ourselves to mere superficial observation, the fact will not strike us so forcibly ; and if Mary now pursued the same kind of life amidst us, as she once led at Nazareth, her virtue would not inspire the deep veneration it deserves. We are ever ready to admire whatever is wonderful and uncommon—brilliant achievements, prolonged prayer, continued fasting and austerity ; and we cannot imagine sanctity to exist apart from these. Let us renounce this erroneous impression ; let us esteem an ordinary, obscure, and laborious life ; let us select it for our own portion, as far as we can, directing our imitation of Mary most particularly to this point.

CHAPTER XXIX.

Mary's application to the study of Jesus Christ.

By the special inspiration of the Holy Ghost, who guided his pen, the Evangelist twice repeats the observation, that Mary, the mother of Jesus, preserved in her heart the record of every word and act which bore reference to her Son. A peculiar motive suggested the repetition of the important remark, on which I deem it advisable to enlarge, although it has already engaged the reader's attention.

From the birth of Jesus, until his death, Mary never for a moment lost sight of him; her mind and heart were continually engrossed by him, as the object not only of her love, but also of her imitation. She knew that he had become man only to be our example; she esteemed herself happy in continually having before her so perfect a model; in conversing with him more freely and more frequently than any other human creature; in being the witness of his conduct and the depositary of his sentiments, and as she was united to him by stronger ties than any other mortal, she justly considered herself under a stricter obligation to resemble him more perfectly. She therefore studied him incessantly;

she observed how he acted on all occasions ; she treasured in her inmost heart and attentively pondered his words; she particularly directed her efforts to the study of his interior dispositions, in order to conform her own thereto. She was equally attentive to the divine communications regarding him conveyed to her through human channels, as Elizabeth, Simeon, and others. In a word, she spared no pains to become a proficient in the only real knowledge—the knowledge of Jesus Christ. She applied to that sacred science, not through curiosity, but in order to make it the rule of her sentiments and conduct, and it was that careful study and assiduous imitation of Jesus Christ which exalted her to the highest perfection ever attained by a creature.

Let us also devote our lives to the study of Jesus Christ, pursuing it with the same earnestness and from a similar motive. Let us study him in himself, and likewise in Mary, his most faithful copy.

Let us devote our life to the study of Jesus Christ. Prolonged as it may be, it will not afford time to exhaust so rich a subject. The more deeply we investigate it, the greater the wonders it will unfold, and in proportion as light increases, we shall find that unexplored depths still lie beyond. Let us study him whatever be our rank and position in life ; whether we be exalted or humble, rich or poor, happy or suffering, whether our pursuits be of a public or a private nature, whether we be afflicted with sickness, or in the enjoyment of health; whether immersed in the world, or dwelling in the cloister. In any condition, we can comply with the duty of true Christians only by the constant and assiduous imitation of Jesus Christ. Every study, every pursuit which diverts us from this, is either useless or dangerous. All other studies will avail nothing in themselves for eternity, unless commanded, directed, and sanctified by this supereminent study.

This was Mary's only object on earth. Even after the death of her Son she occupied herself in recalling his actions, his words, and the various circumstances of his mortal career. She was absolutely ignorant of all beside; profane science had never shed its light on her understanding; she knew nothing of what are termed accomplishments. Yet, although deficient in worldly learning, she was, nevertheless, in the judgment of God, more deeply versed than any other human being in the only science worthy of, or really interesting to, immortal man.

We must not be satisfied with devoting to the study of Jesus Christ a mere superficial attention; so important a subject demands the closest application of which grace can render us capable. In him all is eloquent, all is solidly instructive, all bears an infinitely deep and comprehensive meaning. This observation applies to his doctrine, which even the most enlightened works but imperfectly develope; and it refers with still greater force to his example, which is nothing more than his doctrine perfectly reduced to practice. With the little time and the indolent efforts we devote to the study, can we seriously imagine we shall attain it, not perfectly, but even as far as God requires, and as is necessary for our sanctification? If we are intimately persuaded of the importance, the extent, and the difficulty of this divine science, we shall spare neither time nor pains to acquire it. We shall study Jesus Christ in prayer, not by overtaxing the powers of the understanding, but by following the guidance of the heart. We shall study him in those authors whose pens distil the unction of the Holy Spirit; we shall study him in the divine inspirations which touch the soul, and in the heavenly lessons which, as our interior master, he breathes into the heart.

In studying Jesus Christ, we must be actuated not by curiosity, or by desire to display our superior lights for the direction of others, but by the same motives which influenced Mary, that is, first, for the promotion of our own spiritual advantage, and then of that of our neighbour, if God should please to render our efforts conducive thereto. Truly culpable should we be, and unworthy to receive the light of heaven, if we undertook the study from any but the pure intention of advancing God's glory and our own perfection, as well as that of others, if charged with them.

Our great aim should be to acquire a practical, not a speculative knowledge of Jesus Christ; to this point, above all, should our investigations tend. If we imitate Jesus Christ as far as we know him, we shall merit the happiness of a more intimate acquaintance with him, but if we derive no profit from the lights already received, they can tend only to our condemnation. Unless we make the use of them for which alone they were bestowed, the Almighty will withdraw them, and we shall quickly lose all desire to advance in the knowledge of our Redeemer, for the ardour of the soul's efforts to know Jesus Christ, is always proportioned to her fidelity in imitating him.

It is in himself, first and chiefly, that we should study Jesus Christ, endeavouring to penetrate into his heart, there to discover the source of his doctrine, and the principle of his actions, entreating him to introduce us into that divine sanctuary, and, having once obtained access, frequently resorting to it, or rather, never quitting it. We should also imitate him in his saints, in a St. Paul for instance, a St. John, a St. Francis of Assisium, but, above all, in the blessed Virgin, who so faithfully pourtrayed in herself the features of her Son. She is the great model of her sex, to whom Jesus Christ has given in her person an example of the most eminent virtues. But to the spouses of Christ in particular it belongs to study and to imitate his mother. This is their peculiar duty; they have every facility for doing so, and Mary never refuses to obtain for them a special grace to this effect.

CHAPTER XXX.

The marriage at Cana.

In the beginning of the public career of Jesus Christ, a marriage was solemnized at Cana in Galilee, and Mary was present at the cere- mony, together with Jesus and his disciples. Let us also invite Jesus and Mary to assist in spirit at our rejoicings, and to sanctify them by their presence. Entertainments are not for · bidden by the law of God ; on the contrary, there are occasions, such as marriages, and many others, when he himself authorizes them. He will bless the guests, and diffuse an inno- cent joy among them, provided purity of con- science, temperance and decorum preside at their convivial meetings. How edifying and holy must have been the marriage feast at which Jesus and Mary assisted ! How perfect a model for the festivities of Christians ! At banquets where men expressly meet by mutual consent, harmony and cordiality should most especially prevail. On those occasions, the true Christian, and still more the interior Christian, may easily be discerned amidst the throng, by that holy liberty of spirit, that frank ingenuousness and unaffected gaiety, which result from intimate union with God, and deeply seated interior peace.

"And the wine failing, the mother of Jesus saith to him : They have no wine." (St. John,

ii. 3.) Wishing to spare the newly married couple the confusion arising from so inopportune a circumstance, Mary with considerate kindness mentioned the mischance to her Son, whose omnipotence could so easily provide a remedy. She in fact asked for a miracle, but in terms most cautiously reserved. Jesus was already well aware that the wine had failed, and Mary equally knew the information to be unnecessary. Jesus also penetrated her desire for the exercise of his power, before it had been expressed, having himself inspired it. In fine, he foreknew that he would perform the expected miracle, at the special request of his mother. These observations will help to develop the true sense of the answer of Jesus.

"And Jesus saith to her: Woman, what is it to thee and to me? my hour is not yet come." (Ibid. 4.) Does not the reply seem harsh from a son? and was it not humbling to a mother to be thus addressed before a crowd! These words of Jesus require deep and attentive consideration, that the surprise they at first occasion, may give place to the instruction and edification they are so well calculated to impart. It appears strange that a God-Man should thus publicly repulse his Mother, and that too when she kindly strove to procure an interposition of his power and goodness in favour of men. But it was precisely because he was a God-Man, and because Mary was his mother, that he thus addressed her. He certainly did not mean to reproach her for asking a miracle which he had already resolved to perform; he was not displeased at so discreet an exercise of her maternal influence; nor did he consider her guilty of imprudence or any other imperfection; he on the contrary approved her conduct, and resolved to grant her petition.

In speaking so sternly, he was actuated by many reasons, worthy of himself and his holy mother, to whom those reasons were perfectly intelligible. His first object was partially to manifest his divinity to the assembled guests. By calling his mother *woman*, and asking her what there was in common between them, he clearly insinuated that if he was man, he was also something more than man, and that in the latter sense his mother was nothing to him, and could have nothing in common with him. He thus proposed to prepare the minds of his hearers for future faith in his Divinity.

His second object was to impress on his holy mother herself, that as God, he owed her nothing; that even in the character of a suppliant, she had no authority over him, and that to perform a miracle at her request, was to concede a gratuitous favour as God, not to discharge a debt as man, he himself as man, having no power to work miracles.

His third view was to prove to his mother, his disciples and the spectators, that in one sense, his actions were not under his controul, but dependent on the will of his Father; that the hour appointed for prodigies, being marked out, he should submit to the divine arrangement, performing none in obedience to the suggestion of his own will as man, but solely in submission to the ordinance of heaven; that it would consequently be useless to ask for miracles, either through curiosity, or as a test of his power, as the Pharisees afterwards did—and that even those he should accomplish were to be granted only to the supernatural faith instilled into the hearts of men by his eternal Father.

Finally, he wished to try the virtue of his holy mother, and before granting a favour which only her personal intercession could procure, to entitle her to it by a previous humiliation. " My hour," said he, " is not yet come." As if he had said, " the hour for manifesting my prodigies in favour of others has not arrived, but for you it has ; for, as my mother, you occupy a place and possess privileges peculiar to yourself." The sequel of the history proves this to have been the real meaning of his answer.

Mary's confidence remained unshaken. Favoured with singular light from heaven, she clearly understood the answer of her Son, and, certain of not being refused, " she said to the waiters : Whatsoever he shall say to you, do ye." (Ibid. 5.) •Believe unhesitatingly, and you will behold the visible manifestation of his power.

The first miracle of Jesus was then wrought at the prayer of his mother, but not until he had first put her faith and humility to the test;

thus we learn not to lose courage when he treats us with apparent severity, but to persevere in our faith, and cheerfully to submit to the humiliations he sees fit to send.

The Almighty often performs miracles at the request of interior souls, both in their own favour and that of others. But he usually requires some sacrifice in return, thereby rendering those miracles conducive to the sanctification of the individuals for whom they have been wrought. The humble and persevering faith which in a manner compels him to grant them, is infinitely acceptable; he cannot refuse his miraculous favours to that faith, because he apprehends no danger from yielding to it. Let us not offer rash petitions to God, but, once convinced that he has himself inspired our prayer, and that his glory is interested in its success, let us believe with faith firm as that of Mary; let us endure as she did an apparent repulse; let us not doubt that we shall be heard, and infallibly we shall.

CHAPTER XXXI.

Mary apparently disowned by her Son.

THE three years of Christ's public life were a time of trial to his mother. He left her, to devote himself to the promotion of his Father's glory, to the functions of his ministry, and the instruction of his disciples and the people. During that time, he became in a manner estranged from her, maintaining no more communication with her than if she had been utterly unknown to him. But if he lost sight of her as man, he was ever present to her as God; he continually acted on her heart by the impression of his grace, and taught her to spiritualize and divinize her love for him. The loss of his sensible presence grieved her; yet, far from being a loss, it was in truth a gain, since it contributed to her greater sanctification. Moreover, it was necessary that she should detach her affections from his sacred humanity, gradually to prepare herself for their final parting.

It is, however, probable that she followed her Son in his journeys, in company with the holy women whom the Gospel represents as ministering to his wants. These her saintly associates, no doubt, likewise provided for the temporal necessities of Mary, who, being now bereft of St. Joseph, had no means of subsistence left, and, being likewise disengaged from domestic cares, was free to devote herself to her divine Son. But while she followed Jesus, he in a manner fled from her. From the marriage at Cana, until the moment which preceded his death on the cross, it is not recorded that he once addressed her; on the contrary, he on more than one occasion appeared to disown her, and that publicly.

St. Matthew tells us, that "as he was on one occasion speaking to the multitudes, his mother and his brethren stood without, seeking to speak

to him. And one said unto him : Behold, thy
mother and thy brethren stand without, seeking
thee. But he answering him that told him, said;
Who is my mother, and who are my brethren ?"
As if he had said, I know neither mother nor
brother according to the flesh. " And stretching
forth his hand towards his disciples, he said:
Behold my mother and my brethren. For whosoever shall do the will of my Father, that is in
heaven, he is my brother and sister and mother."
(St. Matt. xii. 46—50.) This is not the moment
to recognize and communicate with those who
are bound to me by natural ties. Acting as I
do, in my public functions, in the name and for
the glory of my Father, who has confided to me
my earthly mission, I acknowledge as my brethren, my sisters, and my mother, those alone
who do the will of that Father : and I admit no
other union with men than a union based on
divine grace and cemented by spiritual considerations.

In these words, Jesus announced to the people
his Divinity and eternal generation, declaring
that he had come on earth only to make known
to men the will of his Father, and to teach them
to accomplish it—that there was no merit in be-
longing to him according to the flesh, and that
he placed no value on any but the spiritual connection subsisting between him and those who,
like him, conform to the will of his heavenly
Father. But knowing, as he did, that from her
infancy Mary had ever perfectly fulfilled the will

of God, this was in itself the highest encomium he could pronounce on her—the strongest expression of his love for her—the clearest testimony to the intimacy of her spiritual union with him. She was never more loudly or more honourably recognized for the mother of Jesus, than on this occasion, when he seemed to assign her a subordinate rank among his disciples and ordinary servants.

Spiritual maternity is a privilege common to all true Christians with Mary, the only one exclusively her own, being that of maternity according to the flesh. But there can be no doubt that even in the spiritual sense, she is the mother of Jesus in a manner peculiar to herself; in this consists her merit and glory, and this, more than her dignity as mother of the Word Incarnate, has God so highly rewarded in her. If Mary, who regulated her opinions by those of her Son, felt herself entitled to glory in the Lord on any subject, it was not for having been chosen as mother of the Messiah, but for having with the assistance of grace always perfectly fulfilled the will of the Almighty.

We may and should aspire to share with Mary the title of Mother of Jesus, in the most exalted meaning of the word. Far from being envious of our dignity, she will herself assist us to bear it worthily. She desires that we should be great before God in the same sense as she herself was great before him, and that we should participate in the union which rendered her so dear to him.

But we must ever remember, that in proportion as Jesus loved Mary, so he afflicted her ; that in proportion as he destined her for an intimate union with himself, so he first detached her from him, and that she was never so truly entitled to the appellation of his mother, as when she accepted with submission to the will of God, the incomprehensibly bitter trials of which her surpassing tenderness for her Son was the source. To belong entirely to Jesus, we must first renounce him; we must consent to forfeit the sweets of his sensible presence ; the delights of his heavenly communications and ineffable consolations. Then we can lay claim in a spiritual sense to a share in Mary's exalted title of mother of God.

CHAPTER XXXII.

Real foundation of Mary's happiness according to the estimation of Jesus Christ.

The following chapter may be considered a partial repetition of the last, yet the subject is one of so much importance, that to enlarge more fully on the maxims already inculcated, may not be useless. " A certain woman," fascinated by his heavenly words, "lifting up her voice said to him: Blessed is the womb that bore thee, and the paps that gave thee suck. But he said : Yea rather, blessed are they who hear the word of God, and keep it." (St. Luke, xi. 27, 28.)

p 3

Thus does Jesus invariably combat the suggestions of nature, opposing to them the spiritual views of faith. The woman mentioned by the Evangelist, proclaimed the happiness of Mary in having borne Jesus in her womb and nourished him with her substance. The congratulation was well-founded, and the Church daily repeats it in her public office, in nearly the same words. But the individual who first gave it utterance, limited her admiration to the least of Mary's privileges, and totally overlooked her far higher prerogatives. The holy Virgin had ever been faithful in hearing the word of God and keeping it, and in this, according to the opinion of Jesus Christ, consisted her real happiness, although of course the honour of the divine maternity must be allowed its full influence in creating it. It was no doubt a great happiness to have borne Jesus in her womb, and fed him with her milk ; but it was a greater happiness still to have been ever interiorly attentive to God's holy word, and punctual in observing it. Her happiness in the first instance was a purely gratuitous favour granted to Mary not for herself alone, but for the benefit of the whole human race ; a favour which abstractedly added nothing to her sanctity, because although her consent to become the Mother of God was demanded, her election to that high dignity depended rather on the free choice of the Almighty, than on her own will. But Mary's happiness in the second instance, was the result of her voluntary correspondence with the inspirations of the

Holy Ghost; it was the fruit of her fidelity to
grace, and of the holy use of her free will, and
this happiness it was, which God most esteemed
in her, and to which he awarded the brilliant
crown she now enjoys in heaven.

In correcting the opinion of the woman spoken
of in the Gospel, Jesus teaches all Christians to
correct the equally erroneous ideas they may have
adopted regarding the nature of Mary's happiness.
We all willingly concede to her the exalted privileges we cannot share; we declare her supremely blessed in being the Mother of God; but
we do not equally esteem the deeper source of her
merit, or equally admire the more imitable feature of her life,—her attention to, and fidelity in
profiting of the word of God, whether addressed
to her interiorly or exteriorly. We find it easy to
eulogize her incommunicable prerogatives; easy
to extol what we cannot comprehend and shall
never be required to copy; but we are not so ready to applaud her practical virtues, because this
would involve an acknowledgment of our obligation to become like her, as well as a condemnation
of the cowardice which shrinks from that duty.

Mary's highest happiness, that on which Jesus
Christ especially congratulated her, may and
should be likewise ours; we are commanded to
aspire to it, and woe to us if we make no exertion
to do so. The privileges exclusively confined to
Mary, do not excite our envy, because we know
them to be beyond our reach, but how many an
emotion of jealousy is aroused by perusing the

record of the supernatural favours granted to the
saints! We esteem them happy in having possessed such gifts, and we desire that a similar
happiness could likewise be ours. But are we
equally anxious to participate in their virtues,
their detachment from created things, their humility, their obedience, their interior abnegation,
their love for the cross, and all the comprehensive
perfection included in attention to the word of
God, and fidelity in executing it? This is the
only foundation of real happiness both for the
present life and that to come. We shall ever be
real objects of compassion; we shall ever misunderstand the meaning of true sanctity; we shall
ever be incompetent duly to estimate the happiness of Mary and the saints, as long as we are
unimpressed with this important truth, and care-
less in reducing it to practice.

CHAPTER XXXIII.

Mary has chosen the better part.

ON the feast of the Assumption, the Church
applies to the blessed Virgin the history of our
Lord's visit to Martha and Mary, as narrated by
St. Luke. In conformity with her intention we
shall refer to his holy Mother, the observation of
Christ on Mary, Martha's sister. "Mary," said
he, "hath chosen the best part, which shall not
be taken away from her." (St. Luke, x. 42.)

Martha actively exerted herself in preparing a suitable reception for Jesus Christ, and she was mortified, that instead of taking a part in the domestic duties, her sister remained tranquilly seated at the feet of the Redeemer, listening to his words. Jesus, as umpire between them, decided that Martha betrayed excessive eagerness in the preparation of a repast which needed not so much solicitude, and that Mary had made a better choice in reposing at his feet, and calmly imbibing the spiritual nourishment of his heavenly lessons. He added that the part chosen by Mary should not be taken from her, that is, that he would not require her to sacrifice the sweets of his conversation at the request of her sister, for that her pursuits were the better of the two, Martha's although laudable in themselves, being accompanied with reprehensible, because excessive eagerness and impetuosity.

To understand the application of these truths to the mother of God, we must consider in what consists the better part she has chosen. First, she chose to renounce herself and live for God. Secondly, she chose so to unite action and contemplation, that exterior labour should prove no impediment to interior peace and recollection. Thirdly, like her divine Son, she chose painful sacrifices, in preference to sweet enjoyment. We shall now examine in detail these three characteristics of the part chosen by Mary, and since it is beyond a doubt the best, let us also select it as our own.

First, Mary chose to renounce herself. She never adverted to herself; she never looked to her own interests, even those purely spiritual; she never desired distinction, and although immeasurably exalted above every individual of her sex from the moment of her conception, she never indulged vanity, or arrogated to herself superior privileges in consequence. Having renounced herself, she existed wholly for God; entirely subject to his grace, submissive to his will, and devoted to his glory. Her heart was undivided; her intention most pure; her thoughts, affections, and actions directed to God alone. With all our efforts, we shall never attain Mary's perfection in these particulars, but we should aspire to it, and may continually advance towards it. Our great object, like hers, should be to renounce self and live for God. Let us not, however, rest satisfied with a vague aspiration after this perfection; let us not feed ourselves with sublime but fruitless desires of sanctity, like so many souls who die to self and live to God only in speculation; but proceeding vigorously to practice, let us exterminate self-love wherever we find it lurking, and sacrifice it absolutely and without reserve to God. In this, we shall ever find something to reform; some new degree of perfection to acquire. To die to self, and live to God, is the affair of our whole life, and of each moment that composes it.

Secondly, Mary combined contemplation with action, so that one was no obstacle to the other. She neglected neither her domestic duties, nor those prescribed by fraternal charity. Being too poor to procure assistance in the care of her household, her toil must have been unremitting during the years of her residence with St. Joseph, as also when at a later period she attended to the temporal concerns of St. John, while he discharged his apostolic functions. But laborious duties never interrupted her prayer, or even slightly disturbed her interior peace. The contemplative life naturally tends to inaction, and unless the soul be on her guard, it induces indolence, inspiring disinclination even for obligatory exterior duties. Many devotees in the world, many persons consecrated to God in religion, have just grounds of self-reproach on this head. On the other hand, a life consecrated to laborious pursuits, feeds activity, eagerness and restlessness; it dissipates the mind, dries up the heart, and gradually withdraws the soul from prayer, to which the embarrassments and distractions of exterior occupation too often pursue her. It is not easy to avoid these two defects, and to combine the love of labour with the love of prayer. Yet it is of obligation both to pray and to labour, and these two duties being commands of God, it is evident they can be reconciled.

Thirdly, Mary preferred the most severe sacrifices to the sweetest enjoyments. We must not imagine that her prayer always overflowed with heavenly consolation. God accustomed her early to the most painful interior trials. Her sufferings in the cause of her Son were inexpressible, and

after he had ascended into heaven, and left her
alone on earth, the remainder of her life was but
a martyrdom of love.   But she accepted that condition; she lived contented in it; she would not
have exchanged it for the heavenly joys to which she
was entitled to aspire.   She never allowed herself to desire that her exile should be abridged,
and the moment of re-union with her Son in the
kingdom of glory accelerated.   Do we thus love
the cross, especially overwhelming interior crosses?   Do we not lose patience if they are protracted? do we not sigh for their termination?
do we not pant for consolation?   How few sacrifice themselves generously, absolutely, and irrevocably!   To make a perfect offering of self, and
never to revoke the oblation, is an event of rare
occurrence in the spiritual life.   We are satisfied
that the victim should endure to a certain point,
but we will not consent that it be entirely consumed.   We wish to burn with the fire of divine
love, but it must be a gentle fire, one to maintain
the life of self, not to divide, to devour and destroy.   Yet, shall we blindly imagine that we can
attain sanctity, if the part chosen by Mary, be
not our selection likewise?

CHAPTER XXXIV.

Mary at the foot of the cross.

MARY had been long prepared for the painful and ignominious passion of her Son. He had frequently foretold it to his apostles, and it was not likely he should conceal it from his mother. Moreover, her fate was so closely interwoven with his, that she must necessarily have received minute information concerning his future lot, as well as clear light regarding the redemption of the human race, which his violent death was to achieve.

From the commencement of his public life, she saw that the heads of the nation were preposses-ied against him; she perceived their jealousy and their hatred ; she was aware of the malicious calumnies they disseminated, and the dark plots they formed for his ruin. She saw the fatal moment gradually approach, and agonizing must have been her feelings in contemplating the ever present scene of future anguish. The expectation of an inevitable affliction, is frequently more diffi-cult to bear than the impending cross itself, and it may in truth be asserted that from the time Mary learned the sad fate of Jesus, she suffered in anticipation all the agony she afterwards en-dured at the foot of the cross.

No less inexorable in regard of the Mother than

of the Son, the Almighty unfolded to her an anticipated view of the principal circumstances of the passion, decreeing that each should pierce her heart with a deep and most painful wound.　As a mother, she must have had a melancholy gratification in endeavouring to learn every affecting particular of her Son's sufferings, and that feeling, natural in any case, was strengthened in hers, by her capability of estimating his passion, by the light of faith, as the effect of his love for his Father and for men.

The apostles who had fled in alarm from the terrible scene, informed her of the treachery of Judas, and the violent seizure of Jesus.　St. John detailed to her the events which had occurred under his own eyes at the houses of Annas and Caiphas, and told her that Jesus had been condemned as a blasphemer, because he had declared himself the Son of God.　The next day, she saw her divine Son led to the palace of Pilate, thence to Herod's, and back again to Pilate's, and the treatment he received at each tribunal she partly witnessed, and partly heard described. She was present when Pilate took his place at the judgment seat; she heard the accusations alleged against her Son, and from the fury of his enemies, as well as the weakness and timid policy of the governor, she quickly inferred that hope was at an end.　She was still present when Barabbas was publicly preferred to Jesus, and her divine Son exhibited to the cruel mob, his flesh all livid and torn; his head crowned with thorns; his shoulders covered with an old scarlet cloak ; his hand bearing the mock sceptre of a reed. She heard the people furiously demand that he should be condemned to crucifixion, the most disgraceful of all punishments. She accompanied the holy women who followed him to Mount Calvary, as he carried his heavy cross, and overcome by exhaustion fell repeatedly beneath its weight. She saw his wounds renewed by the forcible removal of his garments ; she saw him extended on the cross, and fastened to it with sharp nails ; she saw the cross raised from the earth, with a violent shock to his whole frame, and she heard the shouts of the rabble, and their leaders, who derided their suffering victim. What a scene for such a mother! the mother too of such a Son! How excessive, how deep, yet how submissive her grief! how admirable her fortitude! how calm her resignation! Intense as was her agony, it did not crush her heroic spirit, for an extraordinary grace supported her to endure yet more.

As soon as it was possible, she approached the cross, with St. John and Mary Magdalen ; with superhuman strength, she undauntedly stood beneath it, and in that posture, her tearless eyes fixed on Jesus, she waited to receive his last sigh. All her feelings at that trying moment were of a supernatural order. With courage surpassing that of the mother of the Machabees, she offered a full and entire sacrifice of her cherished Son to God, to satisfy the inexorable justice which demanded so noble a victim ; acknowledging the claims of that justice, she voluntarily immolated the new Isaac, who had generously undertaken to blot out the sins of the world; she freely offered his death for the salvation of each of us, and to that offering she united the oblation of her own immense anguish; thus effectually co-operating in our redemption, and indisputably asserting her right to a share in the title of man's Redeemer. The sacrifice of the mother and the Son were so closely identified, that they formed but one; it would have cost her less to give up her life, than to witness the death of her soul's best treasure, and well did she then merit the appellation so justly conceded to her, of the Queen of martyrs.

How sublime are the lessons she here conveys to us! And how truly is she the perfect model of interior souls on whom God inflicts the last extreme of trial. Their pains may be great, yet they are not comparable to hers. They should not sink beneath the cross, but seek support in the contemplation of the mother of sorrows, invoking her intercession for strength to imitate her fortitude, constancy and generosity. After Jesus expiring on the cross, the most eloquent volume to which they can apply for instruction, is Mary standing beneath it.

CHAPTER XXXV.

John substituted for Jesus.

"Now there stood by the cross of Jesus, his mother, and his mother's sister, Mary of Cleophas,
and Mary Magdalen.   When Jesus therefore had
seen his mother and the disciple standing, whom
he loved, he saith to his mother: Woman, behold
thy Son.   After that he saith to the disciple:
Behold thy mother.   And from that hour the
disciple took her to his own."   (St. John, xix.
25–27.)

The crowning trial of Mary's life, was to see
herself in a manner renounced by her Son.   At
the very moment when she most strongly testified
her love, braving all dangers that she might cling
to him until his last sigh;   at the very moment
when she might naturally have looked for a peculiar manifestation of his tenderness, as an evidence
of his sympathy in her grief, he withheld from
her the sweet, endearing name of mother, and
addressed her by the title of *woman,* as if there
had been no particular connection between them;
he declared to her in terms sufficiently plain that
he was no longer her Son, and substituted another
as inferior to himself, as a mere creature could
be to a Man-God.   And it is Jesus who thus
treats his loving mother, and that too at the very
hour when the agonies of death press on him !   It
would be blasphemy to accuse him of cruelty,

or even of indifference ; the circumstance must then conceal a mysterious, and a deeply mysterious meaning.

Although Jesus abandoned himself unreservedly to his Father in death, his sacrifice would not have been complete unless he had also been apparently abandoned by him; so, in like manner, there would have been a defect in the holocaust of Mary, if in consenting to renounce Jesus, she had not also been in a manner renounced by him.   It was necessary that both victims should be immolated without reserve, and the desolation of the mother correspond with that of the Son. The greatest of the sufferings of Christ beyond comparison, was his dereliction by his Father, and the deepest of Mary's sorrows was her renunciation by her Son.   And why did he so grievously afflict her ?   Only to perfect her heroic virtue.

Suffering souls, who are required to sacrifice your dearest interests, by the God who loves you, as Jesus loved Mary, there would be a deficiency in your holocaust, unless the Almighty apparently rejected you.   That trial is indispensable, precisely because it is the most severe of all others ; without it, you would never perfectly die to self. When you find yourselves utterly bereft of support, look at Jesus and Mary ; no other source of comfort can be suggested.

If we consider the matter under another aspect, we shall find that by thus providing for the temporal interests of his mother, Jesus only discharged a filial duty.   She was about to be left without a means of subsistence; without an earthly resource, and he provided her a guardian in the person of his beloved disciple, to whom he bequeathed her with a charge to cherish her as a parent. The prospect thus held out to her was far from brilliant, yet it was well adapted to one who had lived so long in the bosom of poverty ; one to whom existence would henceforth be embittered by the death of her only Son. From that time St. John took her to his own home; he loved, respected, and provided for her as if she had been his mother, and they never again separated, for when he quitted Jerusalem, she accompanied him to Ephesus, and as far as his apostolic labours permitted, he never lost sight of her till death.

The holy Fathers, particularly St. Augustine, here observe, that all Christians were on this occasion represented by St. John, and that Mary was appointed the mother of all the faithful in his person. She became our mother in the hour of her deepest anguish; she gave us birth spiritually at the foot of the cross, and if according to the laws of nature, ordinary mothers love their children in proportion as they have suffered in giving them life, we may conclude how tenderly Mary loves us in the order, and according to the laws of grace. Her divine Son was restored to her after his resurrection, but she did not on that account discard her newly adopted children from her heart; she did not forget that he had substituted them in his own place, and claimed for them a share in the love due to himself. Jesus confided each of us in spirit to her care, and of each he said to her, *Behold thy son*, whom I intrust to thee, as the price of my blood and thine. Let us doubt no more of Mary's love for us, than we doubt of her love and respect for Jesus Christ.

But let us also consider as addressed to ourselves, the words of Jesus to St. John, *Behold thy mother*. Let us love and honour Mary as St. John loved and honoured her; let us confide in her as in the best and tenderest of mothers, and let us deserve her love by our filial tenderness and obedience. It was because Jesus loved St. John above all his other apostles, that he gave him Mary as his mother. Let us also merit the love of Jesus by our fidelity to grace, and he will grant us a special share in the maternal love of Mary. Virgins have a peculiar claim to that love. 'Jesus,' says St. Jerome, 'recommended his virgin mother to the care of St. John, because he too was a virgin.' Virginity is then a strong claim to the love of Mary; let us rejoice if we have embraced the holy condition, and let us remember that it imposes an obligation to imitate Mary more perfectly than the generality of Christians.

CHAPTER XXXVI.

Mary spiritually dead, and laid in the tomb with Jesus Christ.

MARY had the courage to retain her position at the foot of the cross until her divine Son had expired. She heard him exclaim, "My God, my God, why hast thou forsaken me?" (St. Matt. xxvii. 46); and from the words she inferred the extreme rigour with which he was treated by his Father, and the intensity of his interior sufferings, compared with which, his exterior pains were as nothing. How deep a wound to the mother's loving heart, to hear the doleful lamentation of the Victim of overwhelming justice! What a trial to her faith to see the Man-God, the object of the Eternal Father's complacency abandoned, and in a manner rejected by him, because, to repair the glory of the God-head, he had generously undertaken to cancel the sins of men! The interior desolation of Jesus, was a mystery incomprehensible to Mary herself; one too of which she could scarcely support the bitter thought, even endowed as she was with superhuman fortitude.

She heard the noble act of resignation and confidence pronounced amidst the horrors of that desolation, " Father, into thy hands I commend my spirit." (St. Luke, xxiii. 46.) I voluntarily submit to thy extreme severity; I cling to thee with filial confidence, and into thy paternal hands, which now inflict a wound so painful, I commend my soul. In union with that great act, Mary also committed into the hands of God, her tortured, and almost failing spirit. If the Almighty should ever grant us the favour of interior sufferings similar to those of Jesus and Mary;—if he should ever permit us to drink of the same chalice, let us pray to the Son and the mother, for strength and love to produce an act of submission like theirs, were it even to be the last effort of expiring nature.

"It is consummated," (St. John, xix 30.) she heard him say. My sacrifice is complete; the prophecies connected with me are fulfilled; the anger of God is appeased, and the human race ransomed. She saw him bow his sacred head, and with a loud cry voluntarily sink into the arms of death. The feelings of Mary at that moment, surpass the comprehension of mortal mind; she endured the agonies of a spiritual death, incomparably more terrible than those of corporal dissolution. Buried in the depths of her anguish, motionless, apparently bereft of consciousness, she observed neither the miraculous eclipse, nor the unnatural darkness, nor the rending of rocks, nor the resurrection of the dead, nor the universal consternation and terrific convulsion of nature. These prodigies were especially wrought for the conversion of the spectators; but as for the nearly expiring mother, she saw nothing beyond her lost Son, on whom her eyes were rivetted, in whom her soul was centred.

She saw his sacred side wounded with a lance, and that wound, as St. Bernard observes, gave pain only to the mother's heart, which was then in truth pierced through, and the prophecy of Simeon fulfilled.

She saw him taken down from the cross, she saw the nails disengaged from his hands and feet, and the thorny crown from his sacred head ; she saw the pious efforts of his faithful friends to remove from his mangled remains the sad traces of human barbarity, and to restore to comeliness the once lovely countenance now discoloured from bruises, stained with blood, and overspread with the pallor of death. Oh! with what deep love and heart-rending grief, she embraced again and again those adorable features, that open side, those wounded hands and feet! She probably assisted in embalming his sacred body, and wrapping it in its shroud. She accompanied it to the tomb, entering the abode of the dead in spirit, and retiring only at the earnest entreaty of St. John and the other apostles, who earnestly strove to comfort the heart-stricken mother.

Let us attentively ponder each sad circumstance of this tragic scene; let us tenderly sympathize in the grief of the mother of sorrows : if we consider that it was for our sakes she voluntarily endured such excessive anguish, we cannot refuse to mingle our tears with her's. " She loved me, and delivered herself for me." She offered a greater sacrifice than if she had actually resigned her life for me. Who now can refrain from loving

Mary? Who can deny her the justly merited tribute of heartfelt gratitude? But let us proceed farther than mere sentiments, and if it should please God to visit us with the cross, let us unite it to hers; let us bear it as she did; let us walk with alacrity in the footsteps of the Son and the mother, and rejoice at being allowed to share their interior sufferings.

CHAPTER XXXVII.

Mary a participator in the renewed life of Jesus Christ.

JESUS CHRIST, who had frequently foretold to his disciples that he should rise on the third day after his death, had no doubt likewise announced the fact to his mother, whose faith was more lively, though more severely tried than theirs. Every circumstance of the life and death of her son, instead of realizing, seemed to contradict the promises of the angel Gabriel. But those promises were to be understood in their most elevated spiritual sense, and were not to be accomplished until after Jesus Christ had risen from the tomb. Then he was to be great, to be recognized as the Son of God, to establish over all true Israelites the empire of his Church, and to commence here below the reign destined to endure through the ages of eternity. In pursuance with the eternal decree it was necessary that he should rise from the dead before these great ends could be attained. Mary firmly believed on the word of Christ, that he should rise again; but the influence of her strong faith was wholly confined to the superior part of her soul; it produced no sensible comfort or support, and therefore proved no counterpoise to the bitter anguish in which her soul was plunged throughout the passion, and until the very moment of the resurrection.

In like manner, when God first imposes the cross on interior souls, he grants them a foreknowledge of the glory which is to succeed their trials; yet, while those trials last, he does not permit that this foreknowledge should lessen the intensity of their sufferings.

They confidently believe the divine prediction, but at the same time they are deprived of all power to advert to it deliberately as a source of strength and consolation.

Among the many apparitions of Jesus to his apostles, enumerated by the evangelists, there is no mention of even one to his holy mother. The reason is obvious; the apostles were the witnesses of the resurrection of Christ; the object of their ministry was to publish that resurrection all over the earth, it was therefore indispensable that the evangelists should recount the principal proofs which had convinced them of its reality. But as Mary was not destined to preach the resurrection of Christ to the people, it would have been superfluous to mention the visits she received from her divine Son. There can be no doubt that she saw him, and frequently, but her humility concealed a fact which no particular reason obliged her to divulge.

Consoling and delightful as these visits must necessarily have been, she was too perfectly dependent on the will of God to invite them by her deliberate desires; moreover, the cross was to her as welcome a gift as could be the sweetest favours of heaven. To see her Son glorious and immortal, no doubt replenished her soul with overflowing joy, yet she did not eagerly seek that happiness; she would have been equally satisfied if it had been withheld, and the resurrection of her Son intimated to her only through the apostles. As Jesus did not desire his resurrection on account of its connection with his own individual glory, neither did Mary desire it from any personal considerations. Whenever we have no particular document to guide our conclusions regarding Mary's conduct, we have but to inquire what is the highest perfection of which the matter in debate is susceptible. That perfection we may unhesitatingly decide to have been her practice. In the present instance the detachment just described embraced the sublimity of virtue.

Souls destined for spiritual holocausts, are gradually conducted by the power of divine grace to this exalted degree of sanctity. When they have attained perfect spiritual death, all desire becomes extinct within them, and, if it pleased God, they would submit for a whole eternity to that state of interior death. This appears incomprehensible to the soul which still retains a remnant of self-love and self-will. To her, it seems strange to desire spiritual death as a great good, and to renounce the wish to rise once more from the tomb. Yet it would be more extraordinary still to connect the idea of death with the possibility of forming a desire, since the very fact of forming a desire necessarily pre-supposes life.

Mary arose from the dead with her Son, and her spiritual resurrection was so much the more perfect, as her spiritual death had been entire. God was the author both of her death and her resurrection, and she submitted freely to his action, neither retarding the hour appointed for the one, nor accelerating, by her desires, the moment marked out for the other. Such should be our dispositions, in whatever condition the Almighty may place us. Few souls attain this degree of perfection, because very few aim at the perfect imitation of Mary. Yet, to rise like Mary, we must die with her; there can be no resurrection unless death precede, and by death is meant the total extinction of life.

CHAPTER XXXVIII.

Mary ascends to heaven in spirit with her Son.

It cannot be doubted, although the Acts of the Apostles do not specify it, that Mary was present at the glorious ascension of her Son. She con-

versed with him, and eat in his company, for the
last time, with the apostles and disciples. She
saw his sacred body resplendent with glory raised
from the earth, and borne on a cloud beyond the
view of the admiring multitude. Unable to separate in heart and thought from her dear Son, she
accompanied him in spirit, and ascended with him
into heaven.

She understood now, more perfectly than ever,
that "Christ ought to have suffered these things,
and so to enter into his glory." (St. Luke, xxiv.
26.) She applied the words to her own case also,
and, on those terrible sufferings of which her Son
alone had been the cause, she founded the sweet
and confident hope of being one day re-united to
him in the kingdom of his glory.

What attraction had this earth for Mary after
Jesus had quitted it? What did it contain to
engage her heart? Absolutely nothing. He bore
away to heaven the affections of his holy mother,
whose remaining life was but one sigh of loving
desire to rejoin him. Then commenced her experience of a new description of suffering—a
suffering at once delicious and excruciating—a
suffering gentle, yet violent, which gradually and
imperceptibly perfected her interior death. Oh,
how often she exclaimed, "Wo is me, that my
sojourning is prolonged!" (Ps. cxix. 5.) "What
do I here below? The will of my Son retains
me here, but how much it costs me to submit to
that crucifying will!" Mary loved that divine
will sufficiently to prefer its accomplishment to

her own happiness, thus practically emulating the blessed, whose felicity is identified with the execution of the will of God; and during at least fifteen years that she survived the ascension of Christ, she persevered in that habitual disposition of perfect self-immolation. After having sacri- ficed her Son in this world, she sacrificed him again in heaven, by continually dying to her ardent desire of re-union with him. To form an adequate idea of the agony consequent on Mary's protracted separation from Jesus, we should, like her, be connected with him both by natural and supernatural ties. While her divine Son prolonged her banishment on earth, he at the same time inspired her with a most ardent desire for the enjoyment of his visible presence in heaven, and thus the reciprocal love of the Son and the mother produced a torment which may in some respects be assimilated with the pain of loss.

We are not sufficiently spiritual to comprehend such a species of suffering; some of the saints, who experienced it at the close of life, have averred, that although accompanied with heavenly sweetness, it surpassed all their previous pains, none of which were comparable to that agonizing conflict resulting from the soul's vehement, yet fruitless desire of permanent union with God.

It is humiliating to acknowledge, that, far from having experienced, we have never even formed an idea of the nature of this suffering. Yet we were made for God, and to love anything beside him is mere delusion. If we understood his

amiability—if our hearts were perfectly detached
from all beside him, how irresistibly would they
tend to God! How would they be consumed by
the glowing flames of divine charity! How
would they languish at finding their bliss de-
ferred!—at beholding it apparently within reach,
and still eluding the grasp! Why is not this
our enviable condition? What fruit do we derive
from prayer and communion, if they fail to produce this effect? Why do we not dispose ourselves for so great a happiness, by disengagement
from creatures and from self—by esteem for, and
submission to the purifying trials which must
precede it? We wish to possess God, yet we
will not adopt the measures necessary for attaining union with him; we will not submit to the
divine operations which alone can annihilate the
love of created things, and replace it by the love
of our Creator. That is, we desire the end, and
disregard the means; we aim at reaching the
goal without traversing the allotted course. What
blindness! What folly!

CHAPTER XXXIX.

Mary prepares to receive the Holy Ghost.

JESUS having informed his disciples, immediately
before his ascension, that in a few days they
should receive the Holy Ghost, who would transform them into new men, they disposed them-

selves for that great event by prayer. " All these," says St. Luke, " were persevering with one mind in prayer with the women, and Mary the mother of Jesus, and with his brethren." (Acts, i. 14.) Three observations here suggest themselves : first, the union of prayer among the disciples, an advantage to be also found in religious communities and Christian families, whose members pray in common. Secondly, their constancy and perseverance ; they spent in prayer the ten days intervening between the ascension and Pentecost, abstaining during that period from all unnecessary occupation, observing silence and recollection, and communing with God alone—thus supplying the original model of retreats, which have since proved of such incalculable benefit both to saints and sinners. Thirdly, the advantage of uniting in prayer with Mary, the mother of Jesus. Let us endeavour to engage her interest in our behalf ; let us ask her to pray with and for us ; she is ever ready to do so, and her intercession must ensure the success of our petitions.

Mary prepared to receive the Holy Ghost, in company with the disciples, and far more perfectly than they. Her prayer was neither active nor ardent, nor did it embrace a multiplicity of views ; it was all peace, all love. The Holy Ghost, her spouse, prayed in her, because, acknowledging her incapability of disposing herself to receive him, she earnestly besought his assistance.

Shall we never understand, that it is not we

who are to pray, but the Holy Ghost who is to pray in us; and that our only affair is to yield our hearts to him, that he may produce therein those " unspeakable groanings," (Rom. viii. 26,) of which St. Paul speaks? Mary, the holiest of all creatures, the most perfectly united to God, the most deeply versed in the mysteries of sub- lime prayer, did not pray of herself, but aban- doned her soul to the influence of the Spirit of God, that he might pray in her; and yet, im- perfect, volatile, and easily distracted as we are, we expect to pray by our own efforts; we set in motion all the faculties of the soul, particularly the imagination, which should especially be kept in subjection; we pour out a torrent of words, we heave deep sighs, and then estimate the suc- cess of our exertions by the extent of this mental agitation.

When Mary prayed, she neither moved nor spoke—scarcely was she observed to breathe; her prayer emanated from the heart, so simply and so tranquilly, as to be almost imperceptible— so directly as to exclude all formal considerations. Her prayer was no doubt excellent, yet if ours were similar, we should imagine we did not pray at all; we must clearly perceive and distinctly note our interior acts; we must reflect on them, we must have an internal testimony that they have been well performed. In a word, we look on prayer as the result of our own exertions, and we can scarcely believe that the Holy Ghost should be allowed any influence in producing it, whereas, our sole concern is, on the contrary, to second his heavenly inspirations.

If we desire to receive the Holy Spirit like Mary, let us imitate her preparation, banishing impetuous ardour, placing no reliance on our own weak efforts, and beseeching Him with humility and love to infuse into our hearts the requisite dispositions. It is since the generality of men have become independent of the guidance of the Holy Ghost in prayer, attaching themselves exclusively to printed formulæ, that this Divine spirit has suspended the communication of those gifts and graces which form the true Christian. Mary and the apostles had no books to help them to pray; the source of their prayers was in the heart, which they subjected to the control of that heavenly Comforter whom the Scripture styles the Spirit of prayer.

Prayer of this description pre-supposes habitual recollection, disengagement from creatures, and the love of heavenly things alone. But should not the life of the practical Christian be a life of recollection, of indifference to temporal interests, of lofty and incessant aspirations after eternal goods? Let us endeavour to imitate the example of Mary, that we may share in the immense graces lavished on her by her heavenly Spouse.

CHAPTER XL.

Mary receives the Holy Ghost.

MARY had been declared "full of grace" by the Angel Gabriel; what, then, could be added to that plenitude? Nothing, according to our ideas; yet, in the judgment of God, she had then but imbibed the first elements of that science of the saints in which she was afterwards to attain such pre-eminence. After the Angel's departure, she received into her womb the divine Author of grace, and she was then replenished with grace to a degree compared with which her previous plenitude was but a void. A new increase of grace followed the birth of Jesus Christ. Every change in her condition produced a corresponding alteration in the measure of her holiness. She resembled her divine Son, who from his childhood increased as man in wisdom and grace. The sole object of the Almighty in subjecting her to trials so multiplied and severe, was to add lustre to her sanctity. That sanctity seems to have been consummated by her heroic sacrifice at the foot of the cross, where she exhibited a sublimity of perfection beyond which even imagination cannot reach.

But who are we, to assign limits to the holiness destined for Mary? Before attaining the full measure of sanctity allotted to her, she was destined, if we may so speak, to exhaust the

Divine treasury, wherein were reserved special graces, commensurate with her exalted privileges. The Holy Ghost, intent on dispensing to her his richest gifts, descended on her once more on the day of Pentecost, and dilated her heart almost to immensity, that it might be capable of containing the plenitude of that divine charity which emanates directly from Him who is the Love of the Father and the Son.

Mary was not endowed like the Apostles with the gift of miracles, of prophecy, of tongues, or of knowledge, so necessary for the establishment of the Church; these gifts, however excellent, were inferior to her prerogatives. She was to contribute, more than all the apostles and their successors in the ministry, to extend the dominion of her Son; not, however, by preaching or miracles, but by the ardour of her desires and the incomparable vivacity of her love for her divine Son and for her adopted children. The labours of Christ's ministers were to be limited to a particular sphere, whereas, the agency of Mary was to be universal, although imperceptible; its efficacy demonstrated, not by external evidences, but by interior effects. To assume a more prominent position in the Church, would have deeply wounded the humble and retiring virgin; her prayers were to ensure success to the preaching of the apostles; yet that success, although the result of her influence with her divine Son, was not to be imputed during life to her, who so truly loved obscurity and so com- .

pletely disregarded the approbation of creatures.
How admirable are the dispensations of eternal
wisdom for maintaining the extent and integrity
of Mary's favourite virtue of humility! How
precious must this virtue be in the eyes of God,
when so cherished by his Blessed Mother!

The Holy Ghost, on the day of Pentecost,
diffused among the disciples limited portions of
the sacred fire of charity, but he concentrated all
its intensity in the heart of Mary; in her he
particularly delighted to dwell, penetrating and
inflaming her with his divine ardours; uniting
himself to her once more, and establishing with
her a more perfect and intimate communication
than ever. Without limiting the power of God, it
may be safely asserted that the Holy Ghost never
did or will dispense his gifts so liberally to any
creature as to Mary. On this day, the apostles
were miraculously transformed from gross and
earthly-minded men, into beings altogether spiritual and divine; but a still greater alteration
was effected in Mary—not by the substitution,
as in them, of holiness for imperfection, but by
the exchange of one degree of perfection for
another yet more sublime. This we shall believe
to be literally true, if we reflect that the sanctity
of God, being infinite in itself, nothing can re-
strict its external communications, which with
respect to Mary were limited only by her finite
capacity as a mere creature. And as the capacity
of man may perpetually expand, without ceasing
to be finite, we can have no difficulty in believing

that in Mary it attained an extent surpassing the comprehension of men and angels.

What practical lessons shall we learn from this? That since we may ever increase in sanctity, and are incapable of determining the precise degree of holiness which the Almighty expects from us, we should make strenuous and unceasing efforts to advance in the perfection of Divine love, that at length God alone may live in us.

And in what do those efforts consist? In greater fidelity to grace, more absolute dependence on Providence, more perfect conformity to God's will, a more generous spirit of sacrifice, more perfect resignation to affliction, and more entire self-abnegation. The measure of sanctity demanded from each individual is fixed, and God will assuredly complete it, if we oppose no obstacle to his designs.

CHAPTER XLI.

Life of Mary from that period.

AFTER the ascension of Christ, Mary resided permanently with St. John, who treated her with the love and consideration of a son; she dwelt with him for some time at Jerusalem, and then accompanied him to Ephesus, where she is supposed to have died. At the general Council held in that city, she was solemnly proclaimed mother of God, against Nestorius, who denied her the august title.

She undoubtedly increased in grace during the fifteen remaining years of her life, and her progress in perfection was accelerated by the near approach of the term of her pilgrimage. The love which consumed her, and the intense desire she felt to behold her Son, supplied continual matter of sacrifice, and the merit of those sacrifices was enhanced by the augmentation of her love. Thus, from the beginning to the end of her life, the sufferings of Mary were identified with her exalted prerogatives as a mother. To understand the severity of the last trial, we should be capable of conceiving the love which linked the heart of Mary to that of her Divine Son, as well as the ardour of her desire to be eternally united to him, as to the centre of her affections. The most lively transports and inflamed ardours of the saints bear no comparison with the strength and vehemence of the desires of Mary. Do we endeavour to merit the favour of being one day consumed with love like her? Before the soul becomes a prey to this delicious torment, she must undergo the preparatory sufferings of spiritual poverty and extreme desolation, and be ready, like Mary, to resign, as far as any selfish gratification is concerned, the divine and only object of her happiness. It is only after thus losing, that she can find him, and that he enkindles in her the heavenly flame which gradually consumes the grosser elements of nature.

In what consisted Mary's comfort during the remainder of her mortal career? In daily participating in the adorable body of her Son, and thus consolidating their spiritual union. How ardent was her desire to receive him! How profound her peace after the enjoyment of that happiness! How cold and fruitless are our communions, compared with hers! Oh! let us ask her to obtain for us even a slight share in the purity and fervour of her love! She went to Jesus for his own sake, never seeking to satiate her soul with the sweetness of love, but totally unmindful of personal comfort. Is this our case? Do we approach Jesus for his own sake? Do we believe that we possess all things in possessing him under the veil of obscure faith? Are we not in anguish, on the contrary, when we experience no soft emotions, when we shed no tears of devotion?

Another source of inexpressible comfort to Mary was to witness the flourishing condition of the early Church of Jerusalem; to see her Son recognized and adored by those who had crucified him—his doctrine widely diffused and perfectly practised—his name proclaimed in process of time to the Gentiles—his Divinity loudly acknowledged—the foundation of his kingdom established on the ruins of idolatry, and the true God worshipped instead of the false deities of paganism. The glory of God alone engrossed her mind; nothing on earth but the progress of the religion promulgated by her Son, was capable of engag-

ing her interest or exciting her joy. Do we share
in her zeal? Are we anxious for the promotion
of the Divine honour? Are we not centred in
self? Provided we abound in spiritual helps, of
which, however, we make but little use, are we
not almost indifferent to the spiritual indigence
of others? Mary's zeal embraced the universe;
it extended to all ages, and to each individual in
creation. What is the extent of ours? We have,
perhaps, a little for ourselves, but have we any
for our neighbour or for mankind in general?
After having sacrificed her Son for the redemption of the human race, Mary ceased not to pray
that he might reap the fruits of his death; and,
as already observed, her prayers were more efficacious in the propagation of the Gospel, than the
preaching and miracles of the apostles. When communing with God in prayer, she forgot herself, to
think of us; she recommended each of us to her
divine Son, and implored his graces for the generations to come. Her prayers in heaven are but the
continuation of those she offered on earth; and
in becoming mother of God, she became at the
same time our mother and our advocate. Do we
thus pray for others? Perhaps we do occasionally for our friends and relatives, but where
the momentous question of the soul's salvation is
at issue, should not all men rank as our friends
and relatives? Self-love incessantly reminds us
of our individual necessities; we think we have
never prayed enough for ourselves, and, reversing
the practice of Mary, we neglect to advocate the

cause of others at the throne of grace, because we are totally pre-occupied with our own concerns. " Each," we say, " must think of himself; the affair of salvation is purely personal ; I have to answer only for my own soul." Such is not the language of charity. If I love my neighbour as myself, his salvation cannot be a matter of indifference to me. I owe him at least the aid of my prayers, and those I offer for him, far from being lost for myself, obtain for me a more abundant infusion of grace than the multiplied petitions originating in selfish anxiety about my own interests. Let us endeavour to imbibe from Mary the charity which dilates the heart, and inflames it with zeal for the glory of God, and the spiritual welfare of our fellow-creatures.

CHAPTER XLII.

Death and Assumption of Mary.

MARY died of the effects of divine love, by whose consuming activity her corporal energies had been gradually enfeebled. Her exhausted frame could no longer resist the violent efforts of the soul to disengage itself from its prison, and fly to the embraces of her Son ; the spirit at length triumphed, and was happily released from the fetters which had bound it to the earth. The death of Mary, though apparently very different from that of Jesus, resembled it in fact most closely, the vehemence of love terminated the mortal career of both mother and son, with this difference only, that the son, as absolute master of life and death, sacrificed himself freely for the redemption of mankind, whereas it was Jesus who decreed the termination of his mother's earthly pilgrimage, as a preliminary to their perfect and permanent union in heaven. If she was a martyr at the foot of the cross, she was a martyr also at the closing hour of life, when she became the victim of love, the most inexorable, yet, by a strange contradiction, the most gentle of despots.

It is an article of pious belief in the Church, authorized by a solemn festival, and generally adopted by the faithful, that the holy and incorruptible flesh of Mary was not permitted to remain long in the tomb, but was speedily translated by her divine Son to heaven, there to be re-united to the soul. As God the Father would not permit the flesh of his holy One to see corruption, neither does it seem fitting that Jesus should suffer contamination to approach that of Mary, whence his was derived. She now reigns gloriously in heaven in body and soul, and there possesses all the dignity, happiness, and power which a God can bestow on his cherished mother.

But let us observe that Jesus rewarded her so generously, not precisely because she was his mother, but because she had ever been perfectly faithful to grace, and because she had courageously accepted and endured the trials attached to her dignity as mother of God. The Almighty does not reward in his creatures his purely gratuitous gifts, but the virtues and merits acquired by fidelity to grace. It was not in virtue of the hypostatical union, that an almost infinite reward has been conferred on Jesus Christ as man, but it was because " he humbled himself, becoming obedient unto death, even the death of the cross, that God hath exalted him, and hath given him a name which is above all names ;" (Phil. ii. 8,) and, in like manner, it is not in her capacity of mother of God, but in that of the charitable, faithful, and humble servant of the Lord, that Mary has become entitled to so great honour and glory. Her love for God, her contempt of self, her charity for men were never equalled, therefore is her felicity without a parallel.

While we admire all that God has done for Mary, let us imitate as far as we can all that Mary has done for God. The measure of grace granted to us, is, and ever will be, inferior to her's, consequently the Almighty requires only a corresponding return. He is infinitely just, and does not aim at reaping what he has not sown ; but, on the other hand, he demands that the heavenly seed should produce its appropriate fruit—fruit which may be augmented immeasurably, more by our good will and earnest desires, than by our works—fruit which the sovereign Judge will one day gather into his barn, and according to the abundance of which he will determine our reward.

Most holy Virgin! I place myself under thy special protection, and devote myself with my whole heart to the imitation of thy virtues. I firmly resolve, with the help of divine grace, to reduce to practice the lessons on those virtues imparted to me in the foregoing work, and, above all, to copy thy interior dispositions, thy purity of intention, humility, union with God, and charity to thy neighbour. Beg of Jesus Christ to infuse these dispositions into my soul, and grant that, taking thee for my model, I may daily labour to resemble thee on earth, that I may one day participate in thy bliss in heaven. Amen.

CHAPTER XLIII.

Conclusion.

I SHALL terminate by a few general reflections which may be found useful as forming an epitome of the entire work.

1st. The union of Jesus and Mary is the model of the union contracted between the Redeemer and the interior soul. No sooner has that spiritual union been effected, than its privileged object experiences an immediate and unaccountable alteration in her views and feelings. She becomes familiarized with the divine presence in a manner to which she was heretofore a stranger; she feels herself forcibly attracted, when at prayer, to that profound interior silence which suspends formal reflections and specific acts. Transitory emotions of sensible devotion give place to solid, permanent peace; allured by the heavenly sweetness of that peace, she flies to prayer as to her solace; she would gladly pursue that divine exercise without interruption, and totally forego the society of creatures. Silence and solitude are now her element.

Gradually the mysterious union of Jesus with the soul becomes more intimate; he manifests himself clearly, and in distinct terms he imparts his desire to reign over her without reserve; he grants her many evidences of his love, and receives from her in return strong testimonies of her unbounded devotion. At that period of her career he replenishes her with his consolations, and inebriates her with his divine sweetness.

This season of temporary enjoyment is not altogether free from exterior trials, similar to those which Mary experienced in the early days of union with her Son. But, in progress of time, Jesus diminishes the sensible manifestations of his love, and accustoms the soul to dispense with them. She then begins to adhere to her Saviour for his own sake with more resolution and stability. He has not yet receded entirely from her view, but he is not always present to her, as at the commencement of their union. He goes and comes with perfect freedom, as he did at Nazareth, where Mary enjoyed the happiness of conversing with him only at intervals. Jesus Christ then deprives the soul altogether of his sensible presence; while she pursues, he seems to flee from her, sometimes even feigning not to recognize her. This is the state of obscure faith, and while it lasts, the soul although in reality more strongly attached to Jesus than ever, has to endure many, and most severe trials. But she has within her a powerful, though an imperceptible, support.

She continually plunges more and more deeply into the obscurity of faith, until at last she seems on the point of losing Jesus, and in fact she must eventually consent to sacrifice him, like his most loving mother. Oh, what a pang to lose Jesus! But it is a necessary trial, for he will be restored to her, as to Mary, in a renewed existence, only after she has thus lost him. Finally, he rises in glory, and appears to the soul resplendent and immortal, imparting to her a blessed security of permanently possessing, without ever again incurring the risk of losing him. But while her earthly pilgrimage is prolonged, she languishes with love, until at length she forcibly disengages herself from the incumbrance of the body, and flies to her eternal rest.

2d. Mary never anticipated grace, but waited its coming without eagerness or impetuous ardour. Perfectly satisfied with the will of God as revealed from one moment to another; happy under unceasing vicissitudes of consolation and tribulation, she never wished that her moments of intense spiritual joy should be prolonged, or the hours of her deep anguish abridged. She was ever inviolably faithful to the grace of her actual condition,

entering into, and maintaining herself in the dispositions it suggested. We are not required to
attain such perfection, but only to aspire to it ;
to feel humbled at béing so far removed from it,
and to renew our efforts in the pursuit, when
we perceive any relaxation.

3d. Mary's sufferings were extreme, because
her love was unparalleled. Let us form a correct
idea of the meaning of divine love. It is not by
sensible emotions, or ardent protestations, that we
evince our love for God ; if we content ourselves
with these, they become on the contrary a source
of delusion. The real proof of love is to give to
God what costs us most ; patiently to endure the
sufferings he pleases to inflict ; resolutely to accomplish his holy will, even amidst the most
violent opposition from our own, and generously
to permit him to take what we have not courage
to give. To love God, is to renounce all that
does not appertain to him and to his blessed will.
The extent of this spiritual spoliation can be
estimated only by experience, for God prepares
even the most generous souls for it only by
degrees.

4th. In fine, Mary, though the most crucified,
was at the same time the happiest of creatures,
because she never lost her peace amidst her
sufferings ; because her will was always in unison
with her actual condition. Our unhappiness
arises from our rebellious opposition to the will of
God. The most afflicted soul, if tranquil and
resigned is happy. Her pains increase ; the

sacrifices required of her become more difficult, but her peace and submission augment in proportion, and it is certain that the closing trials of her spiritual career are less intolerable than her first afflictions. Mary at the foot of the cross was more calm, more courageous, more resolute, than Mary fleeing into Egypt.

Reader, peruse the foregoing pages occasionally under the guidance of the Holy Spirit; the more you advance in virtue the more intelligible will become the maxims they inculcate.

THE END.

Thomas I. White, Printer, 45, Fleet Street, Dublin.

www.ingramcontent.com/pod-product-compliance
Lightning Source LLC
Chambersburg PA
CBHW031043120726
47905CB00007B/2282